Elena Gross

P9-DFP-283

A NOVEL BY MEGAN SHULL

BOUNCE

KT KATHERINE TEGEN BOOKS
An Imprint of HarperCollins Publishers

Also by Megan Shull
The Swap
Amazing Grace

Katherine Tegen Books is an imprint of HarperCollins Publishers.

ISBN 978-0-06-231172-6

Typography by Aurora Parlagreco
16 17 18 19 20 CG/RRDH 10 9 8 7 6 5 4 3 2 1
❖
First Edition

"The world is full of magic things,
patiently waiting for our senses to grow sharper."

—W.B. YEATS

PART ONE

1.

"I'M NOT TRYING TO BE mean or anything, but..."
Alexis Wright stops midsentence just long enough to
scrunch up her nose and share a huge smile with her two
best friends. "Do you even *wear* deodorant?" she asks.

All three girls burst out laughing.

Alexis Wright is not talking to me.

She doesn't even really know me.

I just happen to be the lucky girl sitting beside her,
three rows from the very back of the bus, squished
between her gigantic paisley backpack and the window.

"Dirty Smelly," Alexis starts back up.

That's what they call her. The girl sitting one seat up
and across the aisle with pale skin, long, tangled, white-
blond hair and wild blue eyes. I am trying not to watch
and trying not to listen, but I can't really block it out. It's

all going down right in front of me.

"Dirty Smelly," Alexis says with a smirk. "Hellooooo, I'm talking to you." She giggles.

I turn and glance at the girl. Her head is down and her eyes are closed as if she's wishing she were someplace else, or maybe was *someone* else. And right at this moment, I am suddenly feeling very bad that I don't even know this girl's name. She's in seventh grade, just like Alexis, and just like Alexis's stupid friends, and just like me. We all go to Redwoods.

"Hey." Alexis reaches out her hand across the aisle and pokes the girl. "Yoo-hooooo, Dirty Smelly! I'm talking to you. Hello? Seriously, um, like—" Alexis stops again and shoots another grin at her two friends. Both of them are smiling.

My shoulders tighten.

Alexis leans forward in her seat. "Dirty Smelly, are you listening? Seriously, do you not believe in washing your clothes? Or do you just like to wear the exact same disgusting outfit every single day?"

I start to feel sick.

I don't know what to do.

I wish I had the courage to say something.

What I want to say is, *Stop!*

What I want to say is, *Leave her alone!*

But what I want to do and what I do are two very different things, and so I keep my mouth shut and the side of my face mashed against the cold bus window. A steady rain is falling, and I focus on the drops of water hitting and sliding down the glass. The only good news—if there is any—is that today is Tuesday, December 23, which means tomorrow is Christmas Eve, which means we won't have school for a whole ten days.

When the bus stops and Alexis and her pack of friends stand up, I work very hard at not making eye contact. The last thing I need is for Alexis to turn on *me* next. I'm sure she'd have something to say about the huge gap between my two front teeth or my messy, long dark hair, or the fact that I have a zit the size of a small city on my forehead. I wait for Alexis to grab her bag and move toward the narrow aisle of the bus before I lift my head and watch.

Alexis Wright and her friends are the sort of girls boys notice. If you saw them in the yearbook, they would be:

Best hair! (Whitney Miller)

Sweetest smile! (Tay Griffin)

Most popular! (Alexis Wright)

They stand bunched together, almost hugging, as they wait for the kids in front of them to file off the bus. I watch the line and wish it would move faster, because I know they are not finished.

"Merry Christmas, Dirty Smelly!" the three of them sing in unison.

"Oh, and also, pro tip for the holiday"—Alexis whirls

around, tosses her long, straight hair back and flashes a sarcastic smile—"I mean, seriously, Dirty Smelly . . ." She pauses. "Take a freakin' shower!"

When the bus jerks to a start, I jam my knees up against the cracked green vinyl seat in front of me and wish I was brave, and not so scared all the time. I stay just like that when the bus stops again and I watch on the other side of the glass as Dirty Smelly gets off, steps into the rain, and walks with a huge backpack over her shoulders along a narrow patch of wet gravel on the edge of a busy road. Cars are whizzing by. She's wearing only a short-sleeved shirt and jeans. No jacket. She must be freezing.

2.

WALKING UP MY EMPTY STREET through the coldest drizzling rain, I can't stop thinking about the girl on the bus and how she didn't even have a jacket, and I don't even know her name, and how saying *nothing* when you want to say *something* is just about the worst feeling ever.

I look around. The sky is totally gray, and besides three life-size plastic reindeer on my neighbor's muddy lawn, it does not feel like Christmas. My neighborhood is not like those huge mansions where the bus dropped off Alexis Wright. No. Our house is the ordinary two-story fading brick one at the top of the hill. No flickering colored lights, no giant Santa, definitely no trumpet-blowing plastic angels on the rooftop. We don't even have a tree. My mom says we are "too old for that kind of thing!"

"We can't even get a really little one?" I asked.

My mom just, like, snapped. "No! And don't ask me again. I'm the only one who waters it, and I'm the only one cleans up the mess, and I am the one who lugs it out to the road," she said. "So, no. Until you learn how to help . . . no!"

Inside my house, I drop my bag at the door.

"Hello?" I call out.

"Hello?" I repeat.

Wait. Let's back up.

If I'm really being honest, I might as well tell you this: as soon as I turn the key, push open the heavy door, and step inside the front hall, my heart starts thumping like crazy, because it's scary-quiet and kind of darkish (before I turn on all the lights), and I am pretty positive (no matter how many times I come home after school to an empty house) there will be somebody waiting for me who will jump out and _____. (Just fill in the blank with anything that scares you. Chances are I've probably worried about *exactly* the same thing.)

I take small, silent steps, making my way from the hallway into the kitchen.

"Hello?" I say to nobody, because nobody is there.

Nobody is ever here but me.

I am about to go lock myself in my room (like I always do) when I hear the front door scrape open, then—footsteps, and in an instant, panic floods me—my heart begins pounding, and I crouch down behind the kitchen counter.

That's when I hear her.

"Oh my God, Frannie, you're such a little baby!"

I rise slowly and peer over the edge of the counter to see my sister standing in the doorway staring at me. She has on her usual uniform of a black T-shirt and skinny jeans.

She raises her eyebrow at me. "Seriously, though," she says, "what's your problem? You're twelve years old! When I was your age, I stayed at home by myself all the time."

"I, um—" I start, but . . . yeah. I give up.

And for a few seconds the quiet grows until—

Carmen looks me over. "Frannie, seriously, *ew*! There's a toothpaste stain on your jeans. Wait a second. Is that my sweater? Did you go into my room?" Carmen's eyes settle on mine. She lights into me. "One, don't ever do that again. And two? That looks horrible on you. Take it off."

I stand there and look at her like, *Are you serious?*

Carmen's eyes widen and her voice gets louder. "Take it off," she demands. "Now!"

I hesitate only for a second; then right there, in the middle of the kitchen, I take her stupid sweater off and throw it at her. "Fine. Take it," I say.

"Nice bra," she says, laughing. "Really, you're *sooo* mature. And oh, my God, Frannie"—she pauses—"that zit, it's like . . ." Carmen moves closer as if she's examining some sort of science experiment growing on my forehead.

I flinch and take a step backward. "Don't," I say in a small voice.

"You should really do something about that," Carmen says, scrunching her nose. "*So* gross. I'm serious."

My heart is somehow lodged in my throat. I swallow hard, bite down on my lip, and just stare back at her. My sister Carmen is seventeen years old and perfect. She's five feet nine inches tall, with dark long hair, and beautiful.

I stand, frozen, in kind of a daze. I do not know what to say. But that's okay, she says it for me—

Carmen picks up the fuzzy blue sweater from the floor. "Seriously, Frannie," she says, turning to walk away. "I literally can't believe we are even *related!*"

3.

FIVE HOURS LATER I AM sitting at the kitchen table, waiting for some "family meeting." Already this is, like, a very strange thing. My family is *not* the type of family that has meetings. Honestly, nobody really ever talks to each other. We don't even *eat* together. I can't remember the last time we were all home at the same time, let alone in the same room.

I don't know what I'm supposed to do, so I try and sit completely still and just not say anything, so I won't get yelled at before the meeting even starts. My sister is sitting across from me, scanning her phone, which keeps buzzing.

I glance at my father, leaning back in his chair at the head of the table. His hair is shaved close to his skull, and he has a big square jaw. As usual, he is dressed in a crisp white shirt and tie, his sleeves neatly rolled up. His eyes are fixed on the television. He has a drink in one hand and the remote in the other. I watch him and quietly hope he is in a good mood. When my dad is in a bad mood, the slightest thing may set him off, and he will scream and yell so loudly that if you are near him, you will feel it in your body. Your heart will literally shake.

My mother is pacing back and forth in the long hallway, practically shouting into her phone about some real estate deal. She's dressed in all black, head to toe: suede black boots, narrow black skirt, cropped knit sweater. She has glossy dark hair and high cheekbones—just like Carmen, except my mom's hair is shorter and sleeker and cut at a sharp, slanty angle. She's wearing bright-red lipstick. "No, listen to me," I hear her say. She seems angry. "Will you be quiet for a minute?" She pauses. "The buyer has until midnight to counter the seller's offer. The offer you are competing against has *no* contingencies. . . ." My mom is *always* on her phone.

I stare out the kitchen window at the three reindeer planted in our neighbor's lawn, lit up and glowing in the darkness.

"So what's this big meeting about?" I hear.

I turn. My brother, Teddy, has stepped into the kitchen. I can see on his face he doesn't really want to be here. He is tall and handsome with thick dark hair, dark blue eyes, and dimples. Ever since he's been home for Christmas break from college, he has the beginnings of a mustache on his face and some light-brown scruff on his chin.

"Hey, Teddy," I say. "You can sit here," I offer, patting the chair beside me, hoping he'll somehow protect me.

"I'm good." He barely looks at me and plops down next to Carmen. He's changed from his usual sweats and hoodie into jeans, a blue sweater over a white T-shirt, and a Princeton baseball cap pulled over his eyes. He smells like shampoo, fresh from the shower—which usually means he's going out for the night.

For a few seconds we all sit around the table and nobody speaks. My heart starts racing. My stomach clenches with the sense that something terrible is just about to happen.

My mom sits down across from my dad. She seems jittery in the way people do when they are nervous for what they are about to say. She glances at my father, then at us. She folds her arms across her chest.

"So, okay," she starts. She takes a big deep breath. "I have an announcement to make, and I don't know how you're going to feel about it, but I think it's going to be really great and I hope you can understand." She clears her throat. "Your dad and I are going to do something new this Christmas."

Carmen suddenly looks up from her phone. "Wait, what?"

My mother sips a glass of water, then sets it back

down. "At first this will seem like it doesn't involve you, but it does."

Now the three of us are all looking up. Even Teddy.

I watch my mom's face. I can see whatever she's going to tell us is something big, and for a second I get kind of excited. Until—

"So," she starts again. She looks at my dad while she speaks. "We are going to take three days while we have vacation, and we are going to treat ourselves to a last-minute holiday getaway, which is something we haven't done in the nineteen years that we've been parents."

My eyes light up. "Wait, are we going too? Where are we going? Is it warm? Are we going to get to swim? Are we going to a beach!"

"Frannie, *shut up!*" Carmen says. "Let her finish."

My mom flashes an uneasy smile. "Actually, it is somewhere warm, but"—there is a pause, during which my mother glances nervously at my father, then goes on— "you three are going to be here, holding down the fort and having your own Christmas." She looks around the table and continues, "We feel like you are old enough, and your father and I want you to show us that you are responsible enough to have Christmas on your own this year."

I look a little stunned. "You're *canceling* Christmas?"

"We're not *canceling* Christmas. Your dad and I are going to have a wonderful time, and you are going to have a wonderful time too. Look, we need to get away. We've been working hard. We work constantly."

Carmen does not seem disappointed. "So, like, wait— we can have people over?" she asks, raising her eyebrows.

"A few friends, sure," answers my mom. "But you know the rules. So help me if we find out you had a party in this house."

I look at my mom. "No presents?" I say. *I can't help it. I just blurt it out.*

My mom stares at me then shakes her head. "Will you be quiet for a minute?" she says sharply. "Listen, there are plenty of kids worse off than you. And, frankly, I feel like you're all getting too old for Christmas."

"Too old for Christmas?" I repeat. My voice is shaky.

"Frannie." I hear him. It's my dad. And if you knew his voice, you would know this means, *Stop. Talking.* He gives me a silent, seething look and slowly zips his finger across his lips.

My body goes on high alert.

My shoulders tense and I get the worst cramp in my stomach. I look at Teddy for help, but he is looking down—messing with his phone under the table.

My mother turns to my sister. "We expect you three to take care of each other and be responsible."

Carmen's eyes grow huge. "Whoa. Wait. I'm *not* watching *her*! Do you really think I'm going to babysit *her* for three days?" She says this right in front of me, like I'm not even here. Then she stops and smiles this big fake smile. "Unless you want to *pay* me?"

"Carmen," says my mother.

"What? I'm totally *kidding!* Wow. Of course we'll take good care of our little *baby* sister," Carmen groans. She looks at me with her big blue eyes. *Grow up*, she mouths, before turning and grinning all innocently at my mom.

I look back at my sister. I seriously hate her. For a split second I wonder if we'll ever be friends.

Teddy glances up briefly from his phone. "We'll be fine," he says.

I feel sick. My face is heating up. "Please, please, please take me with you?" I hear myself whining. "Please?"

My mom rolls her eyes. "One Christmas where we're not together won't kill you," she says. She glances at me, then at Carmen. "We'll bring you some stuff from Jamaica. And we'll all have so much to tell each other when we get back the day after Christmas."

I turn to my mom. I can feel tears and I swallow hard. "But, I mean . . . it's *Christmas*—" I begin, until out of the corner of my eye I catch a look from my dad, and I immediately freeze. For a second, I stop breathing. My chest feels tight. "Sorry," I say softly. My stomach hurts. Like I told you, he's scary. You never know when he might boil over. It's much safer to just shut down and keep whatever you are feeling in. I just try and, like, not even move, not say a word.

We sit in silence, the five of us. The seconds passing on the clock above the sink sound like a ticking time bomb.

Tick.

Tick.

Tick.

"Three days." My father finally speaks. "No parties," he warns.

I glance sideways. His jaw is clenched. His tie, knotted around his collar, is tilted slightly forward.

Teddy is slowly cracking his knuckles one at a time. "No problem." He shrugs and stands. "So we're done?"

I look around at everyone.

Nobody meets my eyes.

No one is talking.

My father leans back in his chair, stirs his drink, and turns the sound up on the television.

That's it. It has been decided.

Within minutes, our so-called family meeting is over.

My mother slides one seat over into Teddy's empty chair and pulls Carmen in close. "You three are going to have so much fun!"

4.

I HOLD IT TOGETHER JUST long enough to climb the stairs two at a time and run straight into my room, do a face-plant onto my bed, and burst into tears. And it doesn't take long for my tears to dissolve into big, heaving, messy sobs. The kind where your whole body shakes and snot is pouring out of your nose and tears are streaming down your face and you're gulping for air because you can't really breathe. In case you are wondering, this is what is running through my head:

I am alone.

I am alone again.

I am always alone!

The way I know, without looking up, that my mother is standing in the doorway to my room is that I can hear her let out a big, aggravated sigh. "Frannie," she says. "Get ahold of yourself. Calm down!"

How am I supposed to calm down? I think, but I don't say, because I'm crying so hard I'm shaking.

She goes on, but not about anything I wish she would tell me. "This room is a mess!" she says. "I can hardly step foot in here. It's so stuffy. Why didn't you open the window and get some fresh air?"

I don't look straight at her. I keep my face mashed into my pillow and glance sideways just long enough for our eyes to meet. She stays right in the doorway, her arms crossed tightly over her chest.

I turn back and bury my face in my pillow. "Why won't you just let me come with you?" I cry.

"Why are you making this so hard on me?" she says, sounding annoyed. "I can't stand this right now. The world does not revolve around you. Your dad and I need to spend a little time together and—"

"But it's *Christmas*. . . ." My voice trails off. Then I completely break down. I am really losing it. "Who is going to hang the stockings? How am I going to survive without you? What am I going to even eat?"

"Frannie. You have got to be kidding me! I'm so tired," she snaps. "There will be plenty of food in the fridge. Your brother and sister will be here with you and—"

"They hate me!" I cry.

"Frannie, just *stop*. They don't *hate* you."

"Yes, they do. . . ." My sobs grow louder. "Teddy doesn't ever want to do *anything* with me, and Carmen is so mean to me. She doesn't even like me!" I try to catch my breath. "They are going to leave me all alone. I know it. I just know it. What if they both go out and leave me all by myself in this house? What am I going to do? You'll be so far away . . . what if something happens to me?" My voice sounds more babyish than I want it to.

"You know what? You are exhausting me," my mom says, finally stepping into the room and looking down at me. "This is nonsense. You're twelve now, and it's only three days. I am so sick of your crying, Frannie. I don't have the energy for this right now."

I wipe my dripping nose and cheeks with the back of my hand and sit up in my bed and look directly at her. "Please, Mom. *Please, please* take me with you?" I plead, clasping my hands together. I can barely speak, I'm crying so hard.

My mom lets out a deep, huffy sigh. "This is not such a big deal. Pull yourself together, Frannie. Come *on*."

Right at this moment Carmen appears in my bedroom doorway. She's wearing her shiny peach-colored pajamas. She throws her arms around my mom's waist. "Oh my gosh, Frannie, you are a hot mess," she laughs. "Stop being such a little brat! Get it together."

5.

THE NEXT MORNING, I AM half-awake and half-asleep when I hear my mother talking to me. It's early. It's still dark outside. I barely understand what's going on. There is drool under my lips, and the lashes of my eyes are caked with a crusty layer of dried-up tears. I turn my head and look through the darkness of my room. The light is on in the upstairs hallway. I squint at my mom. She is dressed in a long zippered dark coat, her neck wrapped in a loose scarf.

"I'm just saying a quick bye," she whispers from the doorway. "Your dad is already in the car. We're rushing to get to our flight."

I feel tears, new tears, leaking out from my eyes. I turn my head away—I don't want her to see that I'm already crying.

Her voice is hurried. "Try and get along with your brother and sister. Listen to them, okay? And be helpful."

I turn back and look at her standing in the door. "Please, Mom, please don't leave me here all by myself."

She lets out a big sigh. "Really, Frannie? Are you going to do this to me right now? I don't have time for this. Your father's going to be furious if I'm late. I thought we went through this last night. I really wish you would pull yourself together—"

"Well, I *really wish* I had a different family," I mutter into my pillow.

"Well, I have news for you, Frannie," she snaps. "You know what, that's life. You can't *magically* get a new family. You need to figure out a way to deal with the one you have." She pauses. "Maybe you should put *that* on your Christmas list," she adds, then turns and leaves down the stairway.

6.

I DON'T KNOW IF YOU'VE ever been awake in a house where everyone else is sleeping. Like, so awake that you lie in your bed with your eyes wide open, just staring into pitch black. I don't bother looking through the window and watching my parents' car disappear down the hill in the darkness. I glance at the clock next to my bed. It's four fifteen a.m. The house is silent. I curl up into a ball, my arms hugging my knees, my covers pulled up over me. Inside my tent of sheets, I can hear my heart racing.

"Merry Christmas Eve," I say out loud in a whisper. The salty tears sting my cheeks. I close my eyes and wish I somehow knew how to make the hurt, hurt less. And I wonder how long I can stay right here in my room, under my covers. Hiding.

Three minutes later, I just can't take it. I throw my bare feet onto the floor, step over the piles of my not-put-away clothes, and tiptoe down the empty hallway until I'm standing in front of Carmen's closed bedroom door, my hand gripping the doorknob. On the count of three, I bite my lower lip, hold my breath, and slowly turn my hand and push against the door, praying the hinge doesn't creak as I step inside. My feet sink into Carmen's shaggy carpet. I strain my eyes and move toward her bed. All I can make out is a huge lump of blankets. When Carmen turned sixteen, my parents bought her a giant queen-size mattress. She keeps it on the floor, and she has, like, a hundred extra pillows, or, okay, maybe seven, and she has a big cozy down comforter that is so snug and warm it feels like a sleeping bag. Her room is twice as big as my room, and if it wasn't so dark, you could see that she's neat. I mean, like, really, really neat. Everything is put away. Everything is perfect.

I stand frozen, my toes up against the edge of her bed.

"Carmen," I barely whisper.

"Carmen?" I try again.

The room is pitch black. I can't even see my hand. I peel back the comforter and slip into her bed. Underneath the covers, I lie on my side, my face to Carmen's back, and—once my eyes adjust to the shadowy darkness—I watch the outline of her shoulder rise and fall with her breath. Everything about Carmen is better than me. Her sheets are softer. Her blanket is warmer. I can feel the heat of her body lying an arm's length away, and for the first time since I've been crying, I shut my eyes and—

Carmen yanks the covers off me.

"Oh my God! What do you think you're doing?" she moans. "Get out!"

I open my eyes and whisper into the darkness, "Mom and Dad left and . . . um . . . I don't want to be all alone in my room. Please, Carmen, please let me stay."

"Seriously, what is your problem?" she grunts. "Get out of my room!"

"Please," I try again. This time I scoot over just a tiny bit closer. "I won't bother you, I swear. I won't even move."

Carmen pulls the comforter up over her head. "Ugh! You have the worst breath! Get out!!!!"

I shut my eyes. "Please," I whisper, "can I just sleep on the floor? I swear, you won't even know I'm here."

Carmen doesn't say anything.

I lie there on her bed for a few more seconds. "Can I please, just like—"

"Oh, wow, you are so annoying! FINE!" She sighs loudly. "Just DO NOT TALK TO ME."

I slip off the bed and onto the floor. I rest my cheek right up against the scratchy carpet.

Out of nowhere Carmen hurls a pillow at my head.

"Thanks," I whisper.

I close my eyes. "Merry Christmas Eve, Carm," I call out into the stillness.

"Oh my gosh, Frannie!" she hisses. *"Shut up!"*

7.

I WAKE UP ON THE floor of Carmen's room shivering, because I do not have a blanket. It's the day before Christmas, but it's not, like, *snowing*. I've never in my life seen real powdery white snow. But it is rainy and cold and the house is freezing. I run my hand over my arm and feel the goose bumps. It is still kind of dark, because Carmen sleeps with all her blinds pulled down, like a vampire, but slivers of gray morning light are leaking in between the slats. And look, I try. I do. I lay here without moving, not saying a word. But after a good fifteen minutes—or maybe *five*—I peek up and look over at Carmen and her mound of down comforter and pillows.

"Carmen," I lean forward and whisper.

"Carmen," I try again.

I flop back down onto the floor and stare up at the

ceiling. *The quiet is freaking me out.* It's so still, I can hear everything: the clanking of the wind whipping outside, the rain pelting against the windows. Carmen breathing.

"Carmen?" I say in the softest whisper. "Can I please just, like, get on the corner of your bed? I promise I won't take too much of the covers."

Nothing.

"Carmen?" I try again. "Carm?"

"Oh, wow. Are you really doing this right now?" Carmen finally moans. "Fine! You can get in my bed if you just *stop talking!!!*"

"Oh my gosh, thank you, I am so freezing," I whisper into the dim light, and—before she changes her mind—leap up and slip between the super-soft flannel sheets and her gigantic comforter. I curl into the bed and turn toward Carmen.

"Carm?" I ask softly. "Are you awake?"

Carmen's eyes snap open. "Frannie, you are seriously, and I mean, *seriously*, driving me crazy!" She sounds angry. "What about *not talking* do you not get?"

I stay silent for as long as I can, but my thoughts are racing. I watch Carmen closely, staring at her closed eyelids. Then, I just can't hold it in any longer: "Aren't you a little bit freaked out at all that we're by ourselves for Christmas?"

She opens her eyes again. "What is wrong with you!" she says, her voice growing louder. "We're only going to be alone for three days. You need to suck it up and deal. I don't understand what you're so afraid of. Nothing is going to happen in the next three days."

"But, like . . . are we even going to have Christmas?"

"Frannie, listen—" She hesitates, and for just a second, she looks right at me. "It's not the end of the world, okay? I'll even consider hanging out with you if you can try and be a normal human being for the next three days."

"Really?" I break into a smile. "You'll hang out with me?"

"Yeah. I mean, a little." She laughs and turns away, shifting her weight on the mattress.

"Can we order Chinese takeout and watch movies tonight like we always do on Christmas Eve?"

"Fine, I'll watch *one* movie with you." Carmen takes a breath and lets it out so loud I can hear it. "Why do you want to hang out with me? Don't you have friends your own age?"

"I'm just, like, I don't know . . ." I fumble for words. "I'm always really shy when I meet new people. I'm not like you."

"Okay, that's the most stupid thing I ever heard"—Carmen briefly looks away, then spins back to face me—"and FYI, it doesn't come naturally to me either, *duuhhh!* I mean, I'm never super excited to be around people I don't know at first, but you have to just put yourself out there." My sister stares hard at me. "You never go anywhere, or do anything—" She stops and thinks about it for a second, then shakes her head as if she's absolutely disgusted. "It's, like, just do it! Try something! I seriously don't get you. . . ."

There's a long silence.

"What about boys?" Carmen raises her eyebrows slightly. "Any cuties you have your eye on?"

I shake my head and feel my cheeks heat up. I don't tell her that I'm afraid to go near boys. I'm afraid they'll laugh at me.

"Well, maybe you just haven't met the right boy," she teases. Then out of nowhere Carmen sits straight up and stretches her arms over her head in a big yawn. Her fresh-off-the-pillow hair is all crazy, but she's still, like, shining. I look at her and that sparkle in her eyes and try to imagine what it would be like to be that pretty and confident and sure of myself.

She reaches from the bed to the window and pulls the string to raise the blinds, filling the room with dull gray light.

"Here's a thought." Carmen laughs and then rips the covers off both of us and leaps to her feet. She looks down at me lying on her bed in my pink glitter heart pajama bottoms and sky-blue tank top. "Why don't you start with getting out of your room for the next three days—" Carmen stares at me like I am crazy, then shakes her head and turns away. "Conquer your fears, Frances!"

she exclaims, mocking me and laughing as she drags the comforter with her across the room, wearing it like a cape wrapped around her shoulders.

Right before she steps into the hallway, she turns back and lets loose the slightest smile. "Believe me when I say this: one day, it's just going to click and you're going to thank me."

8.

WHEN I WALK INTO THE kitchen, Teddy is standing in front of the microwave, heating up a frozen burrito. We all slept in. It is already after noon.

I flash my brother a huge smile. "Merry Christmas Eve, Teddy!"

"Hey." He nods but doesn't look up. He seems sleepy, and his dark hair is messy and falling into his eyes. His jeans are slung low around his hips, just enough to show the top of his red boxers, and he's shirtless. His abs look like a Ninja Turtle's.

"Aren't you going to say Merry Christmas Eve?" I ask him.

"Merry Christmas Eve," Teddy responds in a voice that is the opposite of merry. I mean, generally speaking, Teddy's not a big talker, but, like, it's Christmas Eve!

I turn to Carmen, already sitting at the table eating a bowl of granola and yogurt. She's still wrapped in her comforter cape. Her nest of dark hair is twisted and tied in a heap on top of her head, secured by a pencil, and she's wearing her black-rimmed glasses.

"That looks good," I say, eyeing her breakfast. "Can I have some?"

"Oh my gosh, Frannie," Carmen groans, and glares at me. "Are you not capable of walking to the counter and pouring yourself some cereal? Can you not do *anything* on your own?" She rolls her eyes and resumes eating, and right at this moment my heart drops, because I gather very quickly the whole being-nice-to-me thing is totally over.

Teddy sits down at the table right beside Carmen. I sink into the empty chair across from them.

Nobody is talking.

The fluorescent light over the table is buzzing.

I watch Teddy squirt half the bottle of Frank's hot sauce on his burrito and take a big bite. He turns and grins at Carmen with his mouth full. "Shane's all in. Did you talk to Jules yet?" he asks, and takes a gulp of juice.

Carmen grabs her phone and immediately begins texting. "I'm so on that, dude," she says. "This is going to be epic."

"What? Wait. What do you mean?" I ask. "*What* is going to be epic?"

Carmen and Teddy, sitting side by side, turn and look at each other like they have some big secret.

Carmen shrugs. "We're having some people over tonight." She shoots me a threatening glare. "And, look, don't be a little baby about it."

My mouth falls open. "But, like—Dad, he said . . ."

Teddy laughs. "Don't sweat it, Frances. You worry too much."

A very bad nervous feeling rises through my stomach and up my chest. "But aren't people going to be with their families for Christmas Eve?" I ask.

"Dude, *relax*," says my brother. "People will do their church stuff and then their family stuff and then—"

"People will come to our house and do their chill stuff," finishes Carmen, nudging Teddy with her elbow, and they both start to laugh.

I begin to panic a little bit. "You guys—um, seriously, this sounds like . . . this sounds like a really bad idea. If Mom and Dad find out—"

Teddy cuts me off. "Nobody is going to find out. Relax!"

"I'll tell you what," says Carmen, raising her eyebrows. "If you keep your mouth shut and just let us do our thing without freaking out, I will go shopping with you and get you some clothes so you don't have to steal mine."

My eyes open wide. "You will?"

Carmen stands up from her chair and carries her bowl to the sink. "Well?" she says, her back to me. "Will you keep your mouth shut and not be a little baby about our party?"

I watch her. "You're not leaving, though, right?" I ask her. "And you'll still watch a movie with me?"

Carmen sighs. "Yes, Frannie," she answers in a voice that's mocking mine. "We're not leaving and I'll still watch a movie with you."

I wait for a second, my eyes going from Teddy to Carmen. *This is the longest we've all actually sat together in a very long time.* "Okay then," I answer. "Fine."

9.

I MAY BE TWELVE, BUT it doesn't take me long to figure out that Carmen is *not* planning on watching a movie with me at all. Carmen is in full-on party mode. Or, I should say, party-planning mode. She's still in her pajamas, minus the comforter, in a heated discussion with Teddy and his best friend, Shane, about rearranging the furniture in the living room to make space for people.

Shane is wearing jeans, a green-and-navy flannel shirt, and one of those funny Santa hats. I don't mind seeing him. To be honest, Shane's the only one in the Christmas spirit. Out of all of Teddy's friends, Shane is my favorite. He has dark brown skin and he's incredibly good-looking, with big square shoulders and a movie-star smile. I watch the three of them move the pale-blue love seat into my dad's study, then push the big leather sofa and the piano up against the windows.

Teddy passes by me on his way to the kitchen. "What's up, Frances!" He plants his hand on my shoulder and squeezes. For Teddy, that is, like, whoa, a lot of communication. For a second my heart feels warm, and I'm a little less nervous.

I sink down to the floor, my back against the hallway wall, and quietly watch them. Teddy returns with two bags of chips, keeps one, and tosses Shane the other.

Shane plunks down on the sofa and looks up, noticing me in the hallway. "Frannie!" he says, his eyes lighting up. He stretches out his hand and waves.

I smile shyly back.

"Come on in!" he says, patting the sofa cushion. "You can help us—"

"No, don't!" Carmen gestures at me like I'm a pesky stray dog. You know, like, *scat*. "Frannie, go away, this is grown-up activity." She looks at me as she says it, arching her eyebrows. "I mean it, go away."

Shane turns to her and laughs. "That's harsh, dude." He glances at me with a look that's like, *sorry*.

Maybe she feels suddenly guilty for being the meanest sister on earth, but for whatever reason, by the time it's dark out, Carmen allows me to sit on the floor of her room and watch her get ready for their party. Her best friend, Jules, is with her; they are both armed with blow-dryers and curling irons and smell like perfume. When their favorite song comes on, the two of them lock eyes and smile at each other.

CARMEN: Oh my God, yes! It's Jasmine's new song!!!! Turn it upppp!

JULES: Oh my gosh, yes! Jasmine! I looooove this song!

CARMEN (*dancing and singing into her curling iron as if it was a microphone*): Jasmine is perfection! I really, freakin' love her!

JULES: Seriously, she couldn't be cuter!

CARMEN: She's so young—she's like Frannie's age, only a thousand times cooler!

After her lip-sync performance, Carmen drops down cross-legged in front of the mirror hanging on the back of her door and begins applying purple-black mascara. She looks at me through the mirror's reflection. "Frannie, do you have to sit there and stare at me? Why don't you go watch a movie in the basement or something?"

I try to keep panic from spilling out of my eyes and just keep quiet—because, well, number one, it is nine o'clock at night and it's pouring and there is no way I am going down to the cold, dark basement in the middle of a thunderstorm to watch a movie by myself and, number two, I don't say anything because, as you probably have guessed by now, there is a 100 percent chance Carmen will bite my head off.

Jules slips into her outfit: a very short red dress. It's sleeveless. "Oh my gosh, a movie might be fun, Carm!" She glances at her phone. "Hey, we actually have some time before everyone gets here." She smiles at Carmen and then at me. "I am kind of obsessed with holiday movies! Let's do it, Carm!"

With Jules's invitation, for just a second I am hopeful. I look back at Carmen in the mirror: she dusts her eyes with smoky bronze shadow before carefully lining her lips with pink shimmery gloss.

"We can watch anything you want," I promise her.

Carmen pops up to her feet and admires herself. She's changed out of her pajamas into a red-hot, body-clinging dress and scuffed black boots. She does a deep forward bend at the waist and runs her fingers through her glossy dark hair, then flips back up straight and plays with it, watching herself carefully in the mirror until strands of long hair effortlessly fall around her face just the way she likes it. The entire room smells like hair spray.

"What do you think, Carm?" asks Jules, turning to me with a wink. "We can get all cozy on the couch in the basement and snuggle up with this little nugget!"

"Um, no! Are you kidding? Sorry, Frannie, you are going to have to solo it tonight. You'll be fine." She stops to grab Jules's hand and pulls her out the door of her room, turning off the light with me still in here.

I can hear her voice all the way down the stairs. "Wow, you picked the perfect dress. We are twinning so hard right now in red! Same, same, and you're rockin' it!" Carmen laughs. "Oh, man. Tonight is going to literally be epic!"

10.

I AM THE ONLY ONE who doesn't change for the party. Until the first guests arrive, I am pacing around the downstairs, still dressed in my pink glitter heart pajama bottoms and sky-blue tank top. A lit-up spinning disco light has somehow materialized and has been hung in the living room, and Teddy and Shane have rearranged the furniture to make space for a dance floor. They brought the fancy speakers out of my dad's study and placed them in the corners. Almost all the lights downstairs are turned off. Of course Carmen has made a party playlist, and in minutes the quiet house is pulsating with music.

Everywhere I look is a disaster waiting to happen: my father's flat-screen television, my mother's expensive vase in the hallway . . . the fact that it's pouring outside and there are already muddy footprints all over the carpet and floor. My mom would flip. My dad? Forget it. *We're toast,* I think, as I plant myself on the top step of the stairwell and start to panic.

The first guests to arrive are Carmen's friends, six girls, all dressed in jeans and cute little tops and Santa hats, squealing and shouting.

GIRL NUMBER 1 *(flipping her hair back and combing it with her fingers):* It's literally pouring out! *(shouting over the extremely loud music)* My hair is soaked!

CARMEN *(grinning):* Did you guys park at the bottom of the hill like we said?

GIRL NUMBER 2 *(high-fiving):* Of course, Carm! I'm all over that!

Next, a carload of Teddy's friends stream in through the open door. I can feel the cold air rushing in, the wind and rain blowing.

"What's up, big man? How's Princeton?" asks a tall, skinny guy dressed in jeans and a polo. I watch as each of them greet Teddy with I-haven't-seen-you-since-the-summertime hugs. My brother is one of those guys who doesn't say much but who *everyone* loves.

Teddy is all smiles right now, dressed in a navy blazer over a T-shirt, jeans, and this funny fedora—he can pull off pretty much whatever. The second Teddy turns away from his guy friends, he is surrounded by a semicircle of girls with flirtatious laughs and gleaming-white smiles.

"Teddy!" they squeal. They fling their arms around his

neck and kiss him on the cheek.

As soon as people move from the front hallway, more kids show up and plow in through the doorway: stampedes of girls in skimpy dresses, guys with colorful plaid shirts under V-neck sweaters. As I watch I just, like, shake my head. I have the worst feeling this is going to end really, really badly.

One hour later it is so loud. So loud! Like, you wouldn't even be able to hear me talking if you were one foot away. You'd have to shout for me to hear anything you said. One hundred people jammed into a house meant for five means one hundred voices bouncing off the walls. Someone spilled a can of soda on the front entryway carpet. I try not to say anything and just, like, keep to myself— until I watch a kid in a dark hoodie and jeans take three uneven wobbly steps inside the front door and vomit into my mother's expensive vase. And so, yeah, what I am thinking as I try to push my way through the crowd is *I need to find Carmen and Teddy now!*

The entire downstairs is packed with kids, and the disco light is glittering. It's hard to see. Not to mention I'm about three feet shorter than everyone here. I stand on my tippy toes, but that doesn't work, so I drag a chair out of the kitchen, step up on it, and peer over the sea of dancing bodies. I finally get a glimpse of Carmen across the room, standing and laughing in her shimmery red dress. You can't miss her. The way the disco light hits her face, her eyelids glimmer. As soon as I spot her, I know what I have to do, and in a moment I am pushing through the crowd. I wriggle and worm my way through a maze of sweaty bodies. I'm getting shoved from every side, elbows knocking against my head as people swing their arms and rock their hips, shouting and laughing. Out of nowhere, some girl wearing a red Santa hat knocks into me and accidentally spills a drink streaming down my back. My feet are bare and the floor is really sticky and already littered with empty red plastic cups. And it's not cold anymore. It's a thousand degrees in here! The air is, like, moist. It smells like hot breath and body odor. It's overwhelming. It feels almost like I might get crushed. I can barely squeeze through or see where I'm going. The closer I get to Carmen, the more relieved I feel until—

She looks up and sees me.

"*What* are you doing down here?" she demands. Her voice sounds scratchy and raw from shouting over the music.

I can tell from the way she looks at me that she wants me to be gone.

She turns to this guy I have never seen before. He is wearing baggy jeans that hang low, unlaced Timberland boots, a backward baseball cap, and a faded T-shirt. He is tall and athletic-looking with big ears. He glances down at me and then walks off.

Carmen looks like she's going to kill me. She grabs my arm and yanks it, her fingers digging in hard as she drags me toward the stairs. "Frannie, seriously, you need to *leave!*"

I look back at her like, *Leave? Where am I supposed to go?* My whole heart feels like it's going to explode. I back away, but Carmen tightens her grip, pinning my arm behind my back and leaning in until she's practically shouting in my ear. The music is so loud, I can hardly hear. "What are you so worried about?" she snaps, and grabs harder and twists my arm. "Stop being such an idiot! What's your deal?"

I feel her wet spit hit the inside of my ear.

"There's too many people here," I tell her, gesturing at the bazillion kids jammed in our living room. "I'm scared something bad is going to happen."

"Oh my gosh, you literally need to learn to chill!" Carmen digs her fingers in deeper. "These are my friends, and we're having fun!"

I am trying so hard not to cry. "But the house—"

Her eyes flash with anger. "Oh my God, everything is fine! Just GO AWAY! You're so annoying. Go find your own friends!" Carmen glares at me and finally lets go of my arm. "You need to get a life!" she shouts. Her raspy loud voice all but stops the dancing around us, and for an instant everyone kind of freezes.

I feel the tears rise up. I swallow them. I somehow

make it through the swarms of totally random people I don't recognize and practically collide with Teddy on the stairs. Teddy does not look up because he is making out with some very tall girl with broad shoulders and long brown hair, in jeans and a clingy red sweater. Have you seriously ever just stood there waiting while people are, like, busy kissing? It's so awkward! I stand on the steps, waiting for Teddy to look up. Then finally, I just blurt it out:

ME: Teddy, the floor is shaking! There's some random guy sitting on top of the piano! There are, like, thirty people in the kitchen! Some guy puked in Mom's fancy vase!

TEDDY: _____. (He says nothing.)

It's like I'm invisible. I'm not even here!

Fine, I think to myself, but I don't say because I have a huge lump in my throat.

As I squeeze past the two of them, Teddy comes up for air. The tall girl giggles.

"Take it easy, Frances," Teddy yells over his shoulder. "Loosen up, have some fun!"

11.

I HATE THIS FAMILY, I *hate them so much*, I tell myself, slamming the door to my room and turning the lock. I step over my clothes and dive, facedown, onto my bed. My ears are ringing. The floor is vibrating with music and voices. I flip over and stare at the ceiling. My hand goes to my face. I have this habit of picking my skin when I'm worried. My fingers find the zit on my forehead and go to work, digging in until there's blood and it hurts. *So gross*—I remember Carmen's words. She's right. *I'm such an idiot. I'm such a mess. Something is really wrong with me.* I have this horrible, hopeless feeling inside, and Carmen's voice is looping in my mind: *Get a life! Go find your own friends.* The way she said it, the look in her eyes.

Two hours later, I wake up feeling puffy. My forehead is throbbing. At first, I don't notice the absolute and utter silence. Then I bolt up in my bed and brace myself with my arms. *Maybe they listened to me and told everyone to leave?*

I get up and walk to my door.

I open it just a crack.

I hear *complete quiet*. I feel a jolt of total panic. I take a few steps. Carmen's door is open and the lights are out in her room. It's empty. I stand at the top of the stairs and look down.

It's dark.

"Teddy?" I call out.

I'm so scared. My heart is pounding. The entire house is motionless.

"Hello? You guys, this isn't funny. Hello?" The downstairs lights are out, but I can make out those bright-red cups all over the rug at the bottom of the stairs. The house is, like—

Trashed.

"Carmen?" I repeat in a really quiet voice. "Teddy? You guys?" The worst feeling spreads through my chest. It's not hard to figure out—

Nobody is here.

They are *gone*.

What do I do? I will tell you what I do: I step into my parents' dark, empty room. It's cold. The bed is made and the lights are out. I sit on the very edge of the all-white sheets, pick up the house phone on the nightstand,

and dial Carmen's cell. No answer. I call back four times. Finally, on the fifth try Carmen picks up.

"What?" she snarls.

I try to sound calm, so she won't get angry. "Where are you?" I ask.

"We went out."

I take a small breath. "When are you coming home?"

"We'll be back when we're back."

"But—" I start, my voice shaking. "Couldn't you just come home now?"

"Oh my gosh, Frannie! You're *fine!* Are you literally kidding me right now? Get over it—" And then?

She hangs up.

I've been trying to ignore the little voice in my head telling me to make sure the front door is locked, but I can't anymore. I go into Teddy's room, flip on the light, and grab one of his lacrosse sticks. I grip it like a baseball bat and take the stairs one step at a time.

"Hello," I whisper. I can hear my heart beating. "Hello?" I repeat.

Downstairs, the entire house is totally dark and quiet. There is garbage everywhere. Red plastic cups, soda cans, a roll of toilet paper strung all over the place. The air smells stuffy and sweaty. I look around and get the feeling they all left in a hurry. I'm so mad at Carmen. *She promised me she wouldn't leave.* I check the front door to make sure it's locked, then set an Olympic speed record running straight up the stairs and back to my room.

Inside, I close and lock the door, pushing my desk up against it, which somehow makes me feel the tiniest bit safer.

This is going to be the worst Christmas anyone can possibly ever have, I think as I crumple into my single bed. The tears that start streaming down my cheeks are not the kind I cried before. They are big and deep and silent tears that spill slowly out, one by one. *I just want to curl up and disappear.* Blinks of lightning illuminate the bare walls of my room. I look out the window into the night—the three reindeer lit up on my neighbor's lawn. I stare at them. I listen to the howling wind, the rain pounding down, and I just keep thinking, *something in me feels like I just don't belong.*

My mom didn't even hug me bye.

I feel so alone.

"Is anyone listening?" I say out loud. My voice is trembling.

I watch a bolt of lightning zigzag across the blue-black sky. I stare at it and whisper out loud, *"Someone please help."*

I cling to my blanket, shut my eyes tightly, and try to picture where I wish I was . . . *I'd definitely want a snowy white Christmas, and a tree! Oh, and also, beautifully wrapped presents—like new clothes, and one of those fuzzy blue sweaters like the one Carmen has and a dog to keep me company, or no, a puppy!* I sniffle back the tears. I cry into my pillow. *More than anything in the world, I just wish I could be someplace warm and cozy with people who love me.*

I flop over and watch the red numbers on my clock change to 12:03. I curl up small and lie very still. I am so sad I can barely breathe.

"Merry Christmas," I whisper. I say it in the softest voice into the dark—to *me*.

PART TWO

12.

AS I AM FALLING, I don't feel like I'm falling, I feel like I'm floating in a kind of slow motion. My arms are spread out, and I can feel the air push against my face . . . it's like time is suspended—all fear just, like, *vanishes*.

I'm not sure how to explain it: if I tell you that I fell from who knows where onto a very soft warm bed, bounced three feet up, and landed facedown with a *THUMP*, you'd think I am crazy! And look, *I don't blame you!*

You know how when you wake up, and at first you're, like, bleary-eyed and totally confused and your head is all foggy and you don't know where you are?

Yeah. Well—

I'm lying on this bed, just flat sprawled out, my chin digging into the mattress, my hands dangling off the sides. Just how you could imagine lying in a bed if you dropped out of the sky! *Splat!* And I'm thinking how, *I'm just not going to open my eyes, I'm not going to look,* when I feel the weight of little footsteps climbing across the length of my body. My eyes pop open only to see: the cutest, most adorable little doggy I have ever seen is all up in my face, licking me! Soft, scratchy licks all over my mouth and cheeks. *This has to be a dream—like, this isn't happening. You know, like in the movies?* The puppy is chocolate brownish-black with a dark nose. His tiny shiny body wiggles when he wags his stubby white piggy tail.

"Are you real?" I ask almost in a whisper, which is exactly when his razor-sharp little teeth sink into my fingers.

"Ow!" I laugh. *Okay, whoa, I totally felt that!*

"Oh my gosh, you are so cute!" I sink my hand into his fur and push back his soft, floppy ears. "Well, hi there. Hi, puppy. Where'd you come from?" The puppy is squirming and licking and nipping my fingers. I have the biggest smile on my face. I mean, it's impossible not to smile when you are snuggling with a puppy! That fur, his wet, cold nose. His breath is hot and sweet. I lift him to my face and inhale. Puppies smell so good, better than perfume.

The puppy pins me on the bed with his big fat paws, licking me all over. "Stop!" I giggle. He pauses for a second and looks right at me. His eyes are like two dark, swirly marbles.

"Hey," I whisper, and smile again. The puppy wriggles and squiggles out of my hands, leaps off the bed like he can fly, and slides across the wide-planked wood floor, skidding to a stop.

I sit up. I look all around and—

Look, this is going to sound crazy, I don't know how to say this, but . . .

I am *not* in my room.

This is *not* my bed!

I have to squint because the brightest light is streaming through the window. I swing my bare feet over the side of the bed and step onto a smooth floor and walk over to the window. *Holy cow! It is snowing!* The most beautiful fluffy snowflakes are cascading like confetti. Everything outside the window looks soft and dreamy, covered by a blanket of snowy white powder.

I don't quite understand how this is happening right now.

I press my forehead to the icy glass, watch my breath melt the frost, then spin back around and try to make some kind of sense of where the heck I am. The room is small and cozy. All of the walls are painted a pretty pale blue. There is a lemon-yellow cushy chair near the window and a mountain of stuffed animals on the floor by the bed: a big-eyed moose, a shaggy dog, a fuzzy fat chicken, a piggy (pink), an orange cat, and a huge bright-green turtle big enough to sit on. There is a bedside table, a lamp, a neat stack of books . . . I go over and pick them up one at a time, reading off the titles in my mind:

Anne of Green Gables

A Wrinkle in Time

Little House on the Prairie

There are shiny, satiny blue prize ribbons pinned on the lampshade and above the head of the bed, and posters of horses plastered to the walls.

I know what you're thinking: *I'm crazy, I'm dreaming!* Yeah. I'm thinking that, too, as I step across the floor and stare into the white-framed mirror leaning on top of the matching white dresser. If this *was* a movie, go ahead and imagine me dropping my jaw. . . . How do I put this?

I am not me!

There. I said it.

No messy dark hair.

No pink glitter heart pajama bottoms and sky-blue tank top.

No dried bloody scab on my forehead.

I take a step back and look myself up and down. I am in the body of a girl who looks about twelve, with thick blond hair that's almost yellow. Two long braids fall over my shoulders. I am dressed in striped red-and-white candy-cane pajamas. I move closer and study my reflection: I have braces on my teeth, with tiny neon-orange elastic bands. My skin is smooth and clear and my eyes are this shocking blue, the color of a swimming pool. There are specks of light-brown freckles across the bridge of my nose. *Oh my gosh!* I lift my eyebrows up and down and kind of giggle. The puppy is going bananas, making yelping sounds and jumping up on my legs and ankles. All I keep thinking is, *This is so crazy! How is this happening?*

I glance out the window at the snow, then turn back to my reflection. There are stickers lining the edge of the mirror:

I ♥ PONIES!

A red heart that says *Horse Crazy!*

A fortune from a fortune cookie: *Follow your dreams!*

Ⓓ Ⓐ Ⓚ Ⓞ Ⓣ Ⓐ spelled out in round lavender-shaded stickers.

"Dakota," I read out loud, and laugh because right this minute it hits me that my voice is *not* my voice at all. It's scratchy and kind of strong. The puppy is jumping and making high-pitched yappy sounds. I bend down and pick him up.

"Hey," I say quietly, lifting his wet nose to mine. "Hey, you," I whisper. His little black eyes are fixed on me. For a second I get the feeling like maybe the puppy senses what is going on. Like, maybe he can sniff me out. Maybe he knows I am not who I seem. "Do you know?" I ask, staring into his eyes. "Am I dreaming? Is this real?"

The minute I set down the puppy and watch him scamper and skid across the floor and yelp adorable puppy yelps, I hear a knock on the door, followed by—

"Dakota . . . honey?"

Oh, snap! If this is a dream, there are other people in it!

I spin around and kind of panic. "Just a sec," I blurt out. My heart starts pounding. My face gets hot. A thousand things shoot through my mind. You know, like, *Who am I? Where am I? What do I do next?* I quickly turn to the bed and try and quiet the debate rattling in my head—*should I stay, should I attempt to leave?* I picture myself standing up on the mattress and jumping up and down like it's a trampoline. I take a big deep breath. . . . *Could I even bounce myself back to real life?* I collapse onto the soft bed and stare up into the ceiling. It all comes washing over me: *the party last night, the darkness, being alone in my room, feeling so hopeless.* I sit upright, and the puppy jumps up next to me on the bed.

I look down into his dark eyes. "Why would I want to be all by myself when I could be with you?" I ask him. I scoop him up and hold him eyeball-to-eyeball. "Puppy," I whisper. "I think I definitely have officially gone crazy!"

I hear another knock at the door. "Honey?"

I feel a twang of jittery nerves.

I glance around the room . . . the old-fashioned bed, the hand-stitched quilt, the blue first-place ribbons, the posters of horses, the snow falling down outside the window. I nuzzle the puppy's velvety nose to mine. As crazy as this sounds . . . I feel safe for once.

"Dakota, sweetheart?" I hear the voice call out.

"Honey?" The voice is warm and reassuring.

I set the puppy down and stand. I have this odd sensation in my stomach that feels like a flock of butterflies are fluttering their wings. *Should I stay? I mean . . . can I really do this?* I take a huge breath and let it back out. Then I find myself moved to do something I'd never thought I'd do—

I reach for the door and open it.

13.

THE DOOR SWINGS OPEN AND a woman walks in. She's wearing faded blue jeans, no socks, big furry slippers, and a pale-pink turtleneck sweater. Her long blond hair is the color of straw and is loosely tied up in a messy bun with flyaway wisps hanging down and framing her face. She has big hoop earrings and this huge shining smile.

"Merry Christmas!" She beams, and before I have time to flinch, she instantly pulls me in close. Her arms are strong and her sweater feels like the fur of a kitten. When I breathe in, she smells like wood smoke and maple syrup. And look, she hugs me and I hug her back, okay? Maybe that sounds funny, but I can't really explain it—except to say, when she holds me, it feels like I can breathe. It's, like, soothing. Those seven seconds feel like total relief.

"Ohhhh, this is my favorite time ever," she whispers gently in my ear, "extra-long Christmas snuggles with my sweet Bear."

With her hands on both my shoulders, the woman steps back and looks at me, grinning. "So, how did you like being woken up by Romeo on Christmas morning?" Her smile is huge. Did I already say that? But I can't not tell you because it's the first time anyone's looked at me like that in, like . . . *ever*. We both look down at the puppy, playfully scrambling around the floor of the bedroom.

The woman laughs. "Your dad and I—we couldn't resist. We thought we'd let the puppy wake you up." She smiles and she's still looking at me, right in the eyes. "How'd you sleep, sweetheart? Are you feeling better?" She reaches out and cups her hand against my face. "Did visions of sugarplums dance in your head?"

I just, like, nod. Because, well. I think you understand. I don't really know *who* or *where* I even am!

The mom walks to the window and gazes into the snowy white blizzard. "Boy, is it gorgeous out!" she says. "We got so much snow overnight, two feet, maybe more! Your dad and I shoveled out to the barn and the chapel." She turns back to me and arches her eyebrows high. "Hey, do you think Santa's reindeer came? Are there any tracks in the snow?"

I know I'm twelve years old and my mom thinks I'm too old for Christmas, but I will admit this: every bone in my body wants to jump up and look to see if there are tracks in the snow! I don't do that, though. Instead, I drop down on the bed and just try not to completely freak out. For a second I consider confiding in Dakota's mom, just blurting it all out. You know, like, *I know I look like I'm Dakota, but inside I'm really Frannie!* Yeah. No. How weird would that sound? Also, the truth is, it feels so good to pretend right now. I have no idea if this is some crazy dream or if I'm really here, but I'm not going to lie: I kind of love Dakota and I kind of love her mom.

She walks back over to the bed and sits down beside me. She is still smiling this big, squinty-eyed smile. I feel her shoulder up against my arm. Normally I get really nervous around people I don't even know, but there's something about her that makes me feel safe, and, like— *calm.* We sit side by side for a long minute. She gazes over at me and breathes in a big breath. I glance sideways at her and I inhale too. She's the kind of person who you instantly want to be like. Do you know what I mean? And, yeah, I think Romeo totally agrees. He jumps up into Dakota's mom's lap, pins his fat paws to her shoulders, and starts licking her face all over.

Dakota's mom begins to giggle. "Oh, you are so cute, those are wet kisses, and your ears, yes, Romeo"—she runs her finger's against the grain of his fur—"your ears are the softest." Romeo loves it. He closes his eyes and pushes his head into her hand, whimpers, then goes right back to licking. "Okay, little Romeo, don't eat my hair!" She pauses to untangle the puppy's mouth from her loose strands of hair and falls straight back onto the bed, looping her arm through mine, pulling me down too. The two of us lie on our backs, bumping shoulders, with Romeo's tickling paws dancing over our chests. He takes turns nibbling and licking our faces. "Oh, those are wet kisses!" The mom giggles. I do too.

14.

APPARENTLY I HAVE—I MEAN Dakota has—a little sister. Her name is Rosie. I pick up on this when she peers mischievously into the door, then runs full steam into my room and jumps up on top of us.

She is *adorable*.

"There she is, there's my sweet girl!" says the mom, sweeping her arms open wide.

We have a group hug on my bed. I just let it happen. I've never had anyone pay me this much attention. It feels better than I could possibly tell you. "Ohhhhh," the mom breathes. She's, like, two inches away from me. "Christmas morning cuddles. Nothing better. My two little monkeys are the *best present ever*."

Rosie buries her face into the mom's hair. "Mama," she whispers the way little kids whisper, which is to say adorably loudly. "Did Santa eat our cookies? Can we go downstairs yet? Can we go see the presents?"

Rosie is maybe three or four years old. She has fair skin, pink cheeks, really, really long eyelashes, curly wild bright-blond hair, and a million freckles. She's basically the cutest little girl in the world. *I am not kidding!* And she talks a lot and she likes princesses and gymnastics and she really, really, *reallllly* wants to open presents!

Right this second I am carrying Rosie down the steep wooden steps. She is wearing pink-and-orange polka-dotted white footie pajamas. Her tiny little arms are latched around my neck. Her chin is resting on my shoulder. "Merry Christmas, Sissy," she whispers, and giggles and clamps her legs tightly around my waist and wiggles, throwing her head back in laughter. Her breath is wet and her raspy little voice tickles my ear.

"Merry Christmas!" I say back. It's seriously impossible not to smile. This little Rosie, she just beams like a lightbulb.

The dad is standing at the bottom of the steps, facing us. Rosie immediately jumps out of my arms and flies into his. "Daaaaaaaddy!" she squeals. The dad effortlessly takes Rosie in his arms. He has blue-gray eyes, curly dark hair, tan outdoorsy skin, and sturdy shoulders. He looks fit, like he climbs mountains. He's wearing faded blue jeans and a black shirt under a red-checkered flannel.

"Hey, sleepyheads," he says, his eyes lighting up. His

face is bright and cheerful. He has a shadow on his jaw of rugged unshaven scruff.

With Rosie in one arm, he reaches out with his other arm and pulls me in too. "Merry Christmas, Bear," he whispers, and kisses me on the head. His breath smells like hot chocolate, and when he talks, his voice is scratchy and gentle. "Oh, my girls, how'd I get so lucky?" he says, pausing to wink at the mom, now standing beside him.

"Okay, lovies," the mom says, looking right at me, "you know the tradition!"

I look back at her like, *tradition?*

She breaks into a gigantic smile. "You know, silly! No peeking at the tree until we get your photo!"

Rosie and I sit together on the stairs.

"No sneaking a look," the dad teases. The two of them face us. The dad has the camera.

I might not be able to see the tree yet, but sitting on the bottom step, I inhale Christmas. It smells like I'm outside in the middle of some magical dark-green forest— only we're inside and it's toasty warm and cozy. Rosie sits behind me on the second-to-last wooden step. She is playing with my braids but pretty quickly changes her mind and climbs right over my head like I'm a jungle gym and drops, giggling, into my lap. I wrap my arms around her. She is a slippery little monkey.

The dad focuses the camera on us. "Say 'Merry Christmas!'"

"Merry Christmas!" we sing.

The dad pulls the mom in and kisses her. The two of them gaze at each other and then at us with big, twinkly-eyed smiles.

I am smiling, too, but inside I'm thinking, *Where am I and what the heck is going on?* I'm sitting with Rosie's little warm hands holding both my cheeks. She is smiling her baby-teeth smile, planting a dozen wet kisses all over my face, giggling and snuggling so close. My "mom and dad" are watching us, their eyes shining. To be completely honest: my heart—it *hurts. It hurts so much.* I don't even know these people, and I don't get how I got here or what is going on, but suddenly, out of nowhere, I am desperately wishing they were *mine.*

15.

WHEN I TURN THE CORNER, it's like I'm stand-ing in the coziest cabin, and I'm instantly filled with a warm, snug feeling. The floors and ceilings are wrapped in solid light honey-colored wood. The living room flows into the kitchen—like, they knocked down all the walls. It's one open space. A simple woodstove sits in the mid-dle of the room. The solid-wood floors are smooth and well-worn—the kind where, if you're wearing socks and you get a running start, you can slide all the way across. And the Christmas tree looks like the sort you'd see in the pages of a magazine! It's big and tall, almost to the ceiling, decorated with twinkly white lights and home-made decorations: gingerbread men, ornaments, pink and red folded origami hearts, felt stars, and strings of popcorn. There are a gazillion wrapped presents piled high beneath the tree.

Rosie sails across the room and kneels in her little pink-and-orange-polka-dotted jammies on her knees, staring at all the presents. "This one is for you, Sissy!" she announces, holding up a red wrapped gift with a white ribbon. "This one is for me!" she sings.

Soon, Rosie and Romeo are both going nuts. Rosie is swinging from a rope hung from a giant wooden ceiling beam, her arms and little legs wrapped around it like a monkey. "Wheeeee! Dakota, look, I can fly!"

I stare at all of it in wonder: Romeo is running in circles, chasing his wiggling tail, the dad is on the couch, strumming a guitar, Rosie—still swinging from the rope—tilts back her head and cheerfully begins humming. I glance at the huge tree covered in lights, the presents, Rosie swaying back and forth from the rafters. *This is the coolest family ever!*

I sit down on a cherry-red sofa piled high with pillows and stare into the strands of white lights wrapped around the tree. I don't get it still. Okay? *How did I get here!!? What is going on?* I look across the room at the mom standing over a long wooden kitchen table, filling a pretty potter's-wheel mug with coffee.

I close my eyes tightly and open them again.

Yep. Everything and everyone is still here: the wood-stove. The lit-up tree. *The presents.* The calming soundtrack of the guitar with Rosie's humming.

I am not dreaming.

And I'm kind of thinking, *This is gonna be awesome,* when—

I hear the mom.

"Hey, Bear," she calls from the other side of the room. "Let's go, my dear, get your jacket on."

I look up at her, confused. Like, you know, *Go? Where are we going?*

She walks toward me, eyebrows lifted. "The girls are going to be *so* happy to see you. You can bring them some treats."

"Girls?" I manage.

For a second she looks at me as if I'm from Mars; then she breaks into that familiar sunny smile. "Oh, lovey, you almost got me," she says, laughing. "The faster you get the girls fed and check on their water, the quicker we can open presents!"

"Uhhh," I say, stalling, and probably look so stupid. Then I just say it—"Check on their water?" I ask. I mean, I have to say *something*. I have no idea what she is asking me to do. I watch the mom walk across the room to the woodstove, crouch down, open the door, and toss in a couple of chunks of wood. She is strong and makes everything look really easy. "Yeah, honey, I bet the water is frozen solid. Dress warmly, it's around *three*—" She pauses, probably because my eyes pop open.

"Three degrees?" I accidentally start talking. It just falls out.

She looks back at me with this big grin. "Put on your muck boots and pull on your big winter coat and a hat and gloves. It is so beautiful, Bear, it's really, really snowy. And the path is all shoveled, right to the chapel."

"Sure, uh—okay . . . ," I say. I have absolutely no idea who the girls are or why their water would be frozen or why they live in a church! But I find myself walking toward the front door and staring into the maze of colorful jackets and coats hanging above a smooth wooden built-in bench. I turn and look back at the mom, who is now standing at the sink. Her eyes light up when they meet mine. "Say hi for me!" She grins.

I hear the dad holler from the couch, "Cass, honey, remind Bear the chapel door gets sticky. Tell her to give it a good shove."

"Did you hear your dad, honey?"

I nod from the doorway. *Her name is Cass. That's kind of cool.*

The water is running in the sink. She's washing out a big, deep pot. "That door does tend to stick." She looks up. "Give it a good shove if it's frozen shut."

I copy the smile on her lips. "Okay," I hear myself say out loud. My heart kind of feels this swell of *good*. There's just something in me that desperately wants to please her.

16.

WHEN I STEP OUTSIDE ALONE, the blast of cold air almost sets me back. I have piled on every piece of clothing I could find hanging by the door that looked like it could possibly belong to Dakota and slipped each item on over my pajamas: a fluorescent orange hoodie, snow pants, a puffy red winter coat, a trapper hat with flappy ears and fur, big thick mittens, and boots that come all the way up to my knees. I feel—and move—like a stuffed sausage. And I'm squinting! It's so bright out here! I close my eyes and then I open them and squint into the winter wonderland. In case you are curious about what I am doing? I'm wondering that too! I mean, I'm totally confused. . . . *Why am I going to a chapel alone? Why is the door sticky? Who are the girls!!?*

There is a narrow shoveled path with mounds of snow

piled up on either side. I make my way one step at a time. The only sound comes from my boots squeaking and crunching down on the snowy packed trail.

Crunch.

Crunch.

Crunch.

I can hear everything.

It's so peaceful.

There is whiteness everywhere I look. Even the big, tall pine trees look like cartoons with their weighted-down snowy branches. I glance back over my shoulder and smile. The cabin looks like a gingerbread house: marshmallows of snow and ice dripping off the steep peaked roof, a green spearmint candy wreath with a sugary red ribbon bow, twinkle lights strung up and outlining the door. *I bounced into some sort of real-life fairy tale,* I think to myself, grinning through the snow. I turn back to the path and keep walking.

Step by step.

It's so dreamy and quiet.

It feels like magic.

And it's almost, like, raining snow! These huge white swirling snowflakes. I tilt my head back and try to catch the falling snow on my tongue. I flop backward into the snow like a cut-down tree—"Timber," I say, laughing, smiling this goofy smile. The snow is an instant fit to my body, like a beanbag chair, but a really, really cold one!

I lie back in my snow throne, my face to the sky, and watch my breath shoot into the air. I stay there for a second and just stare into the beautiful sparkles, tiny little rainbow reflections from the powdered-sugar snowflakes. "Whoa," I whisper to myself into the cold. When the light hits the snow, it looks like a million flecks of glittering diamonds. I have this instantaneous feeling of, like, *amazement*. "I'm sitting in a snowbank!" I announce into the sky, giggling. Then I feel the icy cold seep into my legs and butt, and—you'd laugh so hard if you could see me trying to wriggle and lift myself back up.

The snow comes up to my waist on both sides. Every few crunchy steps I pause and look all around. It's so incredibly quiet. I definitely don't see a chapel and I don't see any girls, so I just keep walking until—

I have to stop.

The shoveled path splits into two different directions.

I stand at the Y, and my heart begins to race. I'm like, *Oh great*. Do I go left, or do I go right? *Who are the girls? Why are they outside?*

My eyes water a little bit, and then the tears freeze instantly. No. For once I'm actually not crying. It's just like, really, really cold out here. And look, I have no idea what I am doing, but I'm pretty sure I'd better keep moving.

17.

I FOUND IT!

I stand outside and stare at the door, and wonder what it is I am about to walk into. There are giant icicles hanging off the wood-planked framed windows, clinking and chiming. This place really does look like the tiniest, sweetest chapel. It's like a little fort, with wood shingles and a snow-covered steepled roof. I lean into the door with my shoulder. It does kind of stick—I have to put my weight into it and ram it. I step slowly inside, shutting the cold out behind me.

Oh, boy. I am not alone!

"Chickens," I gasp, and make a face and scrunch up my nose. It smells *really* bad in here. Seven chickens are at my feet greeting me, clucking and chirping, and just, like, staring at me. It's kind of a little bit scary! They aren't small, fluffy yellow chicks, okay? They come up to my knees! They all have these floppy bright-red Mohawk crowns on their heads and yellow beaks and big eyes that are all looking at me.

"Oh crap," I say, taking one step backward. "Um, hi," I offer. "Merry Christmas," I say weakly. What I'm really thinking is, *Hello, chickens. Please don't eat me!*

I stomp the snow off my feet and take a couple of steps in and look around. The inside of the Chicken Chapel is stuffy and warmer than outside—though it's not *that* warm; I can still see my breath. It's about ten feet long and six feet high. The floor is covered in wood shavings. One side of the tiny room is lined with crayon-colored wooden cubbies—the kind you see in a kindergarten classroom—brightly painted wooden boxes, each one with a little straw nest inside.

"*Buk, buk-buk!*" A pearl-white feathered chicken with knobby legs the color of bright-yellow mustard marches up to me and starts nonstop chatting—"*Buk, buk-buk!*" She looks at me as she talks, as if I can totally understand her! She is making cooing noises and fluffing her pillowy white feathers. Chickens are so funny-looking. Seriously, I've never seen a chicken! Have you? They kind of thrust their necks out confidently and then tiptoe all around me. They're quirky! And they come in all different shades and colors. One is jet-black and shiny. She's tall and big and sturdy. Quiet in a way. I wonder what she's thinking. I peer down at the tiniest one; she's pumpkin and rust, almost peachy orange. Behind her is a fatter reddish-brown one, with a necklace of sleek speckled white feathers. The ringleader—tall and mostly white and bossy—stares at me right in the face with her dark eyes, then up and down, from my snowy hat to my snowy boots, top to bottom, looking at me with this curious gaze like, *Do I know you?* And I immediately feel this sinking doom: it occurs to me that they get it—

The chickens *know*.

I am *not* spunky, strong Dakota, who is obviously *awesome*.

I am Frannie.

You are such a little baby! I hear Carmen's voice snarl in my head. I look down at the chickens. "Can you please tell me what I'm supposed to be doing?" I plead, but they just stare at me.

I stare back.

They scratch and peck at the ground and look up, jerking their heads from side to side. "*Bwaaaaaaaahk,*" says the reddish-brown one with the necklace. That is really the way chickens talk: "*Bwaaaaaaaahk!*"

Ten minutes later, I give up. I'm supposed to feed them, but I can't find any food! I've looked *everywhere*. There's nothing in the Chicken Chapel but chickens. The three metal bowls of water are totally frozen. Each one looks like a mini pond, a skating rink for tiny elves. *How am I supposed to unfreeze it?* I am just totally clueless. *Useless* is another word that pops into my head. My frozen face suddenly feels prickly and hot. And Carmen's voice is getting louder—*You're such an idiot, Frannie, you're so stupid!* I picture her face and see her shake her head and roll her eyes.

The bossy white chicken starts pecking at my boots, then stops and fixes her eyes on mine. I don't speak Chicken, but I'm pretty sure she's talking to me.

"What's your problem?" she clucks. *"You're such a loser."*

I slump down onto the wood-shaving-covered floor, my back to the wall, and hug my knees. I watch the chickens quickly gather around me and have a meeting about how dumb I am. *I know. I agree.* I shrug and drop my head. *I can't do anything. Carmen's right.*

What the heck am I doing?

Who am I fooling?

What is even happening to me right now?

I don't really want to tell you what I do next. I'm so ashamed. They just start falling. Tears. God. I hate it. And it's coming from a place that feels like it has nothing to do with the chickens. It doesn't even matter that I'm a million miles away, slumped on the floor of a Chicken Chapel in the middle of a snowstorm. Everything from last night comes creeping back into my body—and then, this morning, pretending they were all mine—Cass,

Rosie, the dad with the guitar. It was so *relieving*. Now I am remembering: *me*—

The party.

The darkness.

I replay last night over and over again. And then, with the seven chickens looking on, I drop my face into my hands and just start sobbing.

18.

WHEN I HEAR THE DOOR of the Chicken Chapel swing open, I quickly whip off my hat and my gloves and wipe my nose and eyes with my hand and desperately try to act like I'm not the big baby that I'm pretty sure I am.

I take a breath.

I try to focus all my energy on holding myself together. I look up and smile weakly. I don't want anyone to see that I've been crying. I sit up against the wall a tiny bit straighter.

"Hey, honey! Hey, girls!" Cass steps in, and the whole small room instantly brightens.

I watch her shut the door tightly behind her and take a few steps forward. She's carrying two heavy buckets and sets them down, stamps out her big tall rubber boots—identical to mine—and brushes the snow off her arms with her leather work gloves. She's wearing tan overalls with a navy-blue hoodie underneath, and an old beat-up denim jacket lined with woolly fur. She has a bright-orange knit hat under her hood—you can just make out a tiny bit of long blond hair spilling out. She is bundled up, but her face is bright and shiny.

Even across the small space, I can feel the cold coming off her from outside. She stands at the door and smiles really big. She has amazing posture and is just, like, confident, and strong in her body. I watch her unzip her jacket and take off her gloves and place them on an old wooden table in the corner.

The way she looks at me puts me at ease.

"Hey, honey, what's going on? I had a feeling something happened. I noticed you forgot the feed on the porch. Also, water." She rubs her bare hands together as if to warm them.

By the way, as soon as Cass walks in, the chickens desert me. They run over and surround her, their long necks stretched up, looking at her with awe and wonder. I can tell they totally love her.

And I get it.

"Hey, chickies, hey, chicks," Cass says, laughing tenderly. She looks like she is genuinely happy to see them. She bends down and scoops the littlest rust-colored one up with both hands and puts her in the crook of her arm.

"Hey, you," Cass says, cradling her. "How are you doing?" She has a really special way with them. She talks to the chickens like they are people. "Are you having a good Christmas? Are you having fun with Dakota? Yes, she is a sweetheart. I agree! Yes, I know, it's cold!"

As she's talking I suddenly begin to feel more tears come on, and I work to hide them. The second I bite down on my quivering lip, Cass meets my eyes. "Oh, lovey," she says, quickly setting the orange chicken down and moving toward me. "I see some tears. Oh, Bear—" She kneels down so that her face is level with mine and smiles softly. "Oh, honey, what's going on?"

I try to keep it in, but something about the way she looks at me just, like . . . I take a big breath.

"I'm sorry." I hear the words come from my mouth. "There's something really wrong with me." I finally just blurt it out and break down. "I'm, like . . . I'm not—" I start, but then I stop. *What do I say? How do I even begin to explain what's going on?*

Cass moves right beside me. I can feel the heat of her body. I peek sideways and she smiles gently, wrapping her arm around my shoulders, pulling me in, her eyes still on mine. "Oh, lovey, you look like you feel really disappointed, honey. What's going on? What do you need to feel better? How can I help? Is this about last night?"

I can't help wonder what Dakota could be the slightest bit unhappy about. Then. Yeah. It suddenly hits me: *If I am here, is Dakota back locked in my room as me? Is she all by herself? Did Carmen and Teddy even come back?* I burst into bigger tears.

"I'm so sorry," I say. I am barely able to get the words out. I think about how I am afraid of *everything. I can't do anything right.*

For a long stretch Cass just holds me tight, smoothing the back of my head and my shuddering shoulders with her hand. She doesn't seem to mind my big fat tears or the snot dripping from my nose and dampening her sweatshirt.

"Oh, Bear—oh, lovey," she whispers.

"I'm so sorry," I repeat, sobbing.

"Oh, honey, you never have to apologize for telling me how you feel. I'm here for you." She pulls me in tighter. "Sweetheart—oh, Bear . . . I want to be with you any way you want to be . . ."

Pretty soon I melt into her.

I just let go.

We don't even talk for a really long time. When she breathes, I breathe. It makes me feel calm. My ear is pressed up against her chest. I can hear her heart beating. I can feel her breathing. We stay like that for a minute— or five, until the front of her sweatshirt is wet from my tears. My eyes are closed, but when I slowly open them, I see every chicken in the chapel is standing around us, totally staring. When they see me see them, they begin to talk, which makes me kind of softly laugh. Laugh and sit up, wiping my eyes with my hand. Cass laughs too. "Oh, Bear, see, even Macaroni wants you to know she loves you."

It's the tall white one. Her long neck is all stretched out. *Her name is Macaroni.* That makes the edges of my lips turn up just a little bit.

Cass sweeps a wisp of hair out of my eyes. "You know what?" She looks at me with an easy smile. "I wonder if we get up and get these girls fed and change the water and get back and have some pancakes things might feel a little bit better?"

I nod and sniffle. "Pancakes do sound good," I say softly. It occurs to me I haven't eaten since before my mom and dad left. I'm *starving*.

Cass looks at me with the kindest eyes. She's quiet and reassuring, and something about the way she looks at me helps me take a deep breath.

"Oh, honey," she whispers sweetly. "I love your tears. You don't always have to be happy. . . . I'm going to love you always, *no matter what*. That's my job"—she presses her lips to my forehead—"I'm your mama."

Cass moves to her feet and offers me her hand, pulling me up. Her grip is warm and strong and I let her lift me to my feet. "We better get moving," she tells me, breaking into a mischievous grin. "When I left the house, your little sister was ready to burst!" She laughs.

I love her laugh. She's funny without trying to be.

"Okay," I say softly, and smile when I think of Rosie, kneeling at the tree, staring at all the brightly wrapped presents.

"Okay then," she says, her eyes shining—they look a lot like mine. I mean, Dakota's. They are clear blue with specks of green. She hands me a broom from the corner. She grabs one too. We sweep the shavings together. It's quiet for a little bit, except for the chickens. Clucking and cooing.

After a minute Cass looks up. "That's my girl," she says, winking at me.

When she says *my girl,* my heart leaps.

We clean out the nesting cubbies, change the water, make sure there's plenty of food, sprinkle mealworm treats all over the ground—the girls go crazy trying to peck the little worms—and walk back to the house with a wicker basket full of eggs. I even reached my hand into the cubbies and gently gathered each one. The eggs are pale blue, light brown, and white. I have the best feeling as I set the basket down next to a bowl of oranges on the wooden kitchen table. Rosie runs over and climbs up on the picnic-table-like bench and peers into the basket.

"They're so pretty!" she gasps.

"Yeah," I sigh, and I smile at her.

Rosie steps up with her little footie pajamas and

stands on the table facing me. She cups her hands to my cold cheeks and looks at me as if we're having a staring contest, our foreheads touching. I crack up first. We are both pursing our lips and grinning at the same time. Her eyes get big and crazy! I swear they are twinkling.

"Presents!" she squeals, jumps back down to the floor, grabs my hand, and pulls me to the tree. She doesn't have to pull too hard. I go, gladly.

19.

ACTUALLY. HOLD THAT THOUGHT. WE make breakfast *before* we open presents. Cass stands next to me at the sink, and we both wash our hands.

"Let's get some food in our bellies," she says.

She has changed back into her faded blue jeans, kitten-soft pink turtleneck sweater, and big furry slippers. I peeled off all the coats, but I'm still in my candy-cane pajamas. We are making pancakes, using the eggs we just collected. I stand at the sink and carefully run them under the faucet, gently rubbing off a little bit of feathers and dirt.

Rosie climbs on top of a stool and uses her little hands to crack each egg into a blue ceramic bowl. When she's done, she puts her face deep in the bowl, then looks up at me wide-eyed. "They look like suns!"

I laugh softly. It's true, they kind of do. I stare at the bright-orange yolks. *They don't look like the eggs my mom gets at the store.*

Cass slides open a chalkboard wall (covered with Rosie's colorful loopy scribbles) to reveal clean white shelves lined with rows of clear glass jars filled with the essentials. I watch her reach in and collect all the ingredients, loading the glass containers in her arms and setting them down on the counter one by one. A quick trip to the fridge and soon we have everything we need:

flour

baking powder

sugar

salt

butter

milk

eggs

Cass helps Rosie pour the milk and melted butter into the blue bowl with the eggs. I whisk, beating the mixture all together. Then, with Cass's help, Rosie adds the flour, baking powder, sugar, and a pinch of salt. Cass doesn't do it for us, and she doesn't mind the sticky, buttery sugar all over Rosie's little hands. She stands back and helps us figure out each step.

"It's a tiny bit thick," she says, grinning, watching us. "Maybe try adding a little bit more milk."

"I can do it, Sissy!" Rosie says, and so I let her.

I hand Rosie the milk and help guide her hands with mine. Together we stir until the batter is light and smooth.

Cass smiles at me and then at Rosie. "So, what would you monkeys like in our pancakes?" she asks, standing at the fridge.

"Blueberries!" Rosie squeals, clapping, and then she raises her arms high over her head. She jumps down, landing on the floor like a springy frog.

I smile. She's just so cute.

I nod. "Blueberries sound good."

Cass looks surprised, eyebrows up. "Blueberries? Really? I thought that you—" she begins, then stops. "You, my dear, are full of Christmas morning surprises!"

Rosie does the honors, gleefully dumping a small bowl of blueberries into the batter. Cass hugs me to her as we both stand back and watch the action.

"Your turn, Daddy!" Rosie lifts her little stool all by herself and carries it across the kitchen floor over to the stove, then climbs up. The dad—who I hear Cass call *Luke*—is at the stove, cooking bacon in the skillet. Romeo is at his feet, making begging noises and sniffing the sizzling fatty goodness.

Rosie and I both stand back and watch as Luke pours the batter onto the hot buttered griddle. He makes fun shapes like snowmen and reindeers.

The three of us stare at the pancakes until—

"I see a bubble!" Rosie says, getting excited. "Look, Daddy!"

Luke picks up a spatula and hands it to me. "All you." He grins.

I take it in my hand and carefully flip the snowmen and the reindeers over and cook the other side.

Luke's face lights up. "Boom! You got this, Bear. Good work!" He raises his hand for a high five, and when our palms connect, I smile big. *I never knew I could cook!*

I set the table with forks and knives, glossy white plates, red cloth napkins with green stitching, and tall glasses for fresh-squeezed orange juice. Rosie carries the pitcher of maple syrup. I watch her walking, balancing the small ceramic pitcher, and I get a little bit worried that she'll drop it. At my house, oh man, that's just the kind of thing that would make my dad lose it, but that's not how it is here. Everyone is kind of laid-back, relaxed. It's okay to try things, like, even if it went crashing to the floor, I don't think anyone would get really, really angry.

When the four of us sit down at the long wooden table, the kitchen is still messy: bowls, pots and pans, flour, butter, eggshells, crumbs. It's, like, craziness. But every-thing is okay. Nobody is glaring at me or lifting their finger to their lips and telling me to not speak. I look at Rosie sitting up in a booster seat pulled close to the table. She wanted whipped cream and chocolate sauce *and* maple syrup, and she has them all on her face. She loves pancakes!

And I swear—I've never tasted anything better than the first bite. I chew and close my eyes. *Maybe when you make it yourself, it tastes even better.* These are the best pancakes I've ever had in my life.

"You know what?" Rosie announces, staring straight at us with big wide eyes, dark-blue blueberries staining the corners of her mouth. "This is my favorite morning!"

Somehow Rosie says just what I'm thinking.

I smile at her and her tiny blueberry-stained mouth, and her sparkly turquoise eyes, and her crazy, curly blond hair—little kids get right to the heart of things. I love how she says exactly what she's thinking. She doesn't even think about it, she just says it. She's not afraid.

I glance across the table at Luke and Cass. Everyone is eating and talking and laughing. It feels so relaxed and wonderful. That feeling feels so different. I honestly never felt it until just this moment.

20.

I WISH YOU COULD SEE around the tree *before* and *after*. The living room looks like a toy store blew up or a really messy playroom. There is wrapping paper crumpled up and torn off—"Just go for it!"—Cass egged me on. "Tear it off, have fun!" Oh, wow, my pile of presents is huge! Every gift I opened, I didn't quite know what to say or do. I would get up from the floor and hug Cass and Luke, cozied up on the couch. They looked like they were having so much fun just sitting together and watching us. We all took turns until there were no gifts left. Dakota made Cass the best present—it was pretty fun watching her unwrap it. I mean, I obviously didn't know what was inside, right? So I sat and watched in suspense as she carefully unwrapped the paper and took it out and held it in her palm: a little horse and a cowgirl and a lasso all handmade out of papier-mâché and pipe cleaners. Cass had the best look on her face when she unwrapped it. She immediately sprang up, bent down, and hugged me.

"Oooh, Bear," she whispered in my ear, "I *love* it!"

Rosie and Cass and I all presented Luke with a chunky blue wool sweater that I think we all helped knit. He immediately slipped it on over his flannel. Rosie leaped into his lap and hugged his neck. "You look so pretty, Daddy!"

Now there is a calmness, a quiet. Luke is cleaning up the kitchen. He's wearing a denim apron over his sweater. I like the way Luke and Cass seem equal; how they do stuff for each other. Cass is curled up on the couch with one of her presents: a red-striped wool blanket. Her eyes are closed and her lips are smiling this peaceful smile. The heat from the wood-burning stove feels so cozy. Even Romeo is quiet, chewing a toy. Rosie is mesmerized by her new handmade dollhouse, which is bigger than she is! There are little rooms and little beds with tiny pillows and teensy quilt blankets. I can hear her talking to herself in this precious hushed whisper. She's telling a story that is hilarious and awesome. Something about a fairy covered in diamonds and a little baby. She's just so cute. She also got a huge elephant with a floppy trunk, Legos, a puzzle, crazy striped tights, ruby slippers, a tiara, lots of books, and pajamas.

I quietly gather all my treasures, stepping over the stuffed elephant, toys, and empty boxes, and climb the stairs to Dakota's room. I empty my arms of presents on top of the unmade bed. I have so much: a new winter hat, cowgirl boots, clothes, a necklace, books, and something called a Breyer horse, which I have a feeling Dakota wanted a lot. She has a bunch of them on top of her dresser: plastic miniature horses, each the size of a small doll. I add the new one to her collection. It's all black with a white stripe on its forehead—and it came in a gold box, just like a Barbie doll, with a clear plastic see-through window. I carefully take the horse out and set it down beside the others. She has six now. I count them.

I got a new "stuffie"—that's what Rosie calls them— a brown bear that's supersoft and huggable. I tuck him into the bed, right beside the pillow. I fasten my new gold chain with a tiny butterfly pendant, then pull on my new clothes right over my pajamas: a navy Western shirt with snap flap-front pockets and tiny pink-and-yellow embroidered flowers, and tan overalls like Cass wears. I wiggle into them and buckle the straps; they fit perfectly and they're lined with soft red flannel. I tug on my new thick wool socks and sink my feet into the awesome brown cowgirl boots and look into the mirror. It sounds weird to say it, but I like who I see. I smile. Then I remember . . . she's not *me*.

An hour later I hear Cass. "Bear? Are you ready for our ride?"

Ride? I think, and kind of panic. "Uh—yeah," I call down, and wonder what I just agreed to. A minute later Cass appears in the bedroom doorway. She's dressed like she's going to do chores: navy hoodie, tan overalls just like mine. Her hair is still swept into a twisty bun, wispy strands hanging down. Her face lights up when she connects with mine.

"Oh, good, you have on your new coveralls. It's going to be cold, but it's going to be beautiful!"

Romeo leads the way, and it's hysterical. The snow is still falling and the stuff on the ground is way over his head. He is amazed and confused and he moves kind of like a dolphin in the water as he tries to figure out the fluffy white stuff. Cass and I can't stop laughing as we watch his little ears come up, then disappear down. Then we see his tiny tail, up and down. Soon he's exhausted. Cass scoops him up and zips him into her jacket like a baby kangaroo. The two of us walk together hand in hand, or, well, Cass's tan leather work glove and my snowy mitten. We are quiet but also giggling at Romeo, who is peeking his head out of Cass's jacket. We walk on the same shoveled path I took this morning, only when it comes to the Y, we go left instead of right, and soon we're walking down a sloping snow-covered hillside to a big red barn. At first I don't notice until—

Romeo wiggles out of Cass's jacket and bounds ahead, barking.

"Horses," I say, and my mouth falls open.

21.

I TAKE MY FIRST STEP toward the horses. There are two—both gigantic. One is dark brown all over, with a black mane and tail and a white stripe down his nose and face. The other is a big gray one. His legs are black and his body is dark gray that fades into a light gray, and he's got a lot of different shades in him and a jet-black mane. Both horses have their ears turning toward us, and they're following us with their eyes.

Luke is standing in between them right outside the barn. He has on a beaten-up tan work coat, jeans with a big silver belt buckle, and worn-out leather boots.

"I thought my girls might want to go for a ride," he says. His eyes are shining. He's got this warmth. Except for his red baseball cap tugged down over his curly dark hair, he looks like he could be a cowboy or guy who rides bulls.

Cass immediately breaks into the hugest smile. "Honey," she tells Luke. "You are the best!" Then she turns to me. "Oh my goodness, Bear, what an awesome present. We don't have to tack up for our ride!"

"Uh—I, um—" I sputter. *Our ride.* I'm scared to even get *on* a horse, let alone *ride* one. My mind is already racing to think of some way to explain how I cannot possibly ride a horse! I mean, like, *I don't know how!*

"I'm, uh—" I try again, but Cass is too excited.

"Oh my gosh," she says throwing her arms around Luke and giving him a big kiss. "Honey, this is the sweetest thing ever. I wasn't expecting this. That is *so* nice! I cannot believe you did this for us. Thank you so much!"

"Um, yeah, thanks," I manage, and try to sound grateful. I look past Luke and Cass and the horses. The huge barn doors are pushed wide open, and the inside of the barn is all lit up. Rosie is in her little snowsuit with a white fur-lined hood tied snug around her face, playing on the barn floor with the puppy.

Cass is already buckling a helmet onto her head. "Bear, honey, why don't you go get your helmet and gloves."

I look at Cass, and then I look at Luke.

They are just smiling at me like this is the greatest news.

"Um—I . . ." I stall and try to fake a smile.

I watch Cass effortlessly get up on the big gray horse: gathering the reins in one hand and grabbing hold of the mane. She steps up into the stirrup and slowly swings her right leg over and really gently lowers herself into the saddle. She's smooth and strong. Her whole face is smiling. I can tell she's really good at this, and I think I'm staring.

I take a big circle around the horses and enter the barn. Inside, it's cozy and protected from the cold. I instantly smell hay and horses and leather.

Rosie is busy with Romeo—giggling and chasing him around. "You can't catch me!" she squeals, and shrieks with laughter.

I look around the barn until I spot a helmet and tan leather gloves hanging from a hook above two saddles. I take a deep breath and look back over my shoulder at the horses and Luke and Cass talking. The snow and the cold wind blow in through the open barn doors, and Luke's eyes meet mine with an encouraging smile—he doesn't have to say anything, he just looks at me like, *You totally got this.*

Okay. Wow. I can't believe I'm trying this! I mean, seriously, this is going to be a disaster. I try and remind myself that I'm not really fearless Dakota, I am *Frannie, remember!!!?* I do NOT know what I'm doing. Just last night I was hiding in my room under my covers. But . . . I don't really have a lot of other options, and also? There is a tiny part of me that *does* think this all looks kind of amazing in a totally terrifying I-have-no-idea-how-to-ride-a-horse kind of way.

Cass is sitting up on her gray horse, draping her body over his neck, reaching down and giving him hugs. I can hear her talking, calm and sweet: "What a pretty boy you are. How are you doing today, Gussy? How are you feeling? Are you feeling a little stiff?" She stops and gives him a nice little scratch on the top of his face. "Did the cold get in your bones a little bit?" I can tell Cass understands the language of horses. The way she snuggles into his neck. The way she gently strokes him.

Luke is standing, holding the reins of the massive chocolate-brown horse that I'm pretty sure is mine. Luke has this easy way of being. I've never been around a guy who's so gentle and at the same time strong. Just really sweet and really kind.

I glance back inside the barn. Rosie is shrieking and giggling, chasing Romeo all over the stable. I slowly strap the helmet on over my head. I stare at the horse I'm supposedly riding and feel my throat tighten and my hands start to sweat under my leather gloves. *Oh my gosh.* Have I mentioned how big horses are? They are really, really huge, with muscular legs, and they are making huffing sounds and blowing air out of their nostrils. *Oh God. I'm pretty sure horses sense fear.*

Cass looks back at me. "Come on, let's go, Bear—what are you doing?"

What should I do? My heart is trembling. I try to have courage, but what comes out of my mouth is, "Um, no, it's okay. I changed my mind."

Cass doesn't seem to think I'm serious. She just nudges her horse sideways and says, "What's wrong, honey? Do you need a leg up?"

Before I can answer, Luke is right beside me, interlacing his fingers together to make a step. "Let me give you a boost," he says.

Oh my gosh, I think this is happening. I gather my reins and reach up like Cass did and grab onto my horse's mane.

Luke focuses on me with his blue-gray eyes. "Okay, honey," he says. "Step up."

I take a deep breath and set my boot into his hands. *Oh, wow. It's too late now!*

"Get ready," says Luke. "One, two, three—" As Luke says "three," he lifts me up, and I swing my leg right over and just like that settle into the saddle.

Oh my gosh! I am sitting on a horse!!!!!

Cass looks back over her shoulder and shoots me a big *you did it* smile. Rosie has climbed up into Luke's arms.

"Are you ready?" Cass calls back.

The horse, my horse, lurches forward.

"Wait!" I work to make my voice not sound so desperate. I look back at Luke. "Aren't you and Rosie coming, too?"

Luke grins big at Rosie and gives her a tickle. She wiggles and giggles in his arms. "This little monkey and I are going to stay back and get the stalls mucked and put the feed in for the night. Right, Monkey?"

Rosie nods proudly.

Luke looks back up at me. "You and your mom can have a nice long ride." He reaches out and gives the horse a little pat. "Trigger's going to take good care of you, Bear. You trust each other so much. You're a great team." He pauses and looks me right in the eyes. "Ride hard, Bear. Have fun!"

Which is all well and good until Trigger jerks forward again. I'm not ready. My head snaps back. My heart is pounding. I imagine my body flying and spinning over Trigger's head—*I want to jump off, I want to stop.* "Wait!" I shout, but Cass and Gus are already way out past the shoveled front of the barn, stepping into the deep snow.

I sit up stiffly, clenching Trigger's mane. I bend over low and lean into his ear. "Easy," I plead. Also, "Please don't kill me."

Trigger looks at me out of the corner of his eye. He's so big and powerful underneath me.

Cass looks back over her shoulder. "Okay, Bear, are you ready? Trigger's going to take really good care of you, honey." Then she hollers, "Let's go!" and with that, Cass and Gus take off toward the snowy white forest. Thank goodness I am holding on, because in about one split second, Trigger bursts forward through a cloud of glittering snow and—ready or not—we take off too.

22.

HOLY CRAP! I'M DOING IT! My boots are in the stirrups, my hands are gripping the reins, I'm holding on for dear life! It's too late now to change my mind! In a matter of seconds we are careening forward. *Oh my gosh!* My heart is beating like crazy. I am holding my breath when—out of nowhere—I can't explain it, but something just *clicks!* All of a sudden I am squeezing my thighs against the saddle, relaxing my shoulders, sitting up straight: *I can do this!*

"Dakota," I whisper. *She's taking over!*

I move both my hands to the reins; I feel light and move in rhythm with Trigger's shifting weight—It's effortless! It's hard to get this smile off my face!

I look down the sloping hill to the far-off woods. I don't see another human being out here. It's just the horses,

Cass, and me. Nothing but fields of snow. It's so beautiful and so white. I kind of love the wind on my face and the cold on my cheeks. I soften into the saddle. I take a nice deep breath.

When Trigger steps into the woods, everything gets quiet. It kind of feels so dreamy—everything around me is lush and still. The entire woods are like a secret coated with snow, a perfect dusting along every branch and every trunk. And when a low branch snaps against my cheek, and I feel a little hot slice, it feels oddly good—like, I'm alive! I'm doing this! I am riding a horse through a magic forest! It's so silent under the snowy trees: I can hear the saddle creaking as we move, I hear the horse's feet swish into the snow, I hear Trigger huffing through his nostrils. I can see his hot breath in the air. I lean forward and with one hand pat him. *I know I can trust him. He's not going to hurt me.* Trigger perks his ears up, lifts his head, and almost nods. I grin. I get it. I understand what Luke and Cass meant—*Trigger's going to take really good care of you . . . You trust each other so much.* We are doing this *together.*

When I see the giant log ten feet ahead, I don't have time to be nervous. It all happens so fast. My first instinct is to shut my eyes and not look. Then I remember we're a team, and I loosen my grip. I sit up straighter. I feel my feet sink into the stirrups. I lean forward and rise with Trigger. My butt comes out of the saddle a little, my head is up, and in a matter of seconds we are sailing through midair!

On the way back down I get the biggest jolt of adrenaline! *"Wooooo-hooooo!"* I hear my voice echo through the snowy woods. It's the greatest rush!

A second later I hear Cass. "You're doing it, Bear!" she hollers back.

We land on a carpet of snow in one smooth motion, and Trigger opens up, picking up the pace. He sets the beat. I somehow instinctively stand up strong, and my body moves together with his. We are one and I am ducking, snapping branches. Trigger loves running and jumping. He is really, really fast. I am smiling so big right now. Nothing can describe this feeling. It's like I can fly. I feel comfortable in my skin—even though it's not really *mine*. But in this moment, in the woods, galloping through the snowy trees, I know what it feels like to feel strong.

When we emerge from the woods, it is snowing hard. Trigger comes to a gentle stop right at the edge of the forest. It is silent except for the lulling sound of Trigger's breathing. I quickly take off my gloves and tug my wool hat under my helmet down over my ears. The wind hits the side of my face, and I can feel it down my neck. I shiver but it feels kind of good. I bend and give Trigger a hug with my arms, nestle my face against his neck. His hair is so soft. I breathe in his scent.

"What a good boy; that was amazing," I tell him, and give him a pat. I feel the power of his body underneath me, and I feel this special thing that happens when a horse wants to be with a person. Trigger shivers and blows air out his nose. I think he understands me! *I'm in love.*

Trigger and I take a right onto a plowed-flat snowy road with no cars, and soon we are riding side by side with Cass and Gus. The sun has already dipped behind a far-off ridge of trees, leaving the sky a deep, dark blue with streaks of this unreal pink. I can just make out the big red barn in the distance. For a few minutes Cass and I ride together without talking. The only sound is the rhythm of the hooves against the packed-down snowy road. High steps. *Clip-clop, clip-clop.*

I listen to the dreamy twilight.

I breathe in deeply.

Clip-clop, clip-clop.

"Honey, I just love being out here together with you," Cass says, turning to smile at me with a wink.

My heart feels so good. I bite down on my lip and look back at Cass.

The snow is falling all around us.

Clip-clop, clip-clop.

Clip-clop, clip-clop.

Clip-clop, clip-clop.

Right before we turn off the road into the long, curvy

driveway leading to the barn, Cass says to me, "Bear, don't you love how a blanket of snow makes everything feel new? It's like a blank slate—a fresh start."

"Yeah." I turn and look at her and Gus beside me. I hope I never forget this. A *fresh start*, I think to myself. *That sounds good. That sounds right.*

23.

NIGHTTIME: AFTER HER BATH AND stories, two trips to the bathroom, and one glass of water, Rosie tells Cass she would like *me* to tuck her in. When I climb the stairs and walk into Rosie's room, she doesn't see me at first. She's fresh from the tub, and her hair has just been braided into the cutest little braids. She's talking to her new stuffie elephant, whispering in its ear, hugging its neck. Her room is right beside mine and is filled with toys and a little desk. Her scribbly colorful art covers an entire cork wall. The other walls are pale pink with tangerine and yellow polka dots. There is a hanging mobile of cheerful wool felt giraffes over her bed. The room glows with the soft twinkle of a Winnie-the-Pooh nightlight. When Rosie sees me, her whole face smiles.

"Sissy," she gasps, like I'm the greatest thing ever.

She moves over immediately, making room for me to lie down beside her. She's wearing her new Christmas flannel jammies. They're super cozy and white with red and blue starfish. As soon as I curl up next to her, her hand finds my hand under the covers and her tiny fingers wrap around mine.

"Hi," she whispers. She squeezes my hand and giggles softly. She's staring into my eyes, fluttering her lashes. She's so cute. I know I've already said that, but—when I look at her, I get this pang of pain. *Pretty soon, I'm going to wake up, right? Pretty soon I'm going to be me again.* Rosie feels so good to snuggle with. She smells like bubble bath and baby breath.

"Did you have a fun Christmas?" I ask her. We are staring into each other's eyes under the covers.

"Yeah," she breathes, and tries to keep her closing lids open. I can tell she's sleepy. Rosie flops over and snuggles into my body. I watch her little chest go up and down.

"Sissy," she says in the softest tiny voice.

"Yeah?"

"I love you."

"I love you, too," I whisper, and squeeze her.

I close my eyes, but only for a second. I hear Cass and feel the weight of her body lie beside me.

"Oh, my sweet girls," she sighs. I feel her warmth against my back. We are like three peas in a pod, Rosie, me, and Mom.

I feel more at home lying here than anywhere I've ever been. I take my braids out, and Cass runs her fingers through my hair. It feels so good. We stay like that for the longest time.

It's quiet for a few minutes, and I suddenly become very worried. The words come out without me really thinking—"I'm afraid of losing you," I whisper into the hush. My voice gives away the fact that I have tears in my eyes. But I'm just . . . I feel like . . . I can really trust her. I feel safe.

Cass hugs me to her. "Oh, Bear, you can never lose me. I love you so much, and there's nothing you could ever do that would make me leave you."

It's hard for me to swallow, but I soften to Cass's heartbeat, which I can feel against my back. I want time to slow down. I want to press pause and stay right here in this hug with Cass breathing, like, three inches away from me. I feel her hand slide under my arm and pull me in tight.

"Merry Christmas, sweetheart," she breathes.

"Merry Christmas," I say softly, tears trickling down my cheeks. I don't sleep, though. I don't close my eyes. I stay up as long as I can, trying to memorize how I feel right here. Right now.

24.

OH MY GOSHHH, IT'S HAPPENING *again*, is what I'm thinking as I am free-falling through outer space. For a few seconds, time seems to slow down: my body spins—arms and legs flailing—in tumbling, dizzying somersaults. I don't collide with stars or knock into any meteors, but this time my journey through the galaxy isn't quite as smooth as my first! It's clunky. I feel queasy. There's an extremely loud whooshing sound as I drop through the air, then finally bounce hard onto a stiff, cushioned seat.

Okay.

Wow.

As soon as my body is no longer moving, I instantly begin breathing heavily and feeling like I'm going crazy. *Why is this happening to me? What is happening to me?* Also? There's this: I cannot see!

As in: it is totally dark.

I have some kind of mask covering my eyes.

Yes, I begin to panic! I move my hands up to my face and whip whatever is covering my eyes off, and—

Oh, whoa, I think. *Whoa!* My mouth is wide open. My jaw is dropped. I am looking out a small oval window to my left and I see clouds! The big white puffy kind. And I see a whole lot of orange-strawberry-colored sky!

"Oh my gosh," I say, hearing a voice come out of my mouth that is not Dakota's and definitely not mine. It's soft, with a kind of warm, raspy tone. I blink my groggy eyes and squint through the window.

There is so much light.

Light and sky.

About that: *I am on an airplane!*

My heart starts racing. I have never flown on a plane in my life! I swallow and turn my head to the right. I am sitting beside a total stranger: she's young, maybe twenty-five or so, with messy undone deep brownish-black hair, down around her shoulders, long and loose and wavy. She has the same eye mask on that I just took off. She's dressed in, like, laid-back meets totally stylish: a long-sleeved light-gray sweater, a loosely looped lavender scarf, stretchy black yoga pants, sheepskin lace-up furry boots. Her hands are gripping a closed book. I turn back to the window and look out. My heart is seriously racing—I am filled with the most intense fear! I'm like, *Where am I? Who am I?* I feel nauseous. I stare through the oval glass. *Is this really happening?* I watch the sherbet-colored sky and remember last night, snuggling with Cass and Rosie—three peas in a pod, Cass telling me how much she loved me . . . being with them was the best thing that has ever happened to me. I begin to feel my heart in my throat. *I miss them so much.* Does that sound strange? I know I only knew them for, like, one day, but it was just the best day ever! It was so great. Now I'm flying on a plane to who knows where, feeling like I might throw up. My hands are tingling. I glance down and spread my fingers: I have bounced into the body of someone with caramel-brown skin and perfectly manicured fingernails painted bubblegum pink, with tiny nail art designs: a skull, eyeballs, geometric patterns, and polka dots. I look at them up close. They're kind of awesome! I am wearing tight-fitting black leggings with a hooded purple camouflage sweatshirt and bright-white sparkly Converse high-top sneakers. I have huge headphones hanging around my neck. I can hear the music blasting out—it's that same song that Carmen loves! And in an instant my sister's voice rings in my head. *Jasmine is perfection! I really, freakin' love her!* and I get this sudden jolt and it all floods back—

Carmen.

Christmas Eve.

The party.

For the billionth time I try to wrap my brain around what is happening to me, or, like, how I have the sudden ability to travel seemingly through walls and zip through space!

Then I hear a voice.

I look to my right, across the aisle, at a glamorous woman who is talking *very* loudly. She looks straight from the pages of a fashion magazine. She has peachy skin and stained berry lips and she's wearing big, oversize dark sunglasses. I'm pretty sure she's definitely a movie star or a supermodel or something. Her honey-blond hair is cut ultra-short and sleek, and she looks polished and clean in her formfitting navy-blue dress and matching high heels, with a huge mink coat draped around her shoulders. I can't stop staring. No detail is undone. But—

She's in a *terrible* mood!

"Excuse me? Are you listening?" she snaps at the flight attendant guy. "This is quite obviously not cooked! It's cold."

"I'm so sorry, ma'am," the flight attendant responds calmly. "Would you like me to reheat it?"

Movie Star/Supermodel shakes her head. "Oh, God no," she says. "Unbelievable. Did you hear me?" She pushes her sunglasses up and speaks in slow, carefully chosen words. "What I'd like is for you to make me a new one."

"Ma'am"—the flight attendant bends down and lowers

his voice—"the food is not actually cooked in the air, even in first class."

Movie Star/Supermodel rolls her eyes. "Go, then—just take it," she says, shrugging her shoulders. "The sight of this disgusts me."

While I'm staring across the aisle with my mouth kind of open, the girl sitting next to me slowly pushes her mask up to her forehead, opens her eyes, glances toward me, and beams out this huge smile. She is, wow. She is really, really pretty.

"Hey, you," she says. Her eyes are big and sparkly. "Merry Christmas!"

"Wait, it's *still* Christmas?" Yes. I blurt this out.

The girl looks a little puzzled. "What do you mean, *still* Christmas?" She turns her head so we're eye-to-eye. "Hey, how's your headache? Feeling any better?" She studies my face, then gives me another smile. "Why don't you try and get some more sleep? We have such a busy day and our thing tonight."

Oh God. "Thing tonight?" I manage.

She looks at me funny. "Are you okay?"

"Not really," I answer honestly, and bite my bottom lip. I watch her reach down and lift a black leather handbag off the floor and set it in her lap. She glances at me like, *I've got just the thing for you,* reaches in, and pulls out a tiny little bottle with a spray top and holds it right up in front of my mouth.

"Well—" She giggles.

I look back at her like, *Well what?*

"Stick out your tongue, silly!"

I follow her instructions, and she sprays a sweet-tasting mist straight into my mouth.

"A little Rescue Remedy should do the trick." She returns the tiny bottle to her handbag, reaches out, and gently covers my hand with hers. "Hey, so are you feeling a little bit nervous about—" She stops, probably because I look like I'm about to throw up.

My palms are sweaty.

My stomach is nervous and fluttery. I am trying to do everything I can to hold it together.

The girl reaches down into her bag again, pulls out a water bottle, and hands it over to me. "Dehydration can make you feel super tired. We both need to drink plenty of water."

"Thanks," I say softly. I lift the water bottle to my lips and drink it in gulps.

"It's been a rough three days," she sighs. She has the sweetest sympathetic look in her eyes. "You're doing it, though." Her eyes light up. "I'm crazy proud of you."

I hand the water bottle back and try to smile politely. *I wonder what I'm doing and why she's proud.*

My new best friend digs into her bag again. This time she pulls out her phone and checks the time.

"Hey," she says, looking back up. "We have a few more

hours to go. Seriously, why don't you get some rest?" She breaks into a silly smile and raises an eyebrow. "Unless you'd like an in-flight selfie?"

Before I can answer, she stretches out her arm, holding her phone out in front of us, and leans her head against mine. I lean toward her too, our heads tipped together. There's something about her that makes me feel like I can trust her.

"Say Merry Christmas to all your fans!" she says.

All *my fans?* I think, confused.

"Ready? One, two, three . . ."

"Merry Christmas." I play along and I smile straight into the camera and—*OH MY GOD!*

It takes a millisecond for my brain to catch up to *who* I see in the phone's small rectangular screen. "What the . . . ," I begin, sounding totally in shock, because I totally am!

I am *JASMINE!*

The singer Carmen is obsessed with!

I am *Jasmine!* I am in her body!

I reach up and touch my face as I stare in disbelief at the photo on the screen: I have glowing smooth cocoa skin and seriously amazing hair—waves of springy tight brown curls, beautiful lips, and a perfect nose. My eyes are wide-set and dark brown, and my eyebrows are full and expertly shaped.

"Oh my God, it's just so crazy," I say out loud, completely astounded.

"Supercute, right? Except your mouth is wide open!" She giggles. "You look a little bit surprised, but . . . I kinda think that makes it extra awesome." She smiles. "Want to post it?" She hands me her phone.

"Uhhhh, that's okay." I shake my head and push the phone back.

She laughs again and turns to me. "Whatever, but just for the record: I am not playing into that being-mean-to-yourself thing. You're so hard on yourself, Jazz, you really are. I just love everything about you—I'm keeping this one as my Christmas morning treasure!" She flashes me a sly, playful smile and drops the phone back into her big leather bag, then immediately picks my hand up and holds it quietly on her lap.

"Just close your eyes," she tells me. "Try and take some nice deep breaths."

I do. I close my eyes.

I think about breathing. Her hand on top of mine feels soothing.

"With our schedule today, we're going to need some serious endurance." She sighs. "It's a little insane when you think about it."

My eyes pop open, and I turn to her. "Think about what?"

My new friend's whole face lights up. "Oh, Jazz, you crack me up. Christmas Day in London, silly!"

25.

I WAKE UP TO THE captain of the plane speaking to us. His voice is muffled and comes over the PA system through the small circular speakers directly above me: "This is your captain, just giving you an update. We are starting our descent into London's Heathrow Airport. We should be landing in thirty minutes. The current temp is thirty-six degrees Fahrenheit, two degrees Celsius. It's a partly cloudy, cold and windy day, folks. The local time is ten o'clock in the morning, and we hope you have a very merry Christmas."

My new friend shoots me a reassuring smile. She still has my hand in hers. I keep it there. It feels good.

I hear Flight Attendant Guy's voice on the speakers. "Please power down your electronics, we'll be landing shortly. Make sure your tray tables are up, your seat backs are up, your personal belongings are stowed, and your seat belts are fastened. If you have any questions about customs or immigration, please ask your flight attendant."

My friend gently pulls her hand away and fishes her phone out of her bag, glancing down at it, then turns, eyebrows up. "Ready to do this?"

Not really! I want to say. Instead, I nervously smile back and watch her drop the phone back into her bag. It's funny, I haven't seen any phones since . . . I was *me*. The whole time with Cass and Luke and Rosie, my life was electronic gadget free; it was so peaceful. It was so simple.

I look across the aisle. Movie Star/Supermodel is talking too loudly. This time it's into her phone. "I said five. You need to make this happen! No. Listen to me. You need to listen!"

"Excuse me, ma'am." Flight Attendant Guy stands beside her. "No phones until after we've landed."

Movie Star/Supermodel gives the flight attendant an icy glare. "That rule is absolutely ridiculous," she snaps. "I don't give a [*bleeeeeep!*] what the rule is. Is this what you call first class? How is this possible?"

I turn to my friend and whisper, "Oh my gosh, that lady is totally crazy!"

My friend leans toward me with tender eyes. Her smile dissolves. "I know it's not easy—hey, how can we make this work today? What can we do to make it feel a little bit better?"

"Better?" I fish for a clue.

"I heard her. Last night. I could hear the way she was

speaking to you and—"

"Wait. What do you mean?"

"That must have felt really scary, the way she was yelling and—" She pauses and lowers her voice even further. "Look, in no way is this meant to be disrespectful—she is my boss, but . . ." She trails off. "I know it's got to—" She stops. She stops because at this exact moment Movie Star/Supermodel totally loses it. I mean, she *really* flips out!

"No, I will not!" she practically shouts at poor Flight Attendant Guy. "We happen to be paying an exorbitant amount of money to sit in first class, and if I want to talk on the phone, I will!" There's a long, tense pause where everyone in the front of the plane looks up and watches. "Did you hear me?" Movie Star/Supermodel demands. "Okay then, why are you still standing there?"

My new friend reaches for my hand, lacing her fingers together with mine. The two of us exchange nervous, awkward smiles as Movie Star/Supermodel's voice grows louder.

"Oh, fine!" she hisses, finally tucking her phone back into her billion-dollar-looking black leather purse. I hear the snap from the shiny gold buckles.

I watch the whole thing, holding my breath.

The girl sitting beside me leans toward me. "I'm sorry, Jazz. I know this must feel so hard—I mean, she's your *mom* and—"

"Wait. My *mom*?" I blurt this out.

My stomach drops.

My new friend turns and glances at Movie Star/Supermodel, then back at me. "Well, yeah, I mean, I know sometimes you'd like to *pretend* she's not . . . but Jazz, she *is* your mom."

My mom. I stare, bewildered, across the aisle. Movie Star/Supermodel's arms are folded. She looks angry.

My new friend lets go of my hand and leans over me, gazing out the oval window. "Wow," she breathes, "look at those clouds down there. Aren't they amazing?"

I turn and look out too. We are flying though a dazzling sunrise, above a wedge of white pillowy clouds.

"*Mmmmmm*, incredible," she says softly, peering off into the distance.

I nod. "They look like giant cotton balls."

"Yes!" Her eyes light up. "Exactly!"

She sits back in her seat and inches over. She has this twinkle in her eyes that makes me instantly want to be even closer.

She keeps her eyes on the window. "You know, on some weird, deep level, I actually really do *love* flying. It's like, sometimes I picture myself up here looking down—" She pauses. "I try to see anything I'm worried about as passing clouds."

I look out through the window again too.

"Life has so many surprises," she goes on. "That's the beauty of it, right? You never know what's coming."

I stay silent and stare into the clouds, then turn back and smile faintly.

The girl with her mess of shiny long dark hair leans over so close that I can see the light-brown flecks in her eyes. "Hey, we're a team, right?" She looks at me for a second. "I know things have been really hard—" She stops and takes a big breath, her eyes still on mine, and smiles softly. "I'm here with you, okay?" Her eyes sparkle as she says it in a quiet whisper. "I'm right here, and we'll figure this out together."

Finally, we land and after ten minutes of taxiing on the runway, the plane comes to a stop and things around me begin moving fast. Movie Star/Supermodel stands in the aisle and looks down on me. Hard.

"Did you really have to wear that, Jasmine? How could you even begin to think that was okay?" she hisses, and shakes her head firmly, then—"Come on! Let's go! We have a tight schedule!"

I watch Movie Star/Supermodel slip her arms into her enormous brown fur coat. I have never seen someone so perfectly put together: her hair, her face, every detail— everything about her . . . it almost doesn't look real.

Once she has her furry mink on, she stays planted in the aisle and glances my way, then down at the girl sitting beside me. "Jasmine, Dani, come on! Let's go!" She whips her head around and turns and speaks to the man sitting in the seat directly behind us. "Hank? Did you hear me?" She raises her dramatically arched eye-brows. "Let's move! We don't have time to sit around.

We are on an incredibly strict schedule!"

I twist my neck, turn, and look through the thin gap between the seats, and, *okay, wow.* I'm pretty sure I have a *bodyguard!* He is very, very big! He looks like an ex–Navy SEAL or an action film star who does all his own stunts: clean-cut, shaved head, thick dark eyebrows, big neck, and a caterpillar-sized scar right above his top lip. He is wearing an expensive-looking dark suit, an ironed white collared shirt, and a *very* serious look on his chiseled face. He does not smile. Not even at me. His sunken-in sea-green eyes are shifting all around us, assessing the people crowding the aisle.

Movie Star/Supermodel grabs the flight attendant's elbow. "Please, could you let us through? You can't possibly even imagine the time crunch we are in!" She looks back down at the two of us. "Dani, Jasmine, let's go, come on!"

Dani stays in her seat. She doesn't seem at all fazed or worried or in a rush. There's no place to go. There are too many people trying to get up. She winks at me and looks down into her bag, reaches in, and fishes out a small, clear bottle. I watch her open it and shake a little bit onto her index finger, lift her hand, and gently dab some sort of wonderful rose-scented potion on that spot right between my eyes. She puts a dab on her forehead too. "There." She smiles with large, bright eyes. "That, my dear, is to remind us to breathe." Then she takes a big deep breath and slowly, calmly, moves to her feet.

26.

THE SECOND I STEP OFF the plane into the airport, it's a madhouse. The big guy in the suit—Hank, my tough, real-life action hero—does not leave my side. He is like a shield. Everyone who was on our plane seems to be in a hurry, pushing past us. There are a lot of people! Dani stays close, her hand lightly grasping my elbow. Movie Star/Supermodel walks about ten steps ahead. She's tall, and I can see the back of her bright-blond hair and her fur coat. I can hear her speaking loudly into her phone.

Hank, Dani, and I step into the end of a slow-moving line. "Customs and immigration," Dani tells me. "You know the drill. Are you ready?"

The second Dani says that, the lady in front of us spins around. Her eyes are huge. She looks right at me. "Pardon me, I'm so sorry to interrupt, I just have to tell you,

Jasmine, you are my daughter Emmie's biggest idol *ever*! She absolutely *loves* you," she gushes. "Do you mind if I take just one photo?"

Hank begins to step in but—

"Sure," I say with a shrug and a tiny smile.

"Oh my goodness, that is *so* sweet of you!" the lady gasps, then throws her arm around my shoulders, leans in close, and thrusts her phone to Dani.

Dani is a good sport. "Smile!" she says, and snaps the photo.

The lady thanks us about a thousand times and finally turns back around as the line inches forward.

Dani seems surprised. "That was so kind. You don't usually—" She stops and grins big. "That was just—really lovely. You made her day! It's such a gift that we can do that, isn't it?"

I nod. *It kind of really is.*

"And it's Christmas!" Dani beams and with no warning pulls me in for a hard squeeze. "Merry Christmas!" she says. Her silky, long, dark-brown hair falls over my mouth. It smells like peaches and cinnamon. I don't move. I just kind of drop my guard. I'm starting to really be a fan of hugging.

After we go through customs, Dani reminds me that there are going to be a lot of fans on the other side of the tinted sliding-glass doors that open into the airport's public lobby.

"You ready for this, Jazz?" she asks, looking into my eyes.

I nod, like I totally am, even though I am not. I am so *not* ready!

Hank is on one side of me and Dani on the other.

Right before the huge double glass doors slide open, Movie Star/Supermodel appears out of nowhere. She looks me straight in the face. "You are being observed at all times, Jasmine. Get yourself together!" She flashes this unexpected not-sincere perfect-teeth grin. "Let's go! Big smile!" she demands.

When the darkened sliding-glass doors open—*oh my gosh*—I cannot believe it! It's a mob scene! Hundreds of shrieking teenage girls—and guys—going absolutely berserk! "Jas-*minnnn*! Jas-*minnnn*!" they are chanting. A sea of outstretched arms holding up handmade posters, and they're all for *me*! Well, for who I am right now, at least. My eyes scan the crowd. I read the signs:

England ♥'s you!

Your No. 1 fan!

Marry me, Jasmine?

I see so many people waving their hands in the air and shouting:

"Jasmine, happy Christmas!"

"Jasmine, Jasmine! How do you like London?"

"Jasmine, we love you!"

I stop, but Dani pulls me along.

"Keep moving," she tells me. Her voice is firm but calm.

"*Jasmine! Jasmine!*" I hear one girl shriek. "Jasmine, would you sign this, please?"

I turn to Dani in disbelief. "I can't believe all these people are here for me!" I shout over the noise. Within seconds we are surrounded. I feel people pushing and shoving and I stop walking—with Hank keeping a close eye and Dani by my side—and I sign crumpled pieces of paper thrust into my hand. I sign with a black Sharpie pen that Dani slips into my fingers. "Jasmine," I scrawl, and at first I'm shocked at the way my hand moves and signs in script handwriting that I don't recognize. It's big and loopy and I dot the i with a heart and I feel a little thrill as I see the delight in people's eyes. *I'm not used to people noticing me. It's so weird that they suddenly care.* My mouth falls open. I turn to Dani.

"Can you believe this?" I say over the shouting.

Dani looks at me a little funny. "What?"

"Nothing." I shake my head and kind of laugh and sign more autographs as we make our way through the circling fans. We stop right before we step outside the airport's wide glass doors.

"Ready?" asks Dani. "This crowd is pretty crazy! Hold on tight and we'll hustle through the paparazzi."

"The papa what?" I start, but as soon as we walk through the doors into the cold London air I just, like—

Stop in my tracks.

I freeze.

My eyes are huge! There is a mob of photographers camped outside the airport doors, yelling for my attention.

"Jasmine, Jasmine!" the photographers shout as they surround me. "Jasmine, over here, give me a smile!"

I squint into the flashing bulbs.

"Jasmine! Welcome to London!"

"Over here, darling!" they holler at me, and click their gigantic cameras with huge zoom lenses. Very quickly the crowd begins to get out of hand. Reporters thrust microphones in my face.

"Let's get out of here. Now!" I hear Dani tell Hank as he clears a path.

Dani pulls me toward the big black SUV that is parked at the curb. We dart and push through the frenzy. A driver with reddish-blond hair and an all-black suit opens the door. I vault into the seat and Dani slides in next to me and quickly shuts the door. Movie Star/Supermodel is already in the seat behind me, her phone to her ear. She does not look up.

I sit back into the leather seat and stare out the tinted window at the mob of flashing cameras.

"Oh my gosh," I gasp. My heart is racing. "That was totally crazy!"

Dani looks at me. "Yeah, hey, are you okay? Why'd you stop back there?"

"I guess it took me by surprise," I answer, and keep my face to the window.

"I understand, it's a lot," Dani says. "I feel like we've been living in airports the last three months."

As soon as Hank slips into the front passenger seat and shuts the door, the SUV shoots forward. I press my forehead against the cool glass window and watch the pack of photographers chasing after us, running along-side the car for twenty or thirty feet as we speed away.

For a long time we ride in silence.

I hear the driver say something to Hank. "Yes, the center of London overlooking Hyde Park." The driver's British accent is so funny! He sounds like a real-life Sherlock Holmes, so distinguished and proper. Here's another crazy thing I suddenly notice: over here the steering wheel is on the opposite side of the car and we are driving on the wrong side of the road! *Weird.* I turn back to the buildings flashing by my window. We're on some sort of elevated highway above some very modern industrial buildings.

After forty-five minutes or so, we finally exit the expressway and slither down narrow city streets lined with pubs and old brick storefronts. *Yesterday I was on a horse galloping through a snowy forest, and today I'm riding in a chauffeured SUV through the streets of London!* I can't help but laugh softly.

"This is so crazy," I say under my breath.

Dani slips her hand over mine. "I know, right!" she

whispers. "We're in London, and it's Christmas!"

I glance at her sitting beside me. Her eyes are so bright. She is looking past me out the window. "I absolutely adore London. . . . It's so beautiful, so quaint and old and so lovely. What's not to love, right?"

I nod, mostly because everything Dani says sounds cool. She's easygoing. She's just got this glow. She's the kind of person you just want to be near.

When we pass a block full of theaters, a park, and a humongous historical-looking building with a gazillion White House–like pillars, "This is amazing!" falls out of my mouth.

"Oh, come on! Do you have any idea how stupid you sound right now?" I hear from the back.

I glance over my shoulder. Movie Star/Supermodel looks up from her phone, her sunglasses resting on top of her butter-colored bangs. "Really, Jasmine? You act like you've never seen London! Give me a break." She rolls her eyes and then looks back at her phone. "This little naïveté act of yours is getting on my nerves!" She lets out a big, loud, obnoxious hoot. Then—"I'm still incredibly disappointed in your choice of clothing, Jasmine. That outfit is simply *not* flattering," she sneers, "and please work on your posture. I was watching you at the airport. You were slumping like the hunchback of Notre Dame! That's not how I've taught you."

I immediately sit up straighter.

I keep my eyes on the buildings streaking by my window. But . . . I'm kind of surprised—

I'm not holding back tears. To be totally honest, I'm holding back this rising anger in my gut. I don't know if this is the new me who rides horses and signs autographs, but honestly, I feel oddly like turning around and yelling, *Why are you so mean!*

27.

THE SIDEWALK IN FRONT OF the hotel is jammed with more photographers, ready and waiting when our sleek black SUV pulls up to the curb.

"Let's get you in as quickly as possible," says Dani.

Only, as soon as I step down onto the sidewalk, the whole crazy scene from the airport repeats exactly. Cameras are thrust in my face and flashes go off, people are frantically yelling. I start to feel a jolt of panic.

"Dani!" I cry out, and reach for her hand. I am being crushed by photographers and drowned out by shouting.

"Give us a smile, please, Jasmine!"

"Jasmine, what do you want for Christmas?"

"Jasmine, you're gorgeous!"

Dani and I follow close behind Hank, who looks like a Secret Service agent in his all-black suit and serious face, pushing photographers out of our way. I am gripping Dani's hand so tight I'm probably cutting off her circulation— there is a crush of people yelling and shouting—and in a flash, I remember Carmen and Teddy's party: the sticky sweaty bodies, the loud shouting, that awful feeling of a crowd pressing in around me. I glance nervously at Dani and clutch her hand. Hank is still just ahead of us, working his way through the swarm, until—

Dani and I finally step through the hotel doors, and the chaos from outside is instantly gone. There is a gush of beautiful quiet. The all-white ultra-luxurious lobby feels like a tranquil spa. It's bright and airy, and flooded with light. I look back over my shoulder. Photographers are lining the huge glass windows outside, flashes going off.

I turn back to Dani.

"I'd seriously like to kick some of those guys in the—" She stops. "Hey, are you okay?"

"Yeah." I nod. "I mean—I guess."

"That was a little bit scary"—she takes a deep breath and smiles on the exhale—"but we made it!"

I try to force a smile. I'm honestly a little bit stunned. *Being famous isn't so easy!* Ahead of us, Movie Star/Super- model strides up to a reception desk made of glass and topped with rows of tulips. Nothing about the lobby looks like Christmas. It's more like a museum of modern art with oversize funky paintings and hulking sculptures.

And there are other guests. We are not the only ones here. There's a handful of important-looking people, neatly dressed. Some are standing and quietly chatting, others are sitting on long, bright-orange sofas and lime-green lounge chairs—reading, drinking tea, talking into phones, clicking away on laptops. Low-key piano music is floating in the background.

I stand next to Dani and Hank at the bottom of the grand staircase and glance all around.

Dani has the best look on her face. "This place is so super rad." Her eyes get big as she looks up at the gigantic pink glass crystal chandelier hanging over us.

I tilt my head back and stare up at it too. The chandelier is a rainbow of pinks and yellows.

"Whoa, gorgeous," Dani breathes. "So—"

"Fancy," I finish. "I mean . . . this hotel must be so expensive!"

"Are you sure you're okay?" Dani asks, a curious look on her face. "There's something different about you. . . ."

I laugh. I can't help it. "Something different, yeah. You could say that."

I drop onto one of the bright-orange couches.

Dani sits herself down next to me.

She doesn't say a word. She just sits back, silently inhales, and flashes me a radiant smile. Everything about Dani feels so relieving. I've only known her for, like, five hours, but she's honestly one of the most instantly lovable people I've ever met.

For a long minute, I say nothing.

I turn back and look right at Dani and her sparkly eyes.

And then, sitting right here on the bright-orange couch, with Hank standing guard and a few curious onlookers stopping and staring and snapping photos of me, I feel myself take a big, deep, lung-filling breath for what feels like the first time.

28.

THE WOMAN WALKING ACROSS THE lobby right for us is tall and Asian, with shiny black hair parted in a zigzag and pulled back tight, away from her face. She's dressed in a tight, slim lavender dress.

"Ms. Jasmine!" she exclaims in an elegant and formal British accent. She extends her hand, and it takes me a second (and a glare from Movie Star/Supermodel, now standing beside me) to realize that I am supposed to reach out and clasp her hand in mine and shake it.

Our hands meet. "Nice to meet you," I say, trying very hard to be perfectly polite and well-mannered. I immediately stand up stick straight, suddenly very aware of my posture.

"So nice to see you, Ms. Jasmine. It is entirely my pleasure," the lady tells me. She finally lets go of my hand.

"I am Octavia Grace, and I will be serving as your on-call butler at your service, to make your stay with us an unforgettable one."

I look shocked, like, *Butler?*

Octavia Grace's eyes never leave mine. "If there is anything you or any of your party need, I will be delighted to respond to all your requests, Ms. Jasmine. Your bags have already been taken up, so if you please, let me show you to your suite."

All of us—Movie Star/Supermodel, Hank, Dani, Octavia Grace, and I—climb a red-carpeted staircase leading up to two side-by-side gold-encased elevators. Everything that Octavia Grace says sounds so charming. She's cheerful and very positive.

"We've been expecting you, Ms. Jasmine, and the entire staff has been made aware of your incredibly hectic schedule."

When the elevator arrives, the golden doors slide open. Hank stands back until all four ladies—including me—step on, and then he gets on too. For an awkward moment all five of us stand in the elevator and nobody says a word until Octavia Grace glances nervously at Movie Star/Supermodel and says, "We understand this will be an extremely busy Christmas Day, and we will do whatever we can to accommodate you."

Movie Star/Supermodel is too busy scanning her phone to reply. She doesn't even look up.

"Thank you," I quickly blurt out, strangely feeling embarrassed by a mother who isn't even mine. The elevator suddenly starts to rise. I almost lose my balance. I grab onto Dani's arm. It takes me by surprise.

Octavia Grace fills the quiet. "Ms. Jasmine, I understand your press interviews begin in the Queen's Suite at one o'clock?"

I look at Dani, unsure what I should say.

"Yes, that's right," says Dani, jumping in.

Interviews. My stomach drops. I'm not sure what that means, but it doesn't sound good!

We ride up in silence for the rest of the thirty-three floors.

I throw my head back and stare into the mirrored elevator ceiling at Jasmine's reflection. She's so pretty, and I crack a tiny smile at her—or, I guess, *me*—as the elevator rockets up, up, up.

When the elevator stops on the very top floor, Octavia Grace flashes a key card up to a scanner and says, "Welcome to our penthouse suite."

The golden elevator doors open up right into the all-white carpeted room. A few steps later, we are all standing in the sleek, impeccably clean, luxurious suite.

"Whoa!" drops out of my mouth.

"I know, right?" Dani says, as we exchange *holy cow* smiles.

Octavia walks across the suite and draws open the curtains to reveal a floor-to-ceiling wall of glass. "As you can see," she begins, "you have absolutely stunning panoramic views of most of central London and, of course, Hyde Park directly across."

Dani and I both stand in front of the wall of glass and look out at the skyline.

"Wow!" I peer down at the park and the London streets below us. The tiny little cars look like miniature toys. "We're so high above the ground!"

Dani admires the view. "We have stayed at a lot of places in the last six months, but I have to say, this tops them all."

The three of us turn back and face the room.

Octavia nods toward the gigantic bed twice the size of Carmen's and piled high with lavish pillows. "I have it on good authority that these beds are blissfully comfy."

I sit down on the edge of the bed and run my hand over the cool, crisp white sheets and puffy comforter.

Octavia smiles at me. "The sheets and duvet are silk and cotton, custom-made for us in Italy and fabulously lush!"

I look up at the framed modern painting hanging above the bed. I glance across the room at Movie Star/ Supermodel; she has taken her fur coat off and is sitting on a yellow sofa, tapping away on her phone. My eyes move to the glass-top table and the vase filled with long-stemmed hot-pink roses and a white bowl filled with apples, oranges, and bananas. It suddenly occurs to me that I am *starving*. My stomach rumbles. I stand up and follow Octavia and Dani past a writing desk and a light-filled sitting area with a baby grand piano, into the spa-like, gigantic bathroom.

Octavia points out all the features. "State-of-the-art technology," she says, pausing to push a button, and a television screen appears above the bathtub. "This Japanese-style heated soaking tub is your own little oasis of tranquillity."

"Not too shabby," jokes Dani.

"Yeah," I giggle, and step into the all-glass walk-in shower.

Octavia looks at me standing fully clothed in my black leggings and purple camouflage hoodie inside the glass-enclosed shower. "The entire design was really aimed at making you feel like you are in your home away from home." She says, "home away from home" with big eyes and a smile, and I almost laugh. *This place doesn't quite look like any home I have ever been in.*

Octavia opens a cabinet above the tub to reveal a personalized silky white bathrobe with *Jasmine* stitched on the chest pocket in purple script embroidered letters.

"Okay, wow!" Dani smiles. "I am officially impressed."

Dani and I follow Octavia out of the bathroom to the white-carpeted entryway of the suite.

"I'm so glad you're pleased," Octavia says. "Also, Ms. Jasmine, our world-renowned executive chef Élodie Boulleauand and her team are on call at any hour and delighted to respond to any requests and—oh, I almost forgot, one more thing," she says. "If you have time, please enjoy your private rooftop heated relaxation pool accessed just to the right of your balcony terrace."

"A pool!" I say. "Can we go swimming?" I blurt out.

Movie Star/Supermodel, who I didn't think was listening, suddenly pipes in from across the room. "Swimming?" she says, glancing up. "Since when do you like swimming? Please!" She laughs. Then her voice gets sterner and she looks at me hard. "Focus, Jasmine. Do I need to remind you? This is *not* a vacation. We are here on business!"

Octavia shoots me a sympathetic look and walks toward the elevator doors and flashes her key card. "Excellent, ladies. Then I will leave you to enjoy and get some rest."

The elevator doors open and she steps in.

Movie Star/Supermodel stands and strides by me in her towering heels and steps onto the elevator with Octavia. She is facing us as the doors begin to close. "Dani, please, for goodness' sake, make sure she is not dressed like *that* for the press! First impressions are millions of dollars! Look the part. And Jasmine, please go over your talking points."

For a second there is a long, uncomfortable, heavy silence.

Right before the doors shut, Hank sticks his arm in and stops them from closing, holding the elevator from leaving without him on it.

I stay where I am, facing all three of them: Movie Star/Supermodel with her fur coat on her shoulders is already looking down at her phone. Octavia Grace, with her charming smile, has her hands clasped politely in front of her. Hank has one arm on the door and turns and looks back toward me with a warm nod. His voice is soft and kind, not what I expect.

"I will be back to escort you to the press junket in"—he looks down at his watch—"two hours." Then he steps in through the two golden elevator doors, and the three of them are gone.

"Ughh—" Dani looks at me and shakes her head. "I'm so sorry, Jazz. Honestly, sometimes your mom just makes me so angry."

She is silent for a minute. "You know, I just want to say—" Dani stops and smiles at me. "You are just right. There is nothing wrong with you at all."

My heart jumps. *It's such a relief to hear those words.*

I look back at her but I don't know what to say, so I drop down onto the humongous bed and prop one of the fancy white pillows under my head.

Dani collapses onto the bed too. It's massive. She's way over on one side and I'm a mile away on the other. We both are lying on our backs, staring up at the ceiling. For a minute it's quiet. Then she flips over onto her side, props her head up with her elbow, and looks at me. "You know what?" Dani's eyes light up. "We need to fuel up!" She rolls over and reaches for the sleek black hotel phone and looks back at me. "What do you say? Some yummy comfort food, does that sound like a good plan?"

I nod and turn over onto my side, copying Dani, propping up my head with my arm. "But—um . . . Dani, uhhh—there's just one more thing. . . ."

"Yeah?"

I hesitate. But if I don't ask for help, this is going to get much harder. I look back at Dani holding the phone, her long, dark hair spilling around her shoulders. Her eyes are glowing. She radiates warmth. I take a breath, then blurt it out: "Will you help me go over my talking points?"

Dani looks back at me with her crazy big smile. "Oh my gosh, silly, of course I will!"

29.

ONE HOUR LATER DANI IS still prepping me for the interviews as the two of us, and a very serious-looking Hank, ride down the golden elevator to the Queen's Suite for my press interviews. Dani has changed into a simple black dress, leggings, and matching black leather boots. Her long, dark, wavy hair is tied up into a loose thick knot, like she tossed it up in two seconds. Easy. Her lips have a hint of glossy shimmer, and her cheeks are flush and rosy pink.

"So, today we have all European journalists, and first up is that chick from Norway. We had her in Paris, remember? She can be a little intimidating. She asks a lot of questions. Don't let her crush your self-confidence— just be you, okay? Be yourself."

Be myself. I think about that, and let out a soft laugh

until I remember this is not exactly a laughing matter. How am I going to pull this off? I have trouble saying what I think even when I'm *me*! How am I going to do it being someone else?

Dani looks at me. "Hey, I believe in you," she says. "Trust yourself—" She stops and her eyes flash. "This is *your* life. You get to respond however you want. Or not." Dani reaches into her big black leather bag and pulls something out. "Lucky lip balm?" she offers.

I take the cap off the tube and apply it using the elevator's mirrored walls to guide me. I smile as I do it because, well, I can't believe I'm in a gold elevator wearing a candy-pink frilly dress, a leopard-print faux fur jacket, striped tights, and platform leather boots that come up to my knees! I cannot believe I'm *Jasmine!* I have the best hair ever. It's super-duper curly and totally awesome! I move closer to the elevator wall and stare into the mirror at my reflection. I carefully apply the beeswax along my lips and seriously almost start laughing.

Dani lets out a playful giggle as she stands back and watches. "Five interviews in a row, lip hydration is totally key!"

Five interviews! My stomach twists up in a knot. I hand back the lip gloss and look up at Dani. She is calm and cool like she has all the faith in the world in me.

"What if I mess up? What if I say the wrong thing?"

Dani smiles big. "What's the worst thing that can

happen? You have one of those really awkward moments? I kind of love those!" Her voice is bright. "Perfect is boring. I actually prefer people to be real, don't you?"

"Um, I guess?" I say. *I guess I do.*

I glance at Hank, then back at Dani.

"Dani, please," I plead. "Can't you just go instead of me?" I am embarrassed when I hear how desperate I sound. My heart begins to pound so loudly I can feel it in my chest, and my legs are shaking in my platform boots.

Dani plants both her hands on my shoulders and holds them there. She takes a big deep breath and smiles at me for a really long time without speaking.

I copy her again.

I smile.

I breathe.

Dani keeps her eyes right on mine. "Just look at all that sparkly goodness! You are totally amazing," she tells me as the elevator doors begin to slide open. "Just be you, okay? You're gonna rock it!"

Octavia Grace greets us when we step off the elevator, and we follow her down a quiet red-carpeted hallway through a door marked *The Queen's Suite*. The room is smaller than our penthouse but super-deluxe, and there is no bed. It's more like a very proper living room furnished with two red velvet armchairs that sit facing each other. In between the chairs is a polished brass table with two china teacups and a vase filled with a dozen tall long-stemmed pink and yellow roses. Behind the table is a giant blown-up poster of Jasmine's new Christmas album, *Holiday Songs*, propped up and leaning against an artist easel. The walls are painted yellow and the curtains are drawn open, exposing a backdrop of the same floor-to-ceiling sweeping views of London.

"Ms. Jasmine?" Octavia Grace is speaking to me. "Would you care for some tea before your first interview?"

I glance at Dani as if she knows what I want more than I do. But Dani is gazing out the window at the view.

"Um, sure," I answer, turning back and smiling politely. "Tea sounds good."

"Splendid!" says Octavia Grace, pouring tea into my gold-leafed porcelain cup.

I lift the steaming-hot cup to my lips and try to turn up Dani's voice in my head: *Just be you, okay? Be yourself.*

Ten minutes later more people come into the room. Movie Star/Supermodel is here, sitting in the corner, occasionally looking up with a prickly glare. Hank is parked beside the door to the suite. Octavia Grace and three hotel guys dressed in suits and ties are standing with their hands folded in front, no smiles. The room is quiet except for the faint sound of the sirens outside the window. They are not like the sirens you hear at home. They are jolting and they are making my heart quiver.

When the journalist walks across the room to greet me, I awkwardly jump to my feet. I don't know what comes over me, but I somehow know to stand up, walk toward her, look her in the eye, and firmly shake her hand. "So nice to meet you," I offer, and wait for her to sit down, before I drop back into the red velvet armchair and face her.

The journalist is from Norway. It's the first thing she tells me. "*Gledelig Jul*," she says, and explains is "Happy Christmas" in Norwegian.

"*Gledelig Jul*," I fumble back, and laugh because I'm in Jasmine's body, sipping tea and speaking Norwegian at a press interview in the Queen's Suite!!!

"*Gledelig Jul*, yes! Excellent!" the journalist says. She is wearing a pleated green dress and it's supercute. Her English is nearly perfect. She has a charming accent. She reminds me of Tinker Bell from Peter Pan—*a little sweet, a little sassy*—I think to myself, as I watch her. She is small and slight and has short blond hair and light-green eyes. Honestly, she looks almost as nervous as I feel. I watch her fidget with her tan leather briefcase and electronic-looking recording gadget.

"Let me just set this on the table, and then we'll get started," she says from her seat across from me.

"Sounds good," I answer, all cool and calm, like I'm not out-of-my-mind nervous (*yes*) and suddenly feeling extremely hot (*yes*) and pulling and twisting Jasmine's curly ringlets of hair around my finger (*yes*).

I catch Movie Star/Supermodel's no-nonsense eyes from across the room, and I suddenly cross my ladylike legs and sit up, spine straight, like a professional ballerina. I glance at Dani, standing across from me, leaning against the wall, shooting me a steady, soft smile. When Dani's eyes meet mine, I feel it in my heart. It feels so good, like, *maybe I can do this.* And for a quick second I breathe slowly in and out, lift the cup to my lips and take a small sip of steaming-hot tea. Then—

Okay. I think. *Let's do this.*

NORWEGIAN TINKER BELL: Jasmine! So delighted to be speaking with you on Christmas Day! Let's get right to it, shall we? First I must ask: Who are you wearing? You are perfectly adorable, completely stunning!

ME (*looking confused*): Who am I wearing?

NORWEGIAN TINKER BELL: Yes, your clothes, the designer?

ME: Oh, um . . .

NORWEGIAN TINKER BELL: It's okay (*smiling*), we can skip that one. (*She leans in.*) Right now you are one of the most instantly recognizable faces in the world. You've been featured in massively successful campaigns for the likes of Chanel and Estée Lauder! After your first number-one smash hit, you had to contend with overnight stardom.

You have over thirty million followers on social media. What was it like seeing your face on the cover of *Vogue*?

ME: Seeing my face on the cover of *Vogue* . . . is, well, I mean, umm—it's an honor! It's, uhhhhh . . . it's a privilege. (*smiling*) All of this honestly feels like a dream.

NORWEGIAN TINKER BELL: So I don't know about you, but I'm a complete maniac when it comes to Christmas. What's the best gift you have ever received?

ME: Cowgirl boots!

NORWEGIAN TINKER BELL: Fabulous! I'm learning more and more about you! (*smiling*) I have to admit: I'm obsessed with your music. Your new album *Christmas Songs* has already been certified platinum. The opening track is your brilliant remake of Irving Berlin's classic "White Christmas." What an infectious hook, it's impossibly catchy! I can't stop singing that song—I could start humming it now!

ME: I know, right? So could I! I mean (*giggling*), uh— thank you so much!

NORWEGIAN TINKER BELL: "White Christmas" debuted at number one in the UK and across Europe and, of course, the United States. A trifecta! You are a teen-girl pop-star franchise! You may be the richest young woman in music today. Your annual income is estimated to be over forty million dollars. You have performed sold-out shows for three months straight, and now you are catching fire in the UK. You must be one of the hardest-working thirteen-year-olds on the face of the earth!

ME: (*Nervous smile*)

NORWEGIAN TINKER BELL: Oh, you are a modest one! Let's move on. How would you describe your personal style?

ME: Um . . . I guess I really like—uh . . . pajamas? (*Everyone in the room laughs.*)

NORWEGIAN TINKER BELL: Brilliant! Favorite food?

ME: Easy. Blueberry pancakes.

NORWEGIAN TINKER BELL: Oh, yes! (*smiling, long pause*) On a serious note, do you ever just curl up in your bed and have a good cry?

ME: Um. Yes. (*nodding*) You could say that for sure.

NORWEGIAN TINKER BELL: Well, that's a relief to know the amazing Jasmine is actually human! (*pausing and leaning in*) What I really want to know is—what about boys? Any big crushes?

ME: (*Turning red. Cheeks combusting.*)

NORWEGIAN TINKER BELL (*laughing*): Ahhh, my Christmas gift to you—I will let you skip that one too! (*pausing*) Your pop-star life must feel like a roller coaster at times. Are you ever thrilled and terrified at the same time?

ME (*nodding*): Pretty much every minute. (*smiling*) Thrilled and terrified. That's how I feel right now, in fact.

NORWEGIAN TINKER BELL: What do you do? How do you handle that?

ME: I guess I try to, like, remember to breathe?

NORWEGIAN TINKER BELL: Breathe! Yes! Brilliant!

Wonderful. You have been on tour for three straight months. Your mother manages your career, and you are homeschooled, which allows you to tour. Do you ever just want to stop it all and be alone? Do you ever want to be a regular kid and go to middle school? Ride a bus?

ME: Middle school? Um. Yeah, *no!* Definitely not! (*laughter*) I mean, middle school is actually *not that fun!*

NORWEGIAN TINKER BELL: Brilliant! I happen to agree, school is overrated, and you, my dear, are utterly lovely. (*looks at notes, looks back up, smiling.*) One last question. (*leans in.*) What is your advice to girls everywhere? Girls who want to be just like you?

ME: Uhhhh, maybe, just, like, try to be yourself. (*glancing at Dani, who is smiling big*) Trying to be yourself is really actually kind of hard. I'm just sort of learning that right now.

As soon as we are finished, Tinker Bell quickly packs away her special electronic recorder to make room for the next journalist waiting just outside the door.

"I have to say," says Tinker Bell, zipping shut her leather bag, "since I spoke to you last in Paris? It feels like you are a *totally* different person! You were very honest today. You have a natural charm." She stands. "And hey, I will be watching. Good luck tonight!"

Wait. "Tonight?" I say.

"Yes," says Tinker Bell, looking right at me, "tonight's live, nationally televised Christmas night performance!"

30.

WE LEAVE THE HOTEL IN a blur. Everyone is rushing!

We are late!

So, yeah, you can bet I don't mention how tired I am as I follow Dani, Movie Star/Supermodel, Hank, and Octavia Grace onto a private elevator and we plummet down, like a high-speed stomach-churning amusement park ride, to the hotel's lowest level. I step off a little woozy and follow everyone as we herd through a zigzagging maze of basement hallways until Hank pushes open a heavy metal door leading to a cold, damp, empty cement underground parking lot, and just like that, our big black chauffeured SUV pulls up and we hop in. It all goes quickly, planned with precision.

As soon as the SUV turns out of the garage, past the

paparazzi gathered outside the front of the hotel and onto the busy London streets, I rest my forehead against the window and stare out at the zipping cars and traffic and ready myself for Movie Star/Supermodel to tell me how terribly awful I was at the interviews and how I totally blew it. How I said the wrong thing. How I messed up. But to my great surprise, she pretty much says *nothing* the entire way. Not one word. Oh wait, no. She says this: "Dammit! We're late!" Then she takes a big huffy breath and continues scrolling through her phone without looking up.

Besides that?

We ride in silence.

Daylight is almost gone from the sky when the SUV drops us off at the television studio's private back entrance. A chilly gray darkness hits my face as I jump down onto the pavement. As soon as the four of us step inside, we are met by a tall, thin man in a T-shirt, vest, and tan pants, wearing a headset and gripping a clipboard. He looks ticked off. He has nervous darty eyes and gold wire-rimmed glasses.

"You're late," says Clipboard Guy sternly, and immediately turns and begins walking very quickly.

We follow him down a set of stairs through three long, narrow hallways and finally to the edge of a giant stage that has been converted into an ultra-glamorous

Christmas party: a gigantic towering tree lit up with literally thousands of white gleaming lights, huge wrapped presents, and—if you look up—a gazillion glittering stars hanging down and spinning around.

"Unbelievable," says Dani, with a laugh. "It's beginning to look a lot like Christmas!"

I stand right next to her and nod. *It really is beautiful,* I think, as I look at the giant sparkly tree. The lights. The gifts.

"Wow, it's kind of like a fairy tale," says Dani. "You know what I mean?"

I laugh. "Yeah," I tell her, and smile with my eyes. "I sort of do."

Dani nudges me with her elbow. "Hey you," she says, spreading her arms wide and giving me a long, big, warm hug. "You're gonna crush it tonight!"

"Thanks," I say softly, and cling to her like a little kid, my face pressed into her shoulder. The truth is, right now? Right this second. I'm not thinking about singing or remembering the words to Jasmine's hit single. I am thinking about how hugs feel *sooo* good. I close my eyes. I breathe Dani in. For a few seconds I feel my body relax, until I hear a *certain voice* and my eyes pop open and I immediately let go and step back.

Movie Star/Supermodel is standing just a few feet away, her toned arms crossed. Her sunglasses are up and pushing back her blond hair. She's deep in conversation with an important-looking man in a light-gray suit. Her charm is turned up and it's on high: "Great to see you! What a night! This is incredibly impressive, just magnificent," she says, suddenly sounding like the kindest, sweetest person on earth. "Oh yes, the fans have been fantastic! Just lovely, my goodness, we are absolutely wild about London!"

Clipboard Guy walks up to Dani and me, standing side by side.

"Let's go," he says, gesturing for me to come onstage. He has a terrifyingly serious look on his face. "We need to do the camera blocking and the sound check, now!"

Sound check?

A moment goes by and I do not move. "I—uhhh—" But I realize pretty quickly by the fact that everyone is staring at me that Clipboard Guy is not *asking*, he's *telling*.

A young woman in jeans and a dark turtleneck sweater appears and hands me an acoustic guitar. "All tuned up," she says, and loops the strap around my body. I turn to Dani.

"Dani, seriously, I can't do this." I speak in a quiet voice and take a giant step backward. "I'm not kidding, I—um. I'm not who you think I am. I . . . ," I sputter. "I just cannot do this. I really, really, *really* can't."

"Hey, whoa, slow down," says Dani. She looks concerned. "Take a big deep breath."

I do. I take a big deep breath.

But the thing is, I'm still me in Jasmine's body!

And I *can't* sing!

And I *can't* play guitar!

"I can't do this," I repeat, shaking my head.

Dani's voice is calm and her eyes are convincing. "No biggie. You've done this a hundred times. It's just a typical sound check and a run-through so the tech director knows the angles." She pauses, and the corners of her mouth tip upward. "You can do it! You're gonna nail it."

All of a sudden Movie Star/Supermodel looks up from schmoozing with the guy in the suit and connects her eyes with mine. I can read her lips as she turns to the guy and says, "*Excuse me, please.*"

I watch her stride across the stage to me and stop right in front of me.

"Jasmine," she snarls. She is staring at me. "Get it together! Now is not the time for performance anxiety. You heard the man—" She stops as if she's too angry to even speak, shakes her head, and mouths the last three words: *Go. Right. Now.*

Imagine the theater and stage at your school—you know the one where they have the all-school meetings and the musicals and talent shows? Imagine *that* but with bright overhead lights, microphones suspended in the air, and a bunch of people standing behind huge television cameras set up on tripods. Then? Times that by ten thousand and you can pretty much picture me on a splashy new billion-dollar London television studio stage, sitting slouched on a stool with a guitar strapped around my neck and the ultra-glamorous Christmas tree glittering behind me.

Clipboard Guy is barking orders: "When the red light goes on, Jasmine, *ten million* households in Britain will be watching you," he says, pausing to make sure I am paying attention. "There's not a second for hesitation! Not one second." He peers out from behind a television monitor and shoots me an *I'm not kidding* glare.

My breathing gets faster.

My mouth is dry.

I drop my eyes and stare at the floor and try and quiet the voice in my head, which is warning, *This is going to be a disaster!*

"Hi, Jasmine."

I hear a cheery voice and look up.

"I'm Ahmed, your sound engineer for tonight."

Ahmed is holding a bunch of wires and high-tech-looking microphones. He's in dark baggy jeans and a black crewneck sweater and wearing one of those walkie-talkie headsets.

He kneels in front of my feet and begins plugging all sorts of cords into a black box. "The speaker on the floor in front of you is a studio monitor, and you can hear your own voice coming through it—no different than when you play a live concert."

"Oh, okay," I say, like I totally understand what he's saying.

Ahmed smiles. "Do you use in-ear monitors?"

"Um—uh . . ."—*I have no idea*—"No?" I try.

"Old style, baby!" says Ahmed. "Brilliant. This is no different than your normal setup for a concert. Remember not to cup the microphone too much, because these speakers are special for solo acoustic. They're pretty sensitive and prone to feedback."

I nod. *Oh, man.*

Ahmed stands. "It's gonna be great!"

Yeah, probably not, I think, and force a nervous smile, swing the guitar up onto my knee, and grip the neck.

The studio feels kind of cold. We have two hours before the show starts. The seats are still empty. The lights feel hot on my face. It's very quiet. My heart starts to pound. There's a strong chance I might throw up.

I hear a man's voice come over the sound system. "Okay, Jasmine," the voice says. "Can we get a sound check, please?"

I open my mouth, then shut it. My hands are trembling. I lean into the microphone. "Hello?" I say in barely a whisper.

The voice laughs. "Okay, Jasmine. We're going to need you to speak a little louder than that. Can we get a Merry Christmas, one, two, three?"

"Umm. Merry Christmas," I manage. "One, two . . . three."

"Can we get a strum on the guitar?"

I strum. *Oh God.*

A millisecond later, the best words ever: "Okay, we're all set," I hear the voice say. "The blocking is on point. The sound is great. I hear you've had a pretty rigorous schedule today. Let's save your voice for the live broadcast."

31.

WE ARE IN THE DRESSING room, which smells like coconut lotion. And by we, I mean me and Dani. Supermodel/Movie Star is in meetings and cannot be here—*thank you, God*. Just so you know, I am sitting in one of those big styling chairs that swivels, wrapped in a fluffy white robe, facing a sink, a countertop, and a huge mirror lined with a string of white twinkle Christmas lights. The walls are plastered with framed autographed black-and-white photos of famous celebrity rock stars. There is a seating area with an extra-long, funky, hot-pink sofa (where Dani is sitting reading a book), a coffee table with a bowl of fruit and tall blue bottles of sparkling water, and vases placed around the room filled with bright, colorful flowers. You can hear this faint hypnotic hip-hop groove drifting from the speakers, the kind of smooth soft beat you don't really notice until you realize you are tapping your hand on your knee and swaying a little in your seat.

It's like a full-blown music video in here! Or, no—actually, it's more like a car wash, only instead of a car, it's *me*, and instead of giant whirly brushes rubbing and scrubbing, I'm surrounded by a team of three: a tall, thin, redheaded hairstylist named Estelle is currently massaging my scalp; a makeup artist/punk warrior princess, Annika (pink hair, a nose ring, and the word "Believe" in script, tattooed on the inside of her wrist), is dabbing a lavender-scented cool moisturizing cream across my face; and Lily (super-beautiful fashion stylist with gold hoop earrings and a huge white shimmery smile) is busy setting up my potential wardrobe. I have choices! Each dress is hanging on a rack with a photo pinned to the outside of the garment bag with the complete finished look, a fabric sample, and a photo of the corresponding matching shoes.

I sit back in my swivel chair and can't help but grin this big goofy grin into the mirror. I mean, really! This is kind of actually funny. This life could not be more opposite from mine! Somehow I have gone from Carmen making me strip off her fuzzy blue sweater to a tween sensation who has her own glam squad!

If there was a sign outside the door of the dressing room, it would read: *Do Not Enter—Makeover in Progress!*

All three women poke and prod and fuss around me. This is serious business.

I always wondered how girls in magazines and on TV manage to look so, like, flawless and perfect, and now, sitting in this seat—I sort of get it. Pretty much *anyone* can look like *anything*! Everything is art, and I am the painting. *It's sort of like dress-up,* I think to myself as I watch in the mirror: I am transforming into a teen pop-princess right before my eyes. Honestly, I sort of absolutely love the pampering until all at once I suddenly remember one small fact: I have exactly two hours to remember all the words to Jasmine's "impossibly catchy" version of "White Christmas," figure out how the heck to play the acoustic guitar, and step onto the stage and perform in front of ten million people on live TV! When I remember that, I begin to sweat.

When my makeup and hair are done, Dani sets down her book, gets up from the couch, and joins Estelle, Annika, and Lily, all circling behind me, admiring me in the mirror.

"Your hair is fierce!" Estelle says, reaching out and almost petting my amazing curly hair. She has hand-painted streaks of shimmers to a few strands to make it "pop." Her eyes light up as she runs her fingers over my big fluffy curls, ruffling them. "I'm so glad we didn't straighten it. Your best feature is your hair. It's so beautifully, naturally curly! There is truly nothing better than being who you are," Estelle says, grinning. "I kept it natural and glammed it up with just a notch of color."

I sit up in the chair, still wrapped in my robe, and stare at my reflection for a good long minute, and I think, *Wow. I actually love it!* I reach up and push down on my springy curls.

"So dope!" says Dani, smiling at me in the mirror. "Totally love the goldy shimmers!"

Estelle nods and keeps fluffing my big curls with her fingers. "It's so voluminous!" she says, making contact with my eyes in the mirror. "It's almost not fair, Jazz. Your 'fro is on fleek! You seriously have the best hair ever!"

Annika leans in close and with her finger carefully brushes away an eyelash from my cheek. "I love your iridescent eyes! Daaaaaaang, it's all about those brows!" She steps back and folds her arms as if she's admiring a job well done. "That light-catching blue shimmery eye shadow is your signature style, and no lipstick. I stuck with glosses, with just a little bit of glitter. When the lights hit that face. Wow. All sorts of awesome is going on! You are—"

"Absolutely gorgeous!" finishes Lily, flashing her big, magnetic smile.

Five minutes later, I am standing in my white, fluffy bathrobe, realizing I have to change right here in the middle of the room, in front of *everyone*. *Here . . . goes . . . nothing!* I slowly slip out of the robe and drape it over the swivelly styling chair and stand almost totally naked in front of all four women in nothing but Jasmine's frilly purple underwear and bra.

The reason I am standing in my underwear is because we have decided on "the One." The sparkly red amazing dress that everyone—including me—has chosen. Mostly I follow Dani's lead. "Ooh, yes!" she says, her eyes lighting up when Lily takes it off the rack and holds it up in front of me.

"That is 'the One,'" Dani says, sounding excited.

Dani and Lily help me slip the dress on, scooching it very carefully over my hair and makeup. Dani zips it up in the back, and I turn around and face her.

"Oh my God, it's ah-may-zing!" she says with a huge smile. "That's 'the One,'" she repeats, her eyes aglow.

"Totally," says Lily. "That dress is definitely ill. You are on fire!"

"Fierce and fabulous!" says Estelle, nodding.

"I love this dress. It is most definitely 'the One,'" agrees Annika.

"The One" is ruby-red, long-sleeved and tight-fitting, with sparkly sequins at the top. The bottom poofs out fluffy, like a ballerina's shimmery tutu.

Lily stands back and examines me.

"It fits you perfectly," she says, obviously pleased. "It's

really quite striking. It's a fairy-tale dress! Do you feel like a princess?"

I nod, approaching the floor-length mirror, and smile at the sparkles. "I actually sort of do!"

"Hey, what do you think about these Stella McCartney platform oxfords?" asks Lily, holding up a pair of red leather shoes with shiny gold star cutouts and four-inch-thick chunky rubber soles, and then placing them on the floor in front of my feet.

"Sure." I shrug and smile. "Why not?"

"Ohh, I have a little fashionista on my hands! Good call!" Lily says. "Elevated comfort. I absolutely love them."

I balance on one foot, my hand gripping Dani's shoulder, and slip my shimmery stocking-covered feet into the shoes. Instantly I am four inches taller! It feels kind of wild. I have a whole new view! I feel this boost of confidence and pull my shoulders back.

"You're like a Christmas Day Cinderella," Lily says, kneeling down and buckling up the shoes.

"You're a beauty inside and out," adds Dani, eyes flashing.

"Just one more thing," Lily says, slipping behind me and fastening a string of diamonds around my neck. "Oh, you look exquisite! Soooo pretty! It's vintage, one of a kind. On loan from Tiffany's."

I gaze into the mirror at the necklace with amazement.

Lily leans in and whispers into my ear. "Four hundred thousand dollars of bedazzling right here."

"Whoa. Wow!" I say, and smile into the mirror at my gold-streaked dark curls, my blue glittery eye shadow, the red sequined dress, and the diamonds. I turn my face from side to side. *This is the first time I've ever even worn makeup, let alone a billion-dollar diamond necklace!*

I step back and twirl around, spinning.

"That's it! Strike a pose!" Lily says, clapping.

There are lots of nods and grins, and oohs and aahs, and soon the bass-thumping music is turned way up and in a matter of seconds, the hip-hop beat kicks in loudly and we go from admiring my outfit to a full-on dressing-room dance party! The girls all surround me, smiling and laughing. Dani raises her hands in the air. Her shiny long dark hair is whirling around her beaming face. Estelle twirls and twists and dips her shoulders. Lily radiates this inner light as she sways her hips and swings her arms. Even Annika busts out some moves. I stand in my four-inch-high platform shoes and begin to feel this sense of calm as I slowly, rhythmically bob my head and smile this big, silly smile. The music is blasting, and I get this little warm tingling in my chest, like, *Oh my gosh, I'm having fun!*

But around one full minute into our little party, something terrifying happens: the door to the dressing room opens, and the girl from the sound check who handed me the guitar pokes her head in. The music is quickly turned down, and I get a split-second surge of utter panic.

"Hello, lovelies," the girl says, smiling like she has the best news ever. "It's showtime!" She stops and looks at me. "Thirty minutes to air, then *you're on!*"

32.

I'M PRETTY SURE I'M HAVING a heart attack!

"I can't breathe," I tell Dani, as I slouch against the hall-way wall in my ruby-red dress. "Please—I really, really, seriously, honestly *cannot do this*. . . ." I want to blurt out the truth, the facts. I want to tell her: I am not fierce and fabulous at all! I am *Frannie*.

I am Frannie.

And I'm sweating.

I feel dizzy.

I cannot do this.

Oh, don't worry, it gets worse: Movie Star/Supermodel is suddenly in the hallway too. I quickly stand up straight as she approaches. She gets right up in my face, and I flinch.

"Jasmine," she says with this crazy look in her eyes,

"get yourself together. I've told you a thousand times—this is a business." She stops and turns to Dani. "Who picked out this red dress? My God, it's too late now, but frankly, it's just not flattering. It's hideous! It hurts my eyes."

Dani and I just look at each other like, *Really? Did she just say that?*

And then, suddenly, Movie Star/Supermodel's bright white smile switches on. She's like a chameleon. It's scary the way she changes so quickly. "Remember, big, *big* smile. Enunciate and make sure you thank the audience!" She steps toward me and I back away. It's hard for me to even look her in the eye.

"Remember, this can all be gone"—she snaps her fingers—"like that." She begins to walk away and stops, turning back toward me. "For God's sake, Jasmine, get it right. There is a twenty-million-plus-dollar deal riding on this!" She pauses for a moment, gives me a death stare, and then walks away, joining a bunch of nicely dressed men at the edge of the curtained-off stage.

I hear a voice: "Five minutes to air!"

Five minutes! I'm light-headed. My hands are shaking. I turn to Dani and try again. "I really can't do this, I can't!"

Dani looks at me with a soft, sweet smile. "You can. You can do it. And the only way to get over this is to go through it."

With my crazy-tall shoes, we are standing eye-to-eye.

It's calming the way she looks at me. I can't explain it, but it is.

"Hey"—her face lights up—"remember how much you love to sing! Let your passion shine through."

I bite down on my bottom lip. It tastes like strawberry lip gloss. I glance down the hall at Movie Star/Supermodel and all the men in the suits. *I have to do this for Jasmine. I have to find a way to make this happen!*

I glance through the curtain at the hundreds of people sitting in the studio audience. I turn back to Dani and try to stop myself from crying.

Dani looks right into my eyes and reaches out and takes both my hands in hers. "Hey, *you* are the gift. It's Christmas night! The more courage, the more magic, right?"

"The more courage, the more magic." I repeat her words like a mantra, hoping somehow all the brave and light in Dani's eyes will travel through her palms, up my arms, and into my heart, as I stand here, knees wobbling, clutching her hands.

"One minute to air," I hear.

The music starts and the crowd goes crazy. I feel a rush of fear and then my stomach drops. My mind just kind of goes blank. I can hear the announcer's deep, dramatic voice introducing me over the speakers: "And now for the most anticipated performance of the evening . . . America's sweetheart, one of the biggest young stars in music today, singing her smash hit single, 'White Christmas' . . . Heeeeeeeeeere's Jasmine!"

Dani keeps her eyes focused on mine and speaks in a low, smooth voice. "Tap into your courage. You totally got this."

At exactly this moment, lights dim and Clipboard Guy grabs my shoulder and pushes me forward.

33.

I AM WALKING.

I am walking through the curtain into a shining, bright-white heart-shaped spotlight with red and green sparkling confetti raining down on me like pixie dust, and all I hear is the loudest clapping and cheering.

"I love you so much, Jasmine!" one girl shrieks.

I walk across the stage and manage to sit down on the stool. I pick up the guitar and strap it around my neck. The audience is completely dark. The crowd is now practically silent. I cannot see any faces. I cannot see anything but the lights and the camera.

I sit motionless in complete fear. *How am I going to do this?* I take a deep breath and manage the tiniest smile. Red and green glittery confetti is floating in the air all around me. I lean into the microphone and—something just seems to kick in—I feel my hand grip the guitar's neck and my fingers clamp down on the chords. At first I'm like, *How am I doing this?* Then it hits me: "Jasmine," I whisper in awe, "it's like Dakota on the horse!" Yes. I say this, *out loud*—

Into the microphone!

I hear the studio audience's nervous, confused laughter and quickly realize I am having a conversation with myself in front of a live audience and ten million television viewers. *Get it together!* I hear Movie Star/Supermodel snarl in my head. Then, Dani's more gentle whisper—*Tap into your courage. You totally got this!*

I can do this! I think, and I open my mouth. "I'm, um . . ." I sputter. "I'm just a little bit nervous." I speak whisper soft into the microphone.

The entire theater gets very quiet.

There's a hush.

I close my eyes for a second and breathe. "This is one of my favorite songs—and, umm . . . Merry Christmas, everyone."

And the craziest thing happens! The audience starts cheering! First a lady shouts, "We love you, Jasmine!" Then a guy, "You're brilliant, Jazz!" Soon, the whole studio audience is clapping and cheering and my hands grip the guitar, and just, like, start moving! I hear sounds! I am somehow magically playing the guitar! I don't know what is happening or how. . . . All I know is somehow on this stage I have become Jasmine! I am Jasmine sitting, legs crossed, on the wooden stool in my glittery red dress! I am rocking the guitar! This energy rises up inside as I flash the biggest, most relieved smile of my life. I lean into the microphone and I start singing the first verse. . . . I feel the vibration of my voice in my chest, and this pure, beautiful tone comes out of me! I can sing! *I have a voice!*

It feels so good.

So strong.

And soon, the audience begins singing along! Every one of them knows the words!

I'm like, *This is incredible! I can't believe this is happening!*

When I finish the last note, the crowd jumps to their feet, loudly applauding and cheering. I set the guitar down on the stage, and stand and smile. My heart is absolutely pounding, but in a good way. I feel so free on this stage. It's like the crowd is with me. My face is hot and a voice—*my* voice—is in my head: *I did it!* I am saying. *I did it!* I put one hand over my heart, and point, then wave to the whooping, cheering audience. I walk off the stage into Dani's outstretched arms.

"I did it," I say, speaking into her silky-smooth hair as I hug her back and hold on tight.

"You did it! You are amazing. Did you feel all that love out there?" she says. "You gave me tears!"

And as I let go and take a big deep breath, I feel, like, the best feeling of all time. I feel joy. I feel brave.

Afterward, as the other performers of the night are singing onstage, I quickly change back into the clothes I came in, return the diamond necklace safely to Lily, sit in the swively chair while Annika scrubs off my heavy makeup, and finally, sandwiched between Hank and Dani, slip out down the maze of backstage hallways. The entire way, people who work for the show are wanting to pose for selfies, reaching for me, offering me hands to shake. "You were a superstar!" they say. "Wow! Fantastic!"

"Thank you!" I say, and smile back. I'm not gonna lie. It feels good to hear all the compliments and high-five the outstretched hands.

I take the biggest breath when we emerge out the back door into the cool, crisp Christmas night. I hoist myself up into our SUV and sit back and replay it all over and over again in my mind . . . walking out onto the stage, the lights, the glittery confetti snowing over my head, the sensation of the gorgeous tone coming out of me, the audience singing along, the roar of the crowd when I set down the guitar. It's all a blur . . . but it was amazing! *This is crazy! I just sang on a stage in England in front of a live crowd and a TV audience of ten million people!* I lean my head up against the cool, smooth SUV window and close my eyes. Singing in front of all those people. Hearing them whoop and cheer. It just makes me think, *It feels good to sing . . . to let it all out.* That was a rush that I've never felt. That was one of the best feelings in my life.

In the golden elevator, before Movie Star/Supermodel steps off, she turns to me and says this: "Jasmine, your performance tonight was moderately okay. Not spectacularly bad. But far from fantastic."

I look back at her like . . . *wait. What?*

She reaches into her purse and pulls out her phone, stopping for a second to glance at me. "Listen, I don't care how many people are telling you that you're great. My job is to tell you the truth. And the truth is, you were a tiny bit off pitch—" She pauses and shakes her head. "Honestly, Jasmine, if you can't take it, you need to grow a tougher skin."

It's so crazy, she's not even my mom and I just want to cry.

Dani catches my eyes with hers.

I stay silent and cling to the elevator's wall as Movie Star/Supermodel turns, lifts her phone to her ear, and gets off on her floor.

34.

AS SOON AS DANI AND I step off the elevator into the penthouse suite and wave bye to Hank, I immediately just crumple face-first onto the gigantic bed. Dani drops her bag and collapses onto the pillows too.

I kick off my shoes and hear them plunk, one at a time, onto the floor. "I have seriously never been this exhausted in my entire life," I say. "I mean, like, I'm so tired, I can't even think. I can't even move."

"What a day," says Dani. "I'm totally with you."

For five minutes there is this lush, calm quiet. Then Dani stretches her arms and yawns loudly, almost laughing. "Oh my gosh, this is the best bed ever. I never want to leave," she says, turning toward me and smiling. "Can we just live here? Good God!"

"Yeah," I say, and nod, looking back at her from across

the giant mattress. "I actually would not mind that." I laugh.

"Hey," she says, softening her voice. "You just blew me away out there tonight. You tapped into that love-beam heart of yours. You tapped into your courage. You did it!"

"I did it," I say back, smiling.

"You shined tonight. You always do. There was so much love in that room. You made me tear up!"

"I did?" I ask, even though she had already told me. I want to hear it again. It feels *so good*.

Dani smiles at me for a good long time. "Yeah, you really did. You really moved everyone tonight. You always do. It gives me chills every time. And it's so awesome to watch you doing something you love."

After I take the greatest, longest hot shower of my life—in my body, or in anyone else's!—I wrap myself in the silky, long white hotel robe and slide my feet into the cushy slippers. I slather almost half a bottle of the hotel's complimentary lavender-rose nourishing lotion all over my arms and shoulders. It feels warm and soothing. And I think about how it feels good to take care of myself as I massage it into Jasmine's smooth, strong brown legs. And by the time I step out of the bathroom into the suite, I smell like lavender and roses. I take a big deep breath in. I smell so good!

"Hey, you!" says Dani. She has ordered room service

and set up a feast on the table by the window. "I got your favorite: sushi and tempura!"

"Sushi," I say, and look at the colorful platter of Japanese food. I've never had sushi before but . . . I don't even care! I'm starving! I sit down and push back the bathrobe sleeves and dig in and you know what? It's so good! I never knew I liked sushi, but I do!

"You cannot go wrong with sushi," says Dani, bringing a piece to her mouth with her chopsticks. She pauses and smiles and says, "I'm so happy to see you eating! You are totally crushing that tempura!"

I pop a piece of batter-fried shrimp into my mouth. "I guess I didn't realize how starving I was."

"Well, you need to try and remember to eat," she says. "Being totally amazing works up an appetite!"

"Yeah," I say, before I realize that I'm complimenting myself. "I mean, thanks."

After we polish off the best food on the planet, we smear organic clay purifying masks (Dani's idea) on our faces and lie wrapped in our white silky robes in the giant bed while the muddy masks set and watch movies and eat popcorn with lots and lots of butter, and drink blueberry-banana smoothies (room service). I totally love girls' nights, by the way. I've never had one!

A little before midnight I am almost nodding off (mask still on), but Dani jumps up, retrieves something from her bag, and brings me a small silk pouch. It's red and has a little string pull tie at the top.

"It's still officially Christmas," she says, her smile growing brighter as she hands me the present.

"Ooh, Dani—you didn't have to get me anything," I say. I am trying to be polite, but secretly I'm excited! I sit up in the bed, leaning into a tower of pillows.

Dani climbs back onto her side and turns toward me. "So, when I was growing up, in my family we didn't do bought gifts, so, well—" She stops. Her eyes get big. Her smile is huge. "Just open it!"

I untie the top of the small red pouch and pull out the most beautiful red-beaded bracelet, knotted on a natural cord. "Oh my gosh, it's so pretty," I gasp. "You made this?"

She nods. "Do you like it?" she asks, grinning, then we both start laughing so hard, because we still have the dried muddy masks smeared all over our faces and we look like zombies.

"I love it," I say, giggling, and she helps me fasten it around my wrist. "I'm never going to take it off."

Dani holds her gaze on me. "Awwww, I'm so glad it makes you smile," she says. "And I hope those red beads always remind you of how strong you are. There's nothing you can't handle. Nothing at all."

Thank goodness I somehow talk Dani into staying in the suite with me, and *not* leaving to go sleep in her own room one floor down.

"Okay," she tells me, her mask washed off, her face healthy and glowing, as she climbs into her side of the biggest bed on earth. "Sleepover!" she says, and giggles.

After Dani reaches for the light beside the bed and turns it off, it doesn't take much for the quiet to set in. There is the longest wordless hush. I listen to the sirens outside the window, the London night, the fan in the bathroom that I left on when I washed my face. Whatever is happening to me feels so mysterious. I blink back the tears in my eyes and curl up inside the bed, under the covers. I listen to Dani's soft breathing from across the enormous bed. All that's going through my head is the fact that I will probably never see her again, and how much I wish I had someone in my real life like Cass and Dani. Someone safe. Someone who loves me.

"Dani," I whisper into the darkness.

"Yeah?"

"Oh, nothing," I say. My voice is almost too quiet to hear. "I was just making sure . . ."

For a second there is quiet, then—

"I'm here," she whispers. "I'm not going anywhere."

35.

THIS TIME AS I'M FALLING, I know better than to fight it. I am not as terrified as the last time, and when I do have flashes of panic, I just sort of try to let go, try to breathe—and soon it doesn't feel like I'm falling, it feels like I am kind of floating. Weightless. No whooshing. No sound. After a few seconds I even stretch my arms out like wings and feel the wind push against my palms. And when I land? I feel this strange sense of peace. It's not a thud and it's not a splat. No. When I land, I bounce sideways onto a reasonably soft mattress. The first thing I notice when I open my eyes is that there is a boy, who looks to be about five years old, with his little hand on my face. His eyes are closed and his eyelashes are crazy long. His breath is slow and extremely close. He has a lot of dark brownish-black hair, like, *a lot*. The kind that is thick and wavy-messy like a sheepdog. I very gently turn my head until Sheepdog Boy's warm, sticky palm slides off my face and look above me, and then back at the boy. I am in some kind of pointy triangular bed/stowaway cove with a sound-asleep five-year-old who is wearing nothing but red polka-dotted boxers. His skin is tan and smooth and he has muscles. You can even see them while he's sleeping. His little shoulders, his chiseled biceps. There's a blanket, but it's tangled up around both our legs and feet. I take a breath. It smells damp and salty but not like sweat, more like fishy ocean, which is kind of when—

I sit up and whack my head *hard* on the crazy-low ceiling.

"Owww!" I yelp, and stare straight out at the short, narrow gap of space directly in front of me. The exact same moment I realize where I am is the exact same moment I feel instantly terribly sick.

I am on a boat.

I am on a boat and it is rocking back and forth!

It's not a gentle rocking; it's more of a hurricane kind of clanging and banging. My stomach is sloshing. My head is hot. I have a sudden awful queasy feeling. Something does not feel right. I glance down at my hands and my suntanned bronze arms. I am wearing a plain gray T-shirt and candy-striped long underwear almost exactly the same as Dakota's. I have bare feet, and I find that out pretty fast when I try to step down on the wood-planked floor and almost go flying. The ground underneath me is unsteady. I grab onto the edge of a wooden ledge and manage to step over a pair of rubber boots and a rain jacket and make it to a built-in bench before I suddenly feel like . . . oh, man, *sooooo* sick. I am pretty sure I am going to puke. I curl up on the bench. Everything is moving. I feel so dizzy. I feel cold, suddenly kind of clammy. I close my eyes tight and try to wish this I'm-going-to-be-violently-ill feeling away. I try to breathe. I try to not think about the fact that I'm shivering, curled up in a ball on a bench, and that everything is spinning! *Who am I? Where am I? What is going on?* I crack open my eyes: I see a built-in table with a laptop that appears to be bolted in place and radios around it and electrical panels and a lit-up little screen with a lot of green lights. I see a very small, simple kitchen, and a bookcase packed tight with a zillion books. It looks like someone's whole life is here, stored neatly, everything you'd need: pots, pans, containers with labels: *Oats, Beans, Rice, Flour.*

I close my eyes but—no, no, noooo, bad idea—that just makes everything so much worse. *Oh, man.* Puking is definitely going to happen. Soon! I suddenly decide that I maybe need air. No, not *maybe*, it's more like, *do or die.* I slowly sit up. I need to get outside! Only, as soon as I move it's like the whole world is turned upside down, and when I try to stand, it feels like my legs are made of

Jell-O. . . . I stumble to my feet and grab onto the rails of a wooden ladder, step up, and push my hand against the glass hatch above me. I poke my head out into the gray, wet, spitting light. It's sort of like a submarine hatch, except not—because I am not underwater. . . . I am on a sailboat, in the middle of an ocean, and it's raining and windy and there is a man dressed from head to toe in bright-yellow rain gear steering the boat and speaking to me: "We are almost through some big gnarly squalls!" he shouts to me through the wind.

Right when he says "squalls," I turn, look at the rolling waves, and puke all over the boat, and all over *me*. The kind of puke that comes out everywhere: your nose, your mouth, and burns the back of your throat. God, it smells bad. Then? It's weird, but for one blissful second the woozy nauseousness goes away.

I feel so much better—until . . . the boat slams against a wave and it happens *all over again*—

The puking.

The throat burning.

The vomit dripping out my nose and mouth and off my chin.

The man in the rain suit is yelling through the clashing wind. Something about a harness and clipping on.

A *harness?* I think, and wonder what he means. I wipe my face with the back of my hand and slink right back into the cabin and hear the sound of the hatch slamming shut behind me. As soon as I lie flat back on the bench, I just feel like I'm going to throw up all over again. *Oh my gosh, this is how I'm going to die,* is what I'm thinking as I curl up in a tight ball, hugging my knees. I am honestly too sick to even shed a tear. It's bad. It's like, *really, really bad.* After a few moments of moaning, I decide on a plan of action: even though I threw up, it felt much better to be outside . . . to breathe, to see the sky. I stand and gather the rain gear from the floor and manage to pull it on over my clothes: a bright-yellow jacket with clips and buckles, matching rain pants, boots. Then, dressed in my foul-weather gear, I climb the ladder and push the hatch.

"Air," I say as my head pops through.

I take a big deep breath and try to gulp in the wet, windy freshness, which is exactly when the boat rocks and I lose my balance. The jolt throws me. My whole body flies backward. I land hard inside the sailboat's cabin on the wood-planked floor. *Oh, wow.* I just lie there flat on my back and hope the nauseous feeling goes away for even a split second.

Please make this stop, I silently pray as my body rolls with the slamming waves. *Please make this stop,* I say in my head over and over and over again. But after a few minutes of lying still, as soon as I go to move my head, the nausea just comes right back. Boom. The boat is still rolling and rocking. I can barely stand on my feet without being thrown forward. I scramble up and, holding on to the smooth wooden handrails, pull myself up and climb the ladder for my third try.

This time I make it out onto the deck, grabbing onto the side of the boat's railings as I move. The rain has stopped but the wind has picked up. I carefully take three stumbly, drunken-looking, light-headed steps and collapse into a sunken-in seat. My head is spinning so bad.

Without speaking, the man in the yellow jacket, matching bib pants, and a well-worn faded black Baltimore Orioles baseball cap reaches for the harness that's looped around my yellow rain jacket and clips me into a high wire like a dog on one of those dog runs people have in their backyard. Only I'm not a dog, I'm a person with a harness attached to a wire so I don't fall into the gigantic dark ocean. *Oh my God. Where am I?*

The man shoots me a quiet smile. "Need to clip in, Bug. It's been pretty rough wind. Once we get past this last squall, it should smooth out." He pauses and looks at me with a bit of a twinkle in his eyes. "I sure don't want to lose you on Christmas morning."

Christmas, again?!! If I was not feeling so close to death, I would actually seriously laugh out loud right now. *Three Christmas Days in a row!*

I glance at the man. Both of his tan hands are gripped tightly around the round silver wheel, steering the boat through ocean swells. The huge white sail is up. We are moving pretty fast. And look, I'm *not* worried about who I am or where I am right now. The only thing I'm thinking about is *not throwing up!*

I sit still and close my eyes, but every so often I glance at the Baltimore Orioles black baseball hat guy with the light-green eyes and the rain gear zipped up. He has suntanned skin, a thick, reddish-brown lumberjack beard, scruffy dark hair spilling out the back of his cap, and a great, easy smile.

After twenty minutes of me lying motionless, listening to the waves thrash and not moving my head one single solitary inch, the wind finally dies down and the stormy clouds give way to the sun and I get the very, *very* bad idea to try to slowly stand up, and . . . there's that feeling again. It is quick, sudden. A nauseous feeling in my stomach—it doesn't wait for me—I turn and immediately lean over the side of the boat's wire railing, and with my weight on my elbows, stare down into the dark waves rumbling around us. I feel the unmistakable burning rolling up my throat . . . kind of swallow it back, but . . . *Yeah. No.* If there's one thing I have learned: you can't keep those terrible feelings in; you can only hold the bad stuff down for so long. It's going to figure out a way to come up and out, some way, somehow. I can't avoid the pain—no matter how hard I try. And I'm just going to tell you something really gross: I stay like that, perched over the railing, my face hanging out over the water on a fast-moving sailboat, puking into the sea and dry heaving until there is nothing left inside of me, and watch an army of brightly colored fluorescent yellow-and-black-striped fish swim up to the surface and gobble up the green chunks of whatever just came out of me as if it was the best meal ever.

36.

BY THE TIME THE BEARDED lumberjack in the faded black Orioles cap brings up breakfast (pancakes!), I am actually strangely hungry. And in a matter of minutes the weather has totally changed.

The sun is shining!

The wind has calmed.

I see nothing but ocean all around us. The sailboat is cutting through deep blue-green water. Ever since we got out of the windy squalls, the sick, nauseous, I'm-going-to-die feeling has totally vanished.

We must be on some kind of autopilot, because the Baltimore Orioles hat dad disappears down into the cabin and comes back up, climbing the ladder, and tosses me a bright-orange life jacket.

"I know the water has smoothed out, Bug, but you

know you need to have this on," he tells me. He sits down beside Sheepdog Boy (wearing an identical orange life vest) who—with his sleepy eyes and bedhead—has also joined us for breakfast on the boat's sunny deck. I watch the two of them quietly eat their platefuls of pancakes. The dad looks up at me between bites and smiles as I take off the rain gear and slip my arms through the vest and zip it up. It smells like ocean.

The three of us—Sheepdog Boy in his boxers and orange vest, me in my zipped life jacket and candy-striped long underwear, and the Baltimore Orioles dad with the beard (in jeans, and a flannel with the sleeves rolled up) eat together under the bright, warm sunshine.

These pancakes are good! I can't believe he made these in that tiny little kitchen! I wash my last bite down with a bottle of lemon-lime Gatorade. Sheepdog Boy is drinking the same thing. The dad has a mug of hot coffee. There's not a whole lot of speaking, but that's okay. The sun feels so good on my face. After how I felt just a little while ago . . . I feel so grateful to just be here, to not feel so sick. I place the plate down on the floor of the boat, sit back and let the air hit my cheeks, and breathe in slow and deep. And at that very moment, I glance to my right and my eyes pop out! A pack of dolphins shoot up through the water, swim alongside us, then vanish.

The Baltimore Orioles dad takes a long sip of coffee and exhales a big breath. He looks across the narrow boat at me for what seems like a full minute and then breaks into a big warm smile.

"Boy, Sky, you haven't been sick like that in—" He stops. "Since you were a baby. The wind really picked up, the swells were pretty big. I'd say we were moving along at twenty knots."

I nod and pretend to know what he's talking about with the boat lingo.

"You're tough." He winks.

I return his smile and think about how cool the name Sky is. I tilt my head back and look up at the blue. I love that name. *Sky*, I think, and wonder what I look like. I haven't seen a mirror on the boat, and I don't know if I will. I know I have long, dark hair—like the little boy has. It feels thick and is pulled back into a ponytail. I look across at the two of them. They are both lean and fit and handsome. It's like the boy is a mini version of the dad. He's so cute, with his missing-front-teeth smile and his little he-man muscles! I watch the boy shovel pancakes into his mouth and chug down the Gatorade. I wonder where the mom is. She's definitely not on the boat, that's for sure. It's just the three of us out here. I close my eyes again and sit back. This is the opposite pace of Jasmine and Dani. *I wonder how Dani is?* I think, and I imagine they're probably off to some airport in a hurry. I prefer this life to that. I mean, I miss Dani a lot, but . . . wow. The air feels so good. The sun feels so warm. The quiet.

"This is paradise," I say, speaking a full sentence for the first time.

"I think so too," says the dad, smiling at me. "Look," he says, pointing ahead. "Can you see the two mountains?"

"Oh, yeah!" says Sheepdog Boy, springing up on his bare little feet. "I see it, Dad, I see land!"

Ahead of us, off in the distance, is a set of jagged deep-green mountains. They look like two pyramids, side by side, and if I squint, I can make out a thread of white sandy beach along the coast.

The water around us is greenish blue, and the boat cuts through it, with one giant sail powering us forward. It's so calm out here. So peaceful.

The boy jumps up to the upper deck and runs, seemingly with perfect balance, across the length of the boat with his tan bare feet, ducking under wires and beams, until he's at the tippy point of the ship and he's standing at the very front, the wind pushing his dark hair back.

"Ahoooooooy!" he shouts into the bright morning sun.

37.

I CANNOT BELIEVE I'M HALFWAY between South America and Australia, on a sailboat, on our way to New Zealand! This is what I learn as I listen to the dad speak into a handset radio thingie, standing inside the cabin at the table with all the electronic gear and a computer screen filled with charts and maps.

"That's right, we are due east, traveling at around six knots. We should be arriving—" He stops to look down at the big watch on his wrist. "We should be near the pass ready to meet the pilot boat to lead us through the barrier reefs at oh-nine-hundred."

We are heading into a small, remote island port in French Polynesia. Wherever that is! Until this moment I had never even heard of French Polynesia, but the dad, the little boy (who I hear the dad call Max), and I gather around the computer and study a mapped chart.

"Here we are," says the dad, pointing to a tiny green slowly moving dot on the screen. "Here's where we are headed," he says, moving his finger to the left an inch. "It is supposed to be one of the most beautiful and remote islands in the world," he says, pausing to smile and look at me and then at Max. "Your mom always wanted to come here, and now we made it—" He stops for a good long minute, and Max and I sit and sort of just watch him.

The dad takes a big breath. "She'd be so happy we are here together," he says.

I get the feeling by the look in his eyes that the mom is gone. The mom has died. And I suddenly want to hug Max to me and hold him tight. My heart just feels so sad for them. But this sad feeling only lasts in the air for, like, a second. The dad reaches for a clipboard hanging behind the computers and hands me a checklist written in neat handwriting on a sheet of notebook paper.

"Bug, here's the list. There's a very small resupply shop on this island. They're expecting us. They should have everything packed and ready. I need to change the fuel filters. I also need to do some sewing and patching. We'll stay here for the day while I do some repairs and we replenish our supplies. Sound good?"

I nod. "Okay, I guess so, yeah," I answer, take the list, and fold it up.

The dad lifts his hat from his head and runs his hand

through his mop of dark greasy hair. He's handsome, and his eyes are this unreal shade of light green that pop out against his tan skin and his lumberjack beard. He looks like he hasn't slept or showered in a long time, and I guess that's what sailors look like, right? When do you sleep if you have to steer a boat across an entire ocean! He looks like he can handle anything. He looks strong. Smart. Like the kind of guy who can sew, knit, cook, *and* sail a boat around the world. That's what he looks like. He continues talking to me as he straightens up the cabin, hanging up our rain gear on little posts behind the computer.

"Are you feeling a little bit better, Bug?" he asks me.

"Yeah," I answer, and smile slightly. *I am, thank God.*

"Good," he says, and ruffles my hair with his big, strong hand. The dad throws his black Baltimore Orioles hat back on his head and turns to Max with a big smile.

"Okay, pal, let's drop the sails and stow them."

Max's eyes light up, as if this is the greatest job in the universe. The dad doesn't have to ask twice. Max is already following right behind him, bounding up the ladder like a little ninja boy with his life vest on.

"I got it, Dad!" he exclaims, and clips himself onto the wire at the top. I watch him through a skylight above me as he shimmies up the boat's tall mast like a monkey.

Alone inside the cabin of the boat, out of the sun, it's sticky and sweaty down here, and I immediately begin to get kind of hot. I move to the bed area that I woke up in and look around for some clothes that look like they're Sky's. I find a light-blue halter-style bikini top and stretchy red board shorts and squeeze into a tiny—and I mean *tiny*—closet-sized bathroom and slip them on. Yes, it's weird, okay? I know you want to ask. And I'll tell you straight up: Yes, it's kind of a little bit strange—no, make that *a lot*—to suddenly be in someone else's naked body! To be standing inside the world's smallest bathroom, balancing on one leg on a moving boat as I step into the shorts and tie the back of the swim top in a tight double-looped knot. But even though it's strange for a few seconds, all the awkwardness quickly fades away. I mean, after all, this is the third straight time I have bounced into someone else's body. I know the drill. If I don't get comfortable and take care of myself, who will?

When I hear Max shout, "Ahoy, mateys!" I know we must be getting close to land. Inside the tiny cramped bathroom I quickly squat over the toilet and pee and peek into a small round mirror above the sink. It's weird, but Sky kind of looks a little bit like *me*. I mean she has a gap in between her two front teeth just like I do. Okay, wait. Maybe she's more a surfer-girl version of me: her skin is tan and smooth, and she has sun-kissed freckles across her nose, and her hair is thicker than mine. Her eyes are light green and sparkly, like her dad's, and her shoulders and arms are strong and bronzed like Max's. I am in the body of a girl who looks like she can easily do a hundred pull-ups on a pull-up bar or shimmy up a rope using only her arms.

"Hi," I say, and smile at myself in the mirror.

My voice is soft and friendly.

"Hey," I say, this time a little perkier, with more confidence and smiling bigger. "I'm Sky," I say, and giggle to myself. I splash some water on my face and grin even bigger. "Sky," I say, "nice to meet you!" I don't really know why I'm practicing introducing myself. I mean, who am I going to meet on an island someplace in the middle of the Pacific Ocean?

38.

OUTSIDE ON THE DECK OF the boat I stand with my bright-orange life vest over my light-blue bikini top, in my red board shorts, and take in the beautiful surroundings. When I say beautiful, I'm not really sure I have the words to describe it! As we get closer and closer to the island, the water becomes turquoise blue and see-through. Like glass. You can see tropical fish swimming all around us. Ahead are the two hulking mountains— now that we're near them, they look less like pyramids and more like jagged cliffs covered in emerald-green jungle. I can see the white-sand beach dotted with tall, swaying wind-bent palm trees. I look up at Max, stuffing the huge sail into a small case and carefully zipping it, heaving the bag over his five-year-old shoulders and carrying it away. I can tell he knows this boat inside and out.

I glance at the dad as he quietly steers, his Baltimore Orioles hat pulled down shading his eyes as we glide toward the small wooden faded-red fishing boat that is motoring out to meet us.

"Bug," the dad calls out to me, "can you throw these guys a line? And remember, they most likely don't speak English. The official languages of French Polynesia are French and Tahitian."

Okay, so I definitely don't know French and I don't speak Tahitian but—I mean, I can throw something, right? I can do that! I practically rush at the thought of having a job as I walk across the top of the boat, clipped in, carefully stepping my bare tan feet over ropes and bolts, to the front where Max is standing. He hands me a rope with a knot at the end.

"If you miss, can I try?" he asks me in his deep-for-a-little-boy voice. I smile down at him.

"Sure," I say. Max's warm suntanned shoulder rubs against my arm.

"Ahoooooy!" He cups his tiny little hands and yells, and then waves his arms above his head. "Ahoy, mat-eys!" he shouts.

He is *so* cute!

I shade my eyes with my hand and look out ahead. On the boat coming toward us is a shirtless man with a neat buzz cut, shorts, and blue tribal-looking tattoos over his shoulders and chest. To his left, beaming this huge smile at me, is a bare-chested boy around my age with deep brown butterscotch skin and sculpted muscles that make him look like a warrior who can hunt and fish.

More? Okay. Twist my arm!

The boy on the boat has this really wavy, thick dark hair and big brown eyes, and the second he looks up at me, those dark eyes brighten and I get the craziest butterflies in my stomach and I feel this sudden rush of heat. Like, a jolt. It's like everything and anything falls away.

I see him.

He sees me.

Whoa.

I easily hurl the line out and watch it fly across the water and land perfectly in the hands of the boy, who fastens the rope to their boat, looks back up, and flashes that smile again. More butterflies. More *whoa-wow* feeling that I have never ever felt. So, yeah. *Duuuuh!* I stay up in the front with Max. And I am smiling this big goofy smile, not sure what has hit me or *how.*

Max and I dangle our feet off the side, as the small wooden boat motors ahead, guiding us through a maze of gorgeous colorful coral reefs. Soon our long white sailboat is safely nestled up alongside a wooden dock built beside a picture-perfect little hut—a bungalow made of bamboo with a thatched-palm-leaf roof, sitting on stilts and built right over the water. Instead of a driveway with a car, there's a ladder and a wraparound deck to tie up your boat! It's so awesome. *This is the way to live!* I think to myself.

When I step off the sailboat onto the hot wooden dock, I am greeted by an entire French Polynesian family. The mom almost looks like a hula dancer, with a long grass skirt, simple top, and dark, long, wavy hair parted down the middle.

"*Bonjour,*" she says, presenting me with a wreath of flowers strung together. I bow as she slips the strand of blossoms over my head. It's so pretty, and has the most amazing scent, sweet and bright. I never knew flowers could smell so good!

"Thanks," I say shyly and with a smile. "Nice to meet you," I add, even though I can tell nobody understands what it is I am saying.

In addition to the boy from the boat and the two people who I am pretty sure must be his mom and dad, there are six or seven little kids Max's age, all shirtless—even the girls—clearly intrigued by him, smiling and eager to play. Immediately, with no words exchanged, Max takes off for the beach with his new tribe of tiny friends, leaving me and the boy from the boat standing and staring. The butterflies have turned to total heart-pounding I-don't-know-what-to-say-or-what-to-do-or-how-to-act embarrassment. I mean, I've never done this before in my life! Up close the boy is just wow—

He is *cute.*

I glance at his chiseled muscles and his nut-brown skin; he has a shark tooth hanging from a thin cord around his neck. He has extremely white teeth and soft brown eyes that match the color of his shiny dark hair. We are standing about three feet away from each other, and I feel this energy rising in the air between us. I swallow. I breathe. I try not to look as awkward as I feel. My heart is racing but in a good kind of way. After a long minute of me not saying a word and standing and smiling at the sunny sky and the crystal-clear bluest blue water that looks almost not real, the Baltimore Orioles hat dad finally steps down off the boat and shakes the tattooed man's hand.

"Hello, I'm Liam," he says, speaking slowly, and they smile at each other as if they are old friends.

"*Parlez-vous français?*" asks the man.

"No, I'm afraid not." The dad laughs and puts his hand on my shoulder. "This is my daughter, Sky," he says, and then, nodding toward the beach, "and that little one is my son, Max."

The tattooed dad grins, and so does his wife, who is standing beside him. "*Bonjour,*" he repeats, then, "no English," he manages, smiling big. The man points to himself. "*Je suis* Keh-*lah*-nee," he says, sounding out his name. He turns to his wife.

"*Bienvenue, je suis* Lei-*lah*-nee," she says, and unfurls a beautiful smile at me.

Last, we all look at the boy.

That boy.

He looks straight at me and holds out his hand. *"Je suis Niko,"* he says to me. *"Salut!"*

"Sky." I say my name, and when his hand meets mine—oh my gosh, this is kind of like you hear about in books and movies . . . it's true what they say! When our hands connect, my entire body feels it—like, an electric current passes through his palm and up my arm and, well . . . all over the place.

The five of us, me, Niko, his mom and dad, and Liam, stand on the dock just, like, smiling at each other. Everything kind of moves in slow motion until I feel Liam's hand lightly squeeze my shoulder.

"Hey, Bug," he says. "Maybe Niko can take you to pick up our supplies?"

Niko's dad says something to him in another language, not French this time. I think it's Tahitian. Niko turns back to me. *"Je peux! On y va?"* He nods, eyes wide, dimples on.

"Um, okay." I smile.

Somehow, standing on the dock, in front of a small wooden bungalow on stilts, we are all making our way through this conversation.

"Bug," Liam begins, "the shop is down the beach and around the bend—they should have all our supplies packed up and ready. You're going to need to make a few trips, and there will be some heavy boxes. Bring everything back to the boat and"—he stops and looks at me with a smile in his eyes—"hey, you know what? I got it," he says, giving me a wink and taking the folded-up list from my hands. "It *is* Christmas, after all. Why don't you go have some fun?"

I look back at him. "Really, are you sure?"

"Really," Liam answers, grinning through his beard. "Merry Christmas, Bug—don't get lost, and be back by dinner."

39.

I STAND IN MY BARE feet on the dock, watching Liam step back onto the sailboat's deck and disappear down the open hatch into the cabin. A few seconds later he reappears carrying an old-fashioned metal box of tools and heads to the back of the boat and sets up shop by the engine. He whistles as he works quietly, tinkering, with his Orioles cap pulled down and his sleeves rolled up.

Niko's parents go about their day too.

The mom says something to Niko in Tahitian—which sounds a lot different from French—grins at me wide, turns, and slips back inside the simple thatched-roof home suspended above the turquoise water.

Niko's dad says something in Tahitian too, flashes a smile, then carefully lowers himself down the dock's wooden ladder and steps into his fishing boat. He starts up the motor with a cloud of smoke and looks back over his shoulder and waves at the two of us, Niko and me, standing on the sunny dock, suddenly alone, smiling and not saying a word: me in my bikini top and red surfer-girl bottoms, him in his ragged blue shorts, warrior muscles, and shark-tooth pendant.

Now might be a good time to mention it's not exactly very easy to have a getting-to-know-you conversation when two people do not speak the same language. He's fluent in two, and I do not speak either. And so, instead of talking, we move. We head toward the beach, walking down the long, narrow dock. I am nervous. It's a good nervous . . . if you know what I mean. Every step I take seems kind of new and different, like I've reached some better, more complex level in a fun but slightly confusing video game. I'm thinking a thousand things, like, for one, *oh, wow, he's so cute,* and two, *I wonder what we are going to do?* And three—less about the game and more about the scene—*the water, the sky, the entire island just seems like a postcard!* The mountain behind the beach is a jungle—big swaying palm trees, a steep hillside of green.

When I walk onto the hot white sand on the beach, I gravitate close to Max, who is building a turtle made of sand using an old-looking, cracked yellow plastic bucket. There are a pack of kids all working together. They are absolutely adorable, playing and splashing in the gentle see-through sparkling blue water and squealing with giggles and laughter. Max's face is intently focused, like a pint-sized shirtless sandy-shouldered construction foreman. You can't help but love him, his mischievous dancing eyes, and his wild unruly sheepdog hair. He's the type of kid other kids want to play with.

As soon as we step onto the beach, Niko immediately gets right down on his knees and pitches in, too, helping to shape and smooth the turtle's giant sand-carved shell, all while little ones jump and climb over his back and loop their hands around his neck, hanging off him when he stands, giggling as they drop onto the sand. I watch and wonder if they are all his sisters and brothers or, like . . . maybe his cousins? They all definitely look alike—the same thick, curly dark hair, sun-stained deep brown skin, and bright warm eyes. After ten or so minutes of massive sand turtle construction, Niko walks over to me. I stand up, brushing the sand off my arms and hands, and we both kind of just, like, smile and try and talk with our eyes, but that is a little bit hard beyond, you know, "Hi."

Then Niko suddenly begins to act out a question, using animated facial expressions (mostly a huge smile) and stretching his arms out, moving them as if he were swimming, and opening his big brown eyes really wide, like, *Do you want to go swimming?*

"*Tu aimes nager?*" he asks.

I have no idea but I take a guess—

"Do I—" I say out loud, pointing to myself as if I'm playing charades. "Do I want to go swimming?" I say, giddy that I understood what he asked. *Do I want to swim? Heck yeah!* I think, and grin back, a sure and enthusiastic *yes*.

Only one thing: As soon as I nod and smile, Niko turns his back to me and takes off running toward the palm trees, away from the water. I stay right on the beach, a little bit confused, and watch him stop right before he vanishes up a muddy dirt trail into the thick green forest. He pauses, then looks back over his shoulder at me with a dazzling smile, as if to say, *Come on!*

The first five minutes of my hiking-up-a-steep-squishy-muddy-narrow-path adventure in a humid, dripping, hilly rain forest, I'm wondering if I somehow misunderstood Niko's mimed gesture for *swimming*. Whatever this is, it is definitely *not* swimming! This is, like, hot, humid, and straight-up steep. I'm kind of climbing through a jungle! I mean, it's not like Niko is ahead of me cutting out a route with a machete, but each side of the trail is lined with huge palm trees and tickly-wet leaves. My bare feet are quickly stained with red dirt as I jump tree roots and sink my toes into spongy bright-green carpets of moss. My entire body is sweaty and hot. Wet leaves are slapping me in the face, and lizards are darting across my way. It takes me a good ten minutes, but I manage to catch up. Niko looks back over his shoulder, smiling, and we exchange glances, the kind that make me keep going even though I want to stop. He moves easily up his backyard, charging forward unafraid, ducking under overhanging branches, leaping over jagged rocks, every so often stopping to glance back to make sure I'm still back here, flashing me a light-filled quiet smile.

After an hour or so of hiking, my body falls into a rhythm, almost a trance. There is green everywhere, and a kind of deep silence. It's like no place I've ever been. It's like I'm in another world—the smells, the earthy fragrant wet scent, the birdsongs. I can suddenly hear *everything*. The air feels so alive: hidden birds perched high in the trees, insects buzzing, butterflies fluttering, noisy frogs chirping. I notice everything around me. I take it all in. And I walk and walk and scramble up, under a jungly spell, tipping my head back and looking into the green light filtering through the treetops, pieces of blue sky and sunbeams pouring down on me, droplets of water dripping from the ferny leaves.

Oh man, am I happy when I see Niko has stopped and is waiting for me under a gigantic tree. The jungle feels like it's 100 degrees! I'm not going to lie: I'm feeling the heat! My mud-caked feet are scratched and aching. Niko smiles and raises his finger as if to say, *One sec*, then jumps up and, lifting himself using his feet and his hands and his powerful shoulders, climbs like Spider-Man up the tree's trunk. I hear rustling and see Niko's arm outstretched, reaching into the branches.

"What are you doing up there?" I say, even though I know he can't understand.

"Hello-oooo!" I say, trying to spot him in the leaves.

Moments pass before Niko slides back down the trunk with an oval, smooth green fruit in his hand. I watch him as he starts to peel the green skin off. Inside it almost looks like a peach and Niko holds it out and with a big smile hands it to me.

"*Délicieuse*," he offers.

Now *that* I kind of understand! I'm so thirsty and so hot, I gratefully take the fruit, holding it like an apple with my fingers, and sink my teeth in and *ohhhhh* . . . just like the perfect ripe sweetness. I don't know what it is, but it's so good! Every bite I take the juice runs down my face, and it's kind of awesome, because I'm sweaty and caked in mud, and I'm wearing my bathing suit, so who cares if there is sticky juice all over me! I love not having to worry, I love feeling free and doing what I want. I just kind of wipe the drippy sticky sweetness off my mouth with the back of my arm and hand. When I'm done, I'm reenergized, which is good because I look up and see Niko is already moving up the ridge, turning back with a huge smile across his face and motioning for me to follow.

I hear the water before I see it.

This gushing, thundering noise like a river. It gets

louder and louder as I round a bend and—

There's Niko holding out his hand as if to say, *Ta-da*!

I stand beside him, totally mesmerized by what I see. We have hiked to the top of the world! At least that's what it feels like. When I look straight out, I can see forever: the far-off bluest blue ocean, the green treetops all around, and directly in front of us a thundering white waterfall cascading over a cliff, straight down a twenty-foot drop into a perfect beautiful deep, blue pool. The water is crystal clear and coming from higher up the mountain, and the spray of the waterfall creates these tiny light-beam rainbows in front of my eyes. It's amazing! I just never knew places like this really existed. It's like a hidden fairyland, and I stand there squinting into the sun and inhale it all in. Seconds pass as I glance at Niko. The waterfall music sings beside us. Even if we spoke the same language, I wouldn't be able to hear him over the thundering sound of the falling water. Niko smiles at me, his whole face lights up, and then—in one strong, fluid motion—he leaps out, and *jumps!*

40.

I PEER OVER THE LEDGE and watch as Niko plunges feetfirst into the deep, blue pool, and after a few long seconds he reappears, waving for me to jump too. I inch close to the edge, grip the rock with my toes, and look straight down. Niko's a long way away. I watch him swim to the side and hoist himself up onto the smooth black rocks. He looks up and smiles big. My heart is pounding in a what-the-heck-you-only-live-once kind of way. If I stand here and think about it too long, I will chicken out. I look down at Niko grinning up at me . . . and it's weird, but I don't feel like I *have* to do it—

I want to do this.

Not for him.

For *me*.

The rush of the waterfall drowns out my shriek as I

leap out feetfirst, plunging straight down—and there's this moment where I'm thinking, *Oh my gosh, I'm doing it!* It's all so quick, one second, maybe three, and I'm squeezing my feet together, toes pointed down, there's hardly a splash! I shoot into the water and go deep, down, down, down, holding my breath until I swim up to the surface and explode into the bright sunlight. And it doesn't even matter that water goes up my nose, or that I'm coughing and blowing out snot—*who cares!* As soon as my head breaks the surface of the water, I'm like, *I did it!* I have this huge smile on my face and I can't stop. All I can think about is, *That was so amazing! That was so fun! I feel so free!* It's unlike anything I've ever felt in my life. Without thinking, I let out a scream—"Wooooo-hoooo!" It just comes out. Cliff jumping through a waterfall into an icy-cold nature-carved pool—that was insane! I look up at Niko on the wide, flat rocks. It's pretty amazing how you can speak without saying a word. What I want to say is coming out of my eyes—*I kind of want to do that again!*

Niko and I take turns jumping and sliding off slippery black slabs of stone into the secret swimming hole. We splash and laugh as we play some wordless paradise version of Marco Polo. All around us are the green walls of the jungle and blooming reddish-pink fragrant flowers. The only sounds I hear are the rushing waterfall and birds chattering as they dip and fly overhead. The water is cold and feels so good after that hike. It's so clear and fresh, it's drinkable (I tried it!).

A half hour later the two of us, Niko and I, are walking along the shore of a slow-moving stream that flows through a flat valley lined with coconut palms. I'm kind of in post-cliff-jumping la-la land, when we come to a shimmering, light-blue saltwater lagoon. Honestly, it's hard to even describe what I see. It's like something out of a world of make-believe! The turquoise-blue see-through water is calm and wide, circled by soft, sugar-white sand. I don't know where we're going or where it leads to, but I'm right behind Niko as he wades in ahead of me and takes off swimming.

I dive into the lagoon like a dolphin. The water is so clear and warm and beautiful, and I swim underwater on a single breath, a streamlined missile—my hands outstretched in front of me, my legs propelling me forward. When I come up for air and glide across the water, swimming feels as natural as running or walking. I am reaching and pulling my body through the water, turning my head to gulp in air every three or four strokes. Soon I'm all caught up and swimming right alongside Niko—snorkeling with no snorkels—through brilliantly colored patches of coral. All of a sudden a huge school of black-and-yellow fish swarm around me, brushing up against my arms and hands. At first it's almost scary, but then I relax into it and look right back at them. It's like I'm in a giant shallow fishbowl! Every so often I pop up for air and inhale a deep breath, then float facedown. I don't have a mask, so I can't see perfectly, but I keep my eyes open underwater and I can make out colors and fish eyes. Some of the fish get kind of close to me and almost face-to-face. For a second I feel panicky, but then—I glance at Niko a few feet away, his chest skimming the white sandy bottom of the lagoon, and he smiles at me through the clear blue water. It's fun to talk without words in this underwater quiet and dreamy world. I relax and the water holds me up. Everything feels so buoyant and peaceful. I can float easily when I let go.

We stay in the blue lagoon, swimming and floating and talking to fish, until we reach the far end, and I pop to the surface and gulp the air. It's such a good feeling to breathe. I emerge from the water—my long, dark hair shellacked to my face, the taste of salt on my lips, tiny seashells in my swim top, water up my nose—cleaned by the sea, and I collapse onto the sun-warmed sand, completely exhausted and euphoric. Both. And this is what I wonder as I look up into the blue: Was all that strength Sky or *me*?

41.

AFTER THE BEST ADVENTURE OF my life, Niko and I head back to the beach and are greeted like heroes by all the little kids. Max runs up to me and immediately clasps his hand around mine.

"Come see our turtle!" He tugs at my arm. "Come see our treasures!"

A few feet away, lapped by gentle ocean waves, is a giant turtle made of sand and seashells.

"Wow, Max, that's amazing!" I say, and I mean it. It's really cool!

And the wonder continues. On the beach we drink coconut water straight from a coconut (compliments of Niko and his Spider-Man climbing). Then Niko and I and all the kids, including little Max and his sunburned nose, head back to the lagoon on foot. Niko is carrying a long metal spear and a blue rubber diving mask. I get the feeling we are catching dinner—I'm not really sure. Max is beyond excited. He marches right alongside Niko and looks up at him with the cutest, biggest eyes. Max keeps asking him a million questions, as if Niko can understand him, and in some ways I think he does. The way Niko looks back at him and nods and smiles, Max is practically skipping with joy when we get to the lagoon. It is shallow and extremely calm, and all the kids can wade out pretty far in the crystal-clear water, look down and chase pink and translucent-green fish, squealing and splashing. I wade into the water with the kids and look back at Niko as he goes to work. Max won't really leave his side. He stays on the beach and watches Niko as he spits in his mask, wipes the saliva around with his finger, then crouches down and rinses the mask in the water, finally strapping it on tight over his eyes. He looks at me through the mask, eyes bright as he walks into the water carrying the spear in his right hand.

We all kind of stand back and ooh and aah and watch Niko walk out into the lagoon, until the water comes up to his chest. He takes a deep breath of air, then slides in and disappears into the blue.

Max stands in the shallow water in total awe.

We all do. It's suspenseful! Niko can hold his breath for a really long time. It seems like minutes go by until his head finally pops back up and he takes a big, deep breath, then disappears again.

The third time he dives down and comes back up with a fish at the end of the spear.

"Look, he's got a fish! He's got a fish!" Max shouts, and runs right into the water toward Niko as he walks out. Niko pushes his mask up off his face with one hand and grips the long spear with the other. A little bit of bright-red blood drips down his arm. Speared at the end of the rod he's holding up is a beautiful turquoise-green fish with a mouth like a parrot. The fish is still alive and the tail is flapping and the fish is fighting back. I feel kind of bad for a second until Niko walks out of the lagoon and quickly bangs the fish's head on a rock, killing it instantly. Then he turns around, walks back into the water, wades in until he's chest deep, and dives under. He repeats this same scene until soon he has three big fish lined up on the sand. The kids circle Niko and watch as he rinses the fish off in the water, then runs a string through the gills out the mouth, until he has the three blue-green fish hanging from the string like keys, which he lets Max carry in his little hands all the way back to the beach by the dock. One look at Max's face right now, and his huge eyes, and it's safe to say: Niko has a fan for life.

It's amazing how much Niko can do, I think as I watch him walk, a trail of joyful kids skipping and running and following along. I mean, we have supermarkets and just buy stuff . . . he dives into a lagoon and catches dinner with his own hands!

I watch the kids jump and hang off Niko's arm as if they're playing on monkey bars. If I could tell him something, I don't know what I'd say. But the moment I'm staring and watching, he turns and looks back at me and smiles that big, beautiful smile. And in that instant, when our eyes lock, I feel that one single smile right in my chest.

42.

I WALK BY MYSELF BACK down the dock to the boat, practically skipping and humming. In front of me, behind our sailboat, is a movie-screen backdrop of a pink-tangerine sky. You don't need clocks here, and you don't need phones. The sun is just beginning to set. It's almost dinnertime.

When I step back onto the boat and lower myself down the hatch into the cabin, I almost don't recognize Liam. I have to do a double take—the bushy reddish-brown beard is gone! In its place is a smooth, strong jaw and a dimple on his chin and a fresh little cut over his right eyebrow. He's gone from a lumberjack to completely clean shaven. Without his baseball hat or his full, thick beard, something about him reminds me of Dakota's dad, Luke. Liam's hair is darker than Luke's, but they are both fit and strong and gentle when they speak.

"Hey, Bug," says Liam, looking up from the computer and smiling at me. "Did you have a good time? How was your Christmas Day?"

"Oh," I begin. "It was actually pretty fun." I want to tell him more. I want to tell him about the waterfall and the jumping and the lagoon, and the spearfishing and the sticky sweet fruit, and the muggy hot hiking. I give him a shy smile and hope he asks me something else. He's so easy to talk to. A minute goes by and he's just smiling at me.

"Um, I like your haircut," I blurt out.

Liam's eyes light up. "Oh, yeah, beard-haircut combo," he says, and grins, raising his eyebrows. "Had to do it. Thought I'd give a go at a new start on our way to New Zealand and Australia." He pauses and looks at me for a long time, turns the chair toward me on the bench, leans back, and locks his hands behind his head. "So tell me about your day, Bug," he says. His eyes are big and connected to mine, like he really actually is interested, like he really cares. I can't explain it, but it makes me feel special. It makes me feel calm.

"Well," I start, and fold my scratched-up legs under me on the bench. "Niko and I hiked up through the jungle and we jumped off this huge, *huge* cliff into the water. It was seriously, like, the greatest feeling ever. Oh! And there was a waterfall! It was so amazing! And the water in this lagoon, it was like this bluest blue I've ever seen, like, ever, and . . . well, yeah . . ." I smile at him and he smiles at me and for a second neither of us says a word. Then—"But, yeah, I think jumping off the waterfall was the best!"

"Cliff jumping, wow, way to crush it, Bug! That sounds gutsy," Liam says. He sounds proud but not surprised. He leans and just smiles at me—the quiet feels good. Something from the computer suddenly beeps. Liam turns and glances at the green satellite weather maps lit up on the screen, then looks back at me. "Bug, I wish we had more time to hang out here, but there is a storm system approaching, so we need to get moving right after dinner."

My heart kind of pangs.

"We have to leave?" I say. I don't know what I'm thinking. It's not like I would get to *stay* even if we had more time here. If these bounces are happening to me every night, I won't even be here when I wake up. But I am suddenly kind of sad. That we have to leave. That I won't get to be Sky again. That I will never see Niko or Liam or Max after I go to sleep tonight. My stomach suddenly hurts.

"I know, Bug, this place is really special," Liam says, his eyes never leaving mine. "I wish we could stay a little bit longer."

I look back at him with a quiet smile.

"So do I," I say.

* * *

I wash up in the tiny bathroom, splashing my face and scrubbing off the sand as best I can. I look into the mirror above the sink. My nose is peeling and my eyes are a little bit red from swimming in the ocean. When I take off my swim top and change, a hundred tiny seashells and clumps of sand fall out all over the floor and all over me. It makes me giggle. I don't bother taking a shower with a bucket on the deck under the setting sun because I mean, I kind of love the smell of the ocean and the beach and the salty sweat and the hike . . . I want it all on me. I don't want to wash it off. I want to remember every last bit of this day for as long as I can. I study my face—my tan skin, the muscles that pop out of my strong freckled shoulders, the gap between my two front teeth. Out of all the bounces so far, I feel the most like Sky. Or maybe it's that I *want* to be like her. I'm not sure.

I keep the red shorts on and slip a soft gray hoodie over my head, undo the ponytail, and let my dark thick hair fall down around my shoulders. It feels good to not have it back so tight, to let it loose.

"Sky? Let's go, Bug." I hear Liam calling down to me from the deck of the boat. I take one last look into the round mirror above the sink and give myself a tiny smile. Then, I go.

As the sun sinks under the horizon, Max, Liam, and I walk under the most gorgeous violet-orange sky, past Niko's family's small house on stilts, across the long wooden dock to the beach. Max is wearing the cutest white-and-gray Stormtrooper pj's. His nose has white lotion on the tip and he's talking a mile a minute, walking hand in hand with Liam, telling him about the spearfishing and the blood and the fish's head Niko smashed with a rock. It's hard to not completely adore him.

The second we hit the sand, Max drops Liam's hand and takes off running ahead of us to play with his new best friends. The sea turtle made of sand is long gone, washed away by the rolling waves of the ocean. Higher up on the beach is a picnic table and a simple fire pit. There aren't any big shooting flames high in the sky, but I can see the three fish Niko caught roasting over red-hot coals. The wood smoke from the fire smells so good. I am so hungry! Living like this works up an appetite!

We all sit down together, family-style—Niko's little brothers and sisters and cousins, his mom and dad, two aunties, and two uncles—it's kind of like a party. There's a long table lit up by torches anchored in the sand, and while the ladies prepare the food, one of the uncles plays Polynesian songs on a ukulele and all the little kids, even Max, wiggle their hips and giggle and dance as the darkness falls around us. The glimmer from the fire, the rising moon, and a warm, salty breeze off the ocean create this kind of enchanting spell in the air. It's so crazy because even though we don't speak the same language, we are having the best time. So much fun.

When it's time to eat, I am sitting in between Niko's mom and Niko at the very end of the long table, across from Liam and Max. There are platefuls of beautiful-looking exotic dishes: baked papayas, crispy fried shrimp, and something called breadfruit, roasted and soaked in coconut milk, which is so good. And when I take the first bite into the tender, lemony fish that Niko caught, I think it is one of the most delicious things I've ever eaten. I love it. I have a second plateful of everything, but Niko's fish is my favorite. Liam told me that all the things we are eating tonight are harvested from the jungle and from the sea. It's a way of life. They have everything they need.

Every so often I glance sideways at Niko sitting next to me, and he glances back at me. His eyes are shining in the twilight. That's about it for conversation. Oh that, and the funny feeling I get when our elbows knock and touch.

For dessert we eat ripe, juicy passion fruit and mangoes. Niko's dad takes a machete (to Max's delight) and easily splits half a dozen coconuts up into pieces, and we each take a little section in our hands. I copy Niko, scraping the meat from the shell and scooping it with my fingers into my mouth—it's so yummy, slimy and sweet like a pudding. I glance around the table at all the smiles and listen to the singsong voices and the talking, mostly

Tahitian, some French—even though I don't understand a word they say, I am sitting here at the table with the biggest smile on my sunburned face. The stars are just starting to twinkle above us. I don't think I could wish for a better Christmas dinner if I tried. When we clean up, everyone helps.

43.

"NOOOOO! I DON'T WANT TO go. I don't want to goooooo!" Max is screaming, and his face is bright red. It's bad. When he realizes we are leaving the island and not staying, he just melts down into a heap of the biggest tears. It's like a switch goes off. Now he's lying on the dock facedown in front of our sailboat in the fast-falling darkness, his tiny hands gripped tightly to a rope tied around the dock's wooden posts. His little legs are kicking. "I don't want to go!" he wails. "I don't want to gooooo!" He just, like, loses it.

At first I watch him and I'm afraid.

I don't want Max to get in trouble. I don't want Liam to be angry. The night air feels all at once cooler. I try and crouch down beside Max, but his hands just punch and kick, and I stand back up, back away, and feel kind of helpless and scared. But then—

Liam bends down, and with no words, tenderly and gently peels Max off the dock and scoops him up in his arms. Max's wriggling little body softens into Liam's chest.

"Daddy," he says, between big sobbing breaths. "I don't want to go, I don't want to go."

I watch Liam with Max. He just has this calming presence.

He's not angry.

He's not mad at all.

"Oh, Maxi, you're really sad, it's okay, bud. I see you're really upset. I'm here. *Shhhhhhh*," Liam says, stroking Max's shuddering back with his hand. "*Shhhh*, oh, Maxi, it's okay. I know you really want to stay, honey, but we have to get moving." His voice is soft and reassuring. "Let's go for a walk first, just me and you, bud," says Liam. Max's deep sobs slowly get quieter and less frequent as Liam whispers and soothes him.

Max buries his face in Liam's strong shoulder. "Bug, it's time to say your good-byes," Liam tells me across the dock.

I nod and watch Liam—with Max's little hands locked around his neck—fade into the purplish-blue darkness toward the beach, leaving me standing alone in the night. I don't understand it, I don't know why, but watching them together, I have tears in my eyes. I feel this ache in my chest. I guess it's like—

I take a big breath.

I guess, it's . . . well. I guess it's this: *I really, really wish I had a dad like that.*

Ten minutes later, under the nighttime sky, Niko and I are walking to the very end of the dock. We sit side by side, our feet hanging down toward the water. I'm not sure exactly how this is going to go, since we can't really say too much, but at least I knocked on the door and attempted to say thank you—to say *good-bye.* His mom hugged me and his dad smiled and waved from across the small room. Niko seemed surprised to see me standing in the open doorway. He was reading a book on a mat in the corner, and at the sound of my voice, he jumped to his feet, slipped a white T-shirt over his bare chest, and joined me outside. We walked together to the far end of the dock, the only sound the hush of the ocean waves lapping underneath us.

So. That's how we got here.

Sitting on a dock, with the ocean stretched for a thousand miles in front of us, and a sky full of stars. I glance at his deep dimples and his eyes and curly dark hair, and I wait for a moment, trying to think of how to thank someone who doesn't speak the same language as I do. I settle on a smile that I turn and give him.

We aren't, like, touching or anything. There is a good

five inches between his ragged blue shorts and my red ones, but there is a current of energy between us that I'm pretty sure he feels too.

I swallow. "Um, so—thanks," I say. "I had a really fun time. The best day ever." I say this all like he totally gets it.

Niko grins with his eyes and looks at me, then—

He reaches up and lifts the cord from around his neck, slips it off over his thick dark hair—"*Pour toi—joyeux Noël,*" he says, holding the cord out to me in his hand.

It takes me a second, and then I realize. *Oh my gosh. He's giving it to me!* I take the necklace with the shark-tooth pendant. I grasp it between my fingers. The pendant is still warm from his body. I don't know what to say.

Niko looks at me, his eyes widening, like, you know, *Put it on!*

I smile shyly and slip the cord over my head, letting it fall around my neck. The shark's tooth hangs low, inside my sweatshirt. It tickles at first, then it feels kind of good. If it weren't dark, I'm pretty sure you could see my whole face flush. I breathe in. I'm surprised how calm and wonderful I feel.

"Thanks," I say, in a whisper.

He smiles with his gentle dark eyes.

"Thanks," he copies me, speaking in English, fumbling before trying it again. "Thanks."

We both laugh softly. Then—

For a long, hushed moment there is no speaking, or trying to speak—just breathing and both of us staring straight ahead into the shimmering water. I don't move. The ocean is almost glittering from the reflection of the night sky full of freshly born stars. I listen to the gentle waves and the breeze. I feel the heat rising in my head and cheeks. My heart races and, like, flutters. And I'm just thinking, *Wow, this is happening. This is happening right now. To me.*

After a few minutes of staring into the water and stealing glimpses of each other, we finally slowly stand, face-to-face, a few feet between us on the starlit dock.

"Bye," I say, and kind of wave.

"*Au revoir*," Niko whispers back, dimples in full effect.

And that's it.

That's all.

Niko takes one slow step back, a big, shining smile on his face, backpedaling down the dock in his bare feet, then spins around and slips into his bamboo thatched-roof hut.

Yeah. You're right. I'm smiling too.

Five minutes later, I am sitting alone on the gently rocking sailboat, in a daze, or maybe a spell, outside under the stars, wrapping my fingers around the shark tooth like it's some kind of good-luck charm, when Liam steps onto the boat with Max in his arms. Max's heavy little head is sound asleep on Liam's shoulder.

"Someone's exhausted," Liam says in a low, gentle whisper. "This little guy got a lot of sun. It was a big day for all of us. I'm going to put him down, Bug, and then we'll push off."

44.

AFTER WE SET OUT SAILING into the night, I realize pretty quickly that the stars back on the dock with Niko were, like, baby stars compared to the hundreds of thousands of them over my head right now. It's completely dark but kind of not—the night sky is a ceiling of a billion twinkling pinpoints of light.

In the cabin down below, I slip out of my shorts and into my pajama bottoms, keep the hoodie on, then drag a blanket and a pillow up to the deck, zip up my life vest, clip myself into the wire, and settle back, staring up into the starry fireworks show above us.

I'm so happy when Liam appears from below and sits down beside me. I make room for him and the two of us sit. Liam drapes his arm around me and pulls me close. I just let go and let myself snuggle into his warm chest. He holds me like that for a long time. I feel so safe. It's so quiet. I listen to the lullaby of ocean and waves, and the wind against the sails. I feel Liam's heart beating through his sweatshirt. He smells faintly of engine and salty sweat. I take a big breath and wait for a few minutes, hoping he tells me something I can hold on to. Something I can remember when I wake up tomorrow . . . who knows where. We stay like that for what seems like an hour, looking at the stars together. It all just feels so comforting. I have never seen more stars in my life.

"Dad," I manage. It feels weird to call him that at first, but, I mean, that's who he is right now to whoever I am.

"Bug," he says, drawing me in closer.

"Will you tell me a story?" I ask. I don't want this night to end. I have to make it last longer.

"A story, huh?" Silence. "Well, let's see—" He pauses for a long moment. "When you were born"—he speaks in a steady, gentle voice—"it was love at first sight the second your mom and I saw you. And that first day, we looked at your little toes and your little fingers, and we noticed a little freckle on your neck."

I turn and smile at him.

He smiles back.

"When you were three or four, we were looking at all your freckles and you had some on your legs and arms—" He stops and tickles me. And I wiggle and squirm and giggle. "And one day your mom put your little hands together," he continues, "and we noticed your freckles make four bright stars." He pauses and looks at me. "You are made of stars."

"I'm made of stars," I whisper, kind of swept up in the story.

Liam points his finger up into the night. "Not just any stars—your stars make up the Southern Cross. The Southern Cross is *very* special, Bug. It has great meaning. The indigenous people of Polynesia believed it was an anchor. An anchor in the sky—can you see it?" He points again. "See it, there? The four brightest ones?"

"I see it," I say in awe, staring straight up.

Liam pulls me in tight. He lowers his voice to a whisper. "Your mom always used to tell you, you have a star map. That's how you found us. You had the star map to find me and your mom." He stops, his voice breaks, he hesitates. He takes a breath.

Neither of us speak for a moment.

"Your mom and me and you and Maxi—we are all from the same stars and we found each other and so . . ." He trails off, a lump in his throat. "Your mom is out there, Bug. She's with us—" He pauses for a few long seconds and takes a deep breath. "No matter where you are, you can *always* find your way home using the Southern Cross—and we can find each other in the stars."

There is a long, hushed silence, and out of the corner

of my eyes, I see Liam raise his hand to his face and wipe away tears.

A moment later he moves to his feet. "Bug, I'm afraid it's that time." Liam looks at me with tired eyes.

"What time?" I ask, looking back.

"Just like always," he says. "You stand watch the first shift, I will grab—" He stops and fidgets with the high-tech watch on his wrist, setting an alarm. "I will grab three quick hours of sleep and—"

"Wait, what? Where are you going?" I say, sounding panicked and suddenly sitting straight up.

"Bug, you've done this a thousand times," he says, looking a little bit surprised. "The seas are flat and the winds aren't heavy. The self-steering vane is on, and we're safely outside the pass." He shoots me a quiet smile. "You just need to man the wheel, keep us on the compass bearing, stay awake and alert, and keep your eyes open for other vessels."

"Other vessels!" I say, sounding totally freaked out, which is true, by the way. I mean, the night sky is gorgeous and awesome when you are snuggled up to a big, strong dad, but by *myself*, out here in the dark night? My heart begins to absolutely pound.

"Don't go," I beg, reminding me a little bit—no, a lot—of who I was. That terror feeling creeps back pretty fast.

Liam takes a step back. "Bug, I need to get some sleep. I know you can do this. I believe in you. I trust you. I have a lot of faith in you." He flashes me a smile through the breezy night. "You can do this with your eyes closed. . . . Though"—he stops and raises his eyebrows—"that wouldn't be very effective to watch for ships." He winks.

Liam steps toward me, leans over, and kisses me on top of my head.

"Merry Christmas, sweetheart," he whispers. "Thank you for being you," he says, gazing into my eyes. "I feel so lucky to be your dad."

45.

I AM TERRIFIED.

My hands are shaking.

I sit back in the seat and stare out at the night. I am in charge! I am in charge of us living or dying . . . I am in charge of us not smashing into another vessel and sinking to the bottom of the ocean! I suddenly just, like, stand up and grip my hands around the silver wheel. I don't have to turn it or steer it, but I somehow feel better standing here, holding on.

I breathe in and scan the darkness.

No massive tanker ships.

Not another human being. It's just me, and the dark rolling ocean. I hear every single little sound: the wind, the waves, the fluttering sails, creaking pulleys and beams, the boat cutting through the water. I sit back down and hug my knees, then gradually lean back and look straight up at the ceiling of gleaming lights in the sky. The stars keep me company. I watch them shoot and streak across the night.

It's calming.

I can't explain it. It's like a sky full of jewels. It's the most extraordinary thing I have ever seen. "Wow," I whisper. My eyes are wide and my mouth is open and—it's like there are no words for what I am seeing. The world is full of magic. I can't believe this is always here and I just haven't seen it.

46.

ON MY FOURTH DROP THROUGH outer space, there is no floating or flying through the air. Well, wait. There is. I just sleep straight through it.

Completely.

I sleep the kind of deep sleep you sleep after spending all day in the hot sun, climbing a mountain, jumping off a cliff into a natural pool, swimming in fairy-tale blue water, and ending the day under a starry night sky.

When I wake up, it is immediately clear—

Whatever is happening to me is *still happening.*

I am tucked in a cozy bed, buried under a pile of blankets, and I feel like I've been sleeping *forever.* My body feels stiff and achy. My mouth is pressed flat into the mattress, glued to the sheets with dried-up saliva. When I turn my cheek and open my eyes—

There is a dog.

A big dog.

Staring extremely close. And drooling.

He's big and black, with a shiny coat of fur and floppy ears. He's snuggling up next to me, and when he sees that I'm awake, he licks me right across my face with his tongue. "Oh, *yecch!*" I say, scrunching up my nose. "Thanks for the kisses," I tell him, and laugh. The big black Lab opens his mouth and is panting like he's trying to tell me something. I wince again. His breath is a little bit stinky.

I make a face. "You need to brush your teeth," I tease, cradling my hands around the soft velvet of his ears and stroking them. He's so sweet the way he's looking at me, panting. A few seconds go by, and the big black dog lays his heavy head across my chest, comforting me, closing his eyes to rest. He's cuddly. I reach my hand to his ears again and rub them.

"Hey, you," I say in a soft whisper. "What's going on? Merry Christmas. Who am I this time? Do you know? Can you tell me?" I lean in closer. The dog just keeps his eyes closed and lets me rub and nuzzle him. Something about him seems kind of down.

I lift my head and look around—

Everything faraway looks a little bit soft and fuzzy until I reach for a pair of thick black eyeglasses on the bedside table and slip them on. Okay, whoa, much better!

I can see again. That was weird. *Where am I?* I wonder, scanning the room and searching for clues. Whoever's room this is, they share it with someone else. On my side of the room, I have a bedside table with a box of tissues and a window beside me with light pouring in. There is a dresser with the drawers half open and lots of clothes all over the floor—kind of like my room. I turn and look across from me. The bed on the other side of the room is crisply made, right down to the upright pink-and-red-striped pillows and matching sheets. There is a puffy comforter and a purple throw pillow at the head of the bed and a nightstand with a lamp, a few biggish books, and a stash of bracelets in a teacup. Above the bed is a shelf lined with golden trophies. I squint at them through my glasses. I'm pretty sure there are little soccer players at the top. I glance at the posters and pictures on the wall: a USA women's soccer player heading a ball, and ripped-off magazine covers of girl surfers riding crazy-big waves. There is a cork-board in the shape of a heart with newspaper clippings tacked on, a collage of photographs of smiling teenage girls' faces and quotes written in blue marker on index cards covering the closet door. I move to my feet and walk closer to read them:

Ask for what you want and be prepared to get it!
—Maya Angelou

You are braver than you believe, stronger than you seem,
and smarter than you think.
—A. A. Milne

All that we love deeply becomes a part of us.
—Helen Keller

My eyes scan the pictures on the wall, the trophies and newspaper clippings, the photos, the quotes, and then I glance back at my furry friend on the bed and return to him, climbing under the covers. I rub his velvety ears.

"Yes, you like that, don't you?" I say. His ears are so soft and snuggly. "Hey," I say, then look at him hard.

He looks at me back. He looks sad.

"What are you so sad about?" I ask with a little laugh, because on my fourth Christmas Day I am speaking with a dog again! So, yeah . . . maybe it's good that I hear a faint knock, followed by—

"Gracie, honey," a voice says. "It's Tia. Can I come in?"

"Um, uhh—sure," I answer, and sit up in the bed. The dog and I both look up at a young woman who walks in. She is wearing a formal black dress, fitted at the waist. Her long, dark hair is pulled back tight and sleek. She has a little bit of mascara on and pale-pink lipstick.

"Hey, good morning," she says with a soft gaze. She sits down on the edge of the bed, close. "I just wanted to come in and check on you. The family is gathering and we are all getting ready."

I nod.

The woman, Tia, smiles at me with a gentle, warm smile and tired eyes. She has one hand on the dog.

"Hey, Buster, you're taking good care of Gracie this morning," she says to him, then looks back at me. "Gracie, honey, I know the last twenty-four hours have been—" There's a pause; she stares into my eyes. "I just want to let you know I'm here for you," she says.

There is a long silence.

I have no idea what to say, so I decide to say nothing.

The two of us are sitting on the bed connected by Buster, snuggled up next to me. My hand is up by his ears, and Tia's hand is stroking his neck. My fingers graze hers.

She takes a big long breath.

"So, your Poppie and Nonie are here, and they are waiting to see you," she says, and stands. She moves over to the closet, slides the door open, and starts looking through the clothes hanging on hangers. "I think we're all wearing dark clothing—" She stops and pulls two hangers out: a dark-blue dress and a black skirt with a black cardigan sweater. She hangs them up on the back of the closet door. "What do you think about these two?" she asks me. "Which would you like to wear?"

"Umm . . ." I try to stall. *I'm not really sure where we are going. Church, probably—that is if it's still Christmas.* . . . "I

248

guess the skirt and the sweater," I answer with a shrug.

"Okay, and it's not that cold out, but tights would be nice for today." She walks over to the dresser and reaches into the already open top drawer and pulls out a pair of black tights, setting them on the end of the bed.

"These should work," she tells me. "And your black boots, yes?"

I nod. "Okay," I answer.

The woman, Tia, looks at me for a long moment, exhales, and says, "We need to leave in an hour, so you kind of need to get going, Gracie. See you downstairs."

47.

I GET DRESSED IN THE exact outfit Tia chose for me. I wiggle into the tights and pull them up, slip on the black skirt, and find a simple darker gray shirt to wear underneath the sweater. I keep the glasses on—otherwise, I won't be able to see. I slip on the boots and find a full-length mirror behind the door. I stand in front of it and inspect myself: I look around twelve years old, and I have really sweet innocent-looking eyes framed by the glasses, and deep reddish-brown, almost cinnamon-colored hair, with blunt-cut bangs chopped straight across my forehead and grazing my eyebrows. I am not exactly big and not exactly small. I have light peachy skin and freckles on my nose and cheeks. I adjust my skirt and straighten my blouse, and I give myself a little smile. I've always wanted to wear glasses. I look smart. I kind of love them.

About halfway down the family-photo-lined hallway, dressed in my dark fancy outfit, I stop and listen. There are a lot of people talking and sounds of dishes clanging and the strong scent of coffee and something wonderfully sweet and buttery baking in the oven.

As soon as I step into the crowded kitchen, a sweet-looking older woman, wearing an apron over her black dress and washing dishes at the sink, looks up. When she sees me, she immediately turns off the water, dries her wet hands, and hugs me to her pillowy chest. She holds me tight for about a minute. She whispers something that sounds Italian in my ear, kisses the side of my face, then finally pats me on the back, pulls away, and looks into my eyes.

"Graciella," she says. Her eyes are wet and glassy, and in her right hand she's holding a pretty white handkerchief and silvery beads. This must be Nonie. I decide to take a risk—

"Good morning, Nonie," I say, and give her a soft smile.

"Sit," she tells me, pointing to the dining room table next to the kitchen.

I can't sit at the kitchen table because it is covered with huge flower arrangements—the kind that come to the door in a delivery van with notes sticking out the top of them—gift baskets of fresh fruit, cheeses, and salami and platefuls of Christmas cookies covered with plastic wrap. I glance at the dry-erase board covering the fridge with a calendar drawn in blue marker. In red there are days marked with different places to be: *tournament* and *game* and *practice*.

I look through the kitchen into the living room, where the tree is lit up with twinkly white lights and dozens of beautifully wrapped unopened presents underneath it. *It is still Christmas!* I am surprised how relieved I am. *Christmas number four,* I think, and smile inside. It's kind of a good feeling to at least know that much.

The kitchen itself is kind of chaos.

Tia and Nonie stand with their aprons over their dresses, cooking and cleaning up. The older man, Poppie, and I'm pretty sure a guy who must be the dad, are both dressed in dark suits, silently drinking coffee at the far end of the dining room table.

I look around, but I do not see a mom.

I follow Nonie's instructions and sit down at the other end of the dining room table opposite the men. I'm not used to eating with a fancy skirt on. I cross my legs and sit up straight and tuck a red cloth napkin into the front of my sweater so I don't get food on it, and within seconds a plate of eggs and buttered toast and a tall glass of orange juice appear in front of me.

"Gracie, you need to eat before we go to church," says Tia.

"Okay, thanks," I say, and look up at her.

She gently touches me on the shoulder. "You okay?"

she asks, looking into my eyes.

"Yeah," I answer truthfully. "These eggs are really good," I say, and bring the fork to my mouth.

She takes a deep breath. "Well, it's going to be a very long day." She pauses. "I'm glad to see you eating."

Five minutes later as I am sitting at the dining room table, eating the most delicious late-Christmas morning breakfast and wondering why the day is going to be very long, my wondering is interrupted by a tall, muscular teenage boy with a shaved head who suddenly appears standing at the edge of the kitchen, wearing green-striped boxers and a black hoodie with the hood up. The boy is frowning. He looks angry. He is the only one who isn't dressed. This seems to be a problem.

"Look, I'm not going, okay? I'm just not," the boy says.

A woman walks into the kitchen behind the boy. *This must be the mom,* I think. She is wearing a very formal black dress, heels, mascara, and light-rose lipstick. Her long, dark hair is like Tia's, but it is straight and down around her shoulders. She looks totally exhausted but pulled together.

"Dominic," she says to the boy, and shakes her head. "Please, I cannot do this right now."

The boy shrugs.

"Dominic," the mom repeats, and looks at him hard. She has dark circles under her eyes.

The boy sighs and shakes his head. "I'm not going,

okay? Are you seriously going to make me go?"

At this moment, the dad looks up from his coffee and connects eyes with the tall, half-dressed boy in boxers, and with that one glance Dominic—if that's his name—drops his head, whirls around, and stomps back up the stairs.

"Okay, fine! I cannot believe you are making me do this!" I hear him say.

After the boy storms off, I glance around.

Nobody is speaking.

Besides the running water from the sink and the clanging of dishes being loaded into the dishwasher, there is a tremendous amount of silence. You can feel it. Everyone seems on edge and nervous. I stand and clear my empty plate to the sink. The grandfather gets up too. He walks slowly over to the mom, looks at her with a warming smile, and wraps her with his arms. I watch, and for a second she lets him hug her. Then she pulls away and shakes her head.

"Dad, I can't do this right now," she says, and bursts into tears.

Tia comes up to the mom and takes both her trembling hands.

I watch it all from the dining room table, where I sit back in my chair and try and not be in the way. Tia and the mom have to be sisters. They look almost identical—dark hair. Tall. Pretty. Tia, still holding both of the mom's hands, looks at her sister with loving eyes.

"Let's go now, okay, hon? Does that sound good?" Tia is speaking to the mom almost in a way you'd speak to a little child who needs soothing.

The mom takes a big breath and nods.

Tia looks at me across the kitchen.

"Gracie," she says. "Why don't you ride with us."

48.

WE RIDE TOGETHER—THE MOM, Tia, and me, silently in the car. We take the minivan and *not* the bright-blue pickup truck with a surfboard strapped to the roof that was parked in the driveway. Tia is driving as we ride through a neighborhood of houses decorated with Christmas wreaths on the front doors, down winding roads, past fields with cows and barns and old big houses, and then finally down a hill into a small downtown with bigger buildings and storefronts. I am sitting in the back with my forehead pressed up against the window, which I crack open a tiny bit and drink in air. The weather is warmish but not too warm. And the sun is out. I have no idea what town or city or state I'm in.

Tia parks at the end of a quiet, house-lined street. And the mom suddenly panics. "Oh my goodness, the prayer cards. I forgot them," she says.

Tia turns to the mom. "Don't worry, it's okay," she says with a small, soft smile. "I will text George and make sure he brings them. He's coming with Poppie and Nonie as soon as Dominic is ready. Do you want to stay in the car and wait for them here?" Tia asks.

"No," the mom answers, and opens the front passenger door, stepping out onto the curb.

I slide open the back door of the van and get out too.

The three of us stand together for a moment on the sidewalk. The mom suddenly gets a worried look again, turning to Tia. "Someone needs to collect the flowers at the church. We need to get them to the nursing home. I don't want them all just back at the—"

"It's okay," says Tia, gently taking her hand as we begin to walk. "I promise. I will take care of it all."

The mom takes a deep breath and as I watch, I feel Tia's hand slip around my hand too. "You're not too old to hold hands with your auntie, are you?" she says, turning to me and giving me a faint smile.

The outside of St. Mary's Church is made of huge wide, gray stones that look very, very old and topped with a bell tower and a castle-y red steepled roof.

Tia and the mom, who looks like she's in a daze, decide we should wait for the others before we go in. We sit and wait on a bench in a small garden beside the church. I stare at the flowers and the giant boulder with *St. Mary's Church, 1863* chiseled in bold letters. *This church has been here for more than one hundred and fifty years.* I think about how many people must have come here on all the Christmas Days before this one. And the three of us sit quietly, and wait in silence.

When the dad and the grandfather and Dominic and Nonie arrive, there isn't much talking. The dad walks, holding the mom's hand, and I walk beside Tia. Dominic is last with Nonie and Poppie. People are already filing into church ahead of us—families with little children all dressed in their Christmas best—and together we climb the church's big stone steps.

The huge wooden doors are carved with dragons, and when they swing open and we step through the church entrance, the outside world fades away. The church mysteriously quiets my thoughts. I walk in and I get this overwhelming feeling of beautiful, peaceful silence. It's cool inside and very quiet. Older men in dark suits greet us in the church lobby. I watch them all shake the dad's hands and exchange hushed words. People greet the mom and they greet Tia, speaking in soft voices and giving hugs and kisses on the cheek. *Everyone seems to really love them,* is what I'm thinking as I watch people wrap their arms around the mom, holding her just a little bit longer than most hugs usually last.

I watch a dozen adorable little kids the same ages as

Rosie and Max streak past me, giggling—boys in their little white shirts and ties, girls in colorful dresses. They skip and run down a hallway toward a sign marked *Sunday School*.

Soon I am following Tia down the center aisle of the church. My eyes are big and really wide.

"It's so pretty," I say under my breath. The arched high ceilings are built entirely of deep-brown curved wood, supported by posts and intricately carved beams. Huge stained-glass windows filter the sun into slanting streams of shimmery light. Ahead at the very front, where the priest stands, is a curved wall made of more stained-glass windows, an altar, and a pulpit.

The church is full for Christmas Mass. It feels like the entire town is here. People sit tightly packed together. Every single seat is taken. And there are signs of Christmas: a tree at the front and garlands hanging from the ends of the pews. I notice people all look up when our family walks in. Teenage boys dressed in suits—slightly rumpled white dress shirts, black pants, black shoes, girls in dresses, parents sitting quietly beside them. Older people. My family must be important or something, because the entire front row of the left side of the church is saved for us! I slide onto the worn wooden church pew first and scoot all the way down until I can't scoot any farther, then Tia, then Nonie, then Poppie, Dominic—in his crisp dark suit and tie, and finally the mom and the dad on the end farthest away from me and closest to the aisle. I peer over and look at the family, then turn around and glance behind me. There is a very solemn hush. Nobody is talking until—

I feel a hand on my shoulder and turn and look at a lady in a pretty red dress. Her eyes are filled with tears.

"Oh, Gracie," she whispers. "I feel so sad. I still don't believe it happened. I'm still in shock—it doesn't feel real."

Once the lady says that to me, I get a very awful feeling deep in my stomach. And it occurs to me for the first time all morning, whoever I share a room with is not here. She is not with us.

As the priest appears in front of the entire church in a long white robe, I begin to panic about a girl I haven't even met—a girl I don't even know. My throat hurts. My head begins to throb. I have the worst feeling something terrible has happened.

It is so incredibly quiet when the priest begins to speak.

"Let us pray," he says. I bow my head but realize that's not what I'm supposed to do when I notice Tia reaching low, pulling down a wooden step stool that's on a hinge, silently crossing herself with her eyes closed, and kneeling.

I copy her. Not with the crossing. But I kneel on the cushioned stool, drop my head, and close my eyes. For the next half hour there is more praying, kneeling, standing, and repeating, the choir leads the congregation in singing hymns from a book, which Tia thumbs through and holds open so we can both see the words. I don't really sing, though. I just kind of stand quietly and hope and hope and hope that the girl I share a room with is not—

I can't even say it.

Oh God. I just keep glancing up at the beautiful stained glass and quietly wishing that she'll be okay. That what I am thinking has happened is totally wrong. *Please be wrong. Please be wrong. Please. Be. Wrong.* I think it over and over and over again in my head and bite down nervously on my bottom lip.

And for a second, as the priest stands on stone steps in front of the altar and begins to speak, I think maybe I am wrong. Maybe what I think happened hasn't happened. Maybe the dread I feel is . . . I watch the priest's eyes as he smiles softly in his long white robe and takes a deep breath.

"Another Christmas Day has arrived," he says. "The message of Christmas Day is a message of great hope. It is a day of great joy, the realization of a promise of change, the promise of renewal. The promise of a chance to begin again."

There is a long silence.

The priest looks directly at our family, then back at the entire congregation.

"In these times, our gift of love is our greatest gift. As many of you know, our dear friends the Fabianis have suffered a devastating loss."

The priest's words go from my ears into my brain, and my entire stomach immediately drops. I feel the worst tightness in my throat and chest. I just lose my breath.

"Jordan Theodora Fabiani was killed in a bicycle accident early yesterday morning," the priest continues. "Her family is here with us today, and we are here for them." He pauses. "The funeral and visitation for Jordan are set for later this week, but today it seems more important than ever that we share our Christmas Mass together. And so, I'd like to ask Jordan's dear friend Brooke to say a few words."

There is quietness and hushed whispers.

The entire church turns and watches as a tall, very pretty girl in a red dress and white cardigan sweater comes forward and stands before the congregation. I look up at the girl—she looks like she's Carmen's age. She's athletic and strong with long, straight blond hair that falls around her face. I swallow hard and I feel Tia's hand cover mine, and I lace my fingers around hers and hold on tight.

49.

BROOKE TAKES A DEEP BREATH and glances nervously toward our family, then looks out at the sea of people sitting before her. There is not a sound. I look behind me, and there are now people standing in the very back of the church. There must be five hundred people here, but it is absolutely silent.

"I was lucky enough to be Jordan's best friend," Brooke begins. She takes a breath. "But looking out at this gathering, I think many people considered Jordan their best friend. That was just Jordan. I never knew anyone like her. She was such a bright, shining light . . . she collected friends everywhere she went." Brooke drops her head, just for a second, then looks back up. "Jordan was one of the very first friends that I made in middle school. As a soccer player and an accomplished distance runner, she amazed me. But as good as she was, it was her heart that really shined the brightest. Jordan was a ray of sunshine, a beautiful one-in-a-million person. That twinkle in her eyes, it, like, grabbed you." Brooke grins as she says it. "Jordan was one of the kindest and most sincere people that I've ever known. She was smart, curious, a kick-ass surfer, a jokester, and relentlessly positive. I cannot remember any time when she didn't treat others with respect and grace." Brooke smiles at our family. "Jordan," she says, pausing for a bit. "I will remember your amazing fiery thick red hair and how you could rock a miniskirt with your trucker hat and your hair in pigtails and totally pull it off. . . . I will remember you singing country music at the top of your lungs, and how obsessed you were with Harry Potter, how you could be dorky and beautiful at the very same time. How if anyone promised you something, you would make them pinky swear."

There is soft laughter.

"I love how you used to call everyone lady. 'Hey, lady!' you would say. 'Let's go, lady!' I loved that. You could light up a room by just walking into it. People just gravitated to you. You had the best smile and the best sparkly giggle. Sometimes you would just look at me funny and you would make me burst out laughing so hard. I love how you would never leave any place or anyone without giving practically everyone in the room an arms-open-wide hug. You gave the best hugs. . . ." Brooke's voice falls silent. She takes a long, deep breath. "But most of all," she goes on, "I will always remember how you made the people around you feel like they were the most important person in the world. You always saw the best in me, and in everyone. . . ." There is a long minute where Brooke is not talking, a hush. A soft golden light filters through the stained glass and glows on Brooke. "I will never forget the day I met you. . . . It was the very first day of sixth grade. I had transferred to Oak Lake from Saint Ann's. I knew nobody. *No one.* I was small for my age, terribly shy and nervous. I felt so alone. And boom!"—Brooke's face brightens—"There you were, appearing out of nowhere like some kind of redheaded, pigtailed guardian angel. 'Hey, my name is Jordan,' you said, and flashed me your trademark gorgeous smile. 'And if you want,' you said, looking right at me with your shiny eyes, 'you can sit with us.'"

The crowd kind of collectively exhales and smiles.

Then it gets unbelievably quiet again.

"Jordan, I don't think I'll ever meet somebody like you ever again. When you wanted something, there was no stopping you. And on that first day of sixth grade, you waited, holding your tray and smiling as if you wouldn't even take no for an answer. You stood right there in front of me until I stood up too. I stood up and followed you, and honestly, Jordan, I've been so lucky to follow you ever since."

Big breath.

"You were a bundle of determination, totally fearless. You were never afraid to stand up and speak up. You had a quiet way of doing the right thing. That was just you. That's how you 'rolled,' as you liked to say." Brooke stops and breaks into a big smile, and there is a comforting rumble of soft laughter. "Even if it was a little bit scary. You had so much courage. . . I will never forget the last time I saw you. You had this glow in your eyes, and you said what you would always say, 'Keep that smile bright! Love ya, lady!' and you gave me one of your huge heart-to-heart hugs—" She pauses for what feels like a minute. "You would never let go first."

The whole church is silent.

"Jordan Theodora Fabiani—I will never forget your sparkly eyes or your beautiful smile. You were only seventeen and you brought us all together . . . look at this church! You touched so many people . . . It's Christmas and you somehow reminded us . . . the greatest gift of all is love and—" Brooke finally breaks down. She fights to get the words out. Tears are streaming down her cheeks. I feel Tia's grip tighten around my hand.

Brooke looks out at the faces, many of them now crying with her. She speaks through tears. "To everyone who is sitting here. You might think: We are so young. We have so much time," she says, her voice growing stronger and clearer. "To you and to everyone I say: *Do not wait.*

Do not wait to invite someone to sit at your table." She pauses, struggling to hold it together. "Do not wait to do the things you want to do. Do not wait another minute. Be courageous. It doesn't matter who you are or who you were. You can do or be anything you want. Start now— don't put living or loving off. . . ." Brooke stops. Her face is streaked with tears. "Love you, sweet Jordan girl. It was a privilege to have known you."

There is not a single sound as Brooke sits back down. Her parents stand up and hug her to them. She is sobbing in their arms.

The priest steps forward. "Thank you, Brooke. What a deeply powerful expression of the message of Christmas," he says. He does not speak for a long moment. Then he raises his arms and looks out at all of us. "Peace be with you," he says.

The congregation replies in unison, "And with your spirit."

The priest says, "Please turn to your neighbor and greet one another with a kiss of peace."

Right then someone taps me on the shoulder, and I turn.

"Peace be with you, Gracie," says a boy around my age with sandy-blond hair and big blue eyes. He's wearing a red bow tie.

"And with your spirit," I say back softly, because that's what I hear everyone saying. Five hundred voices stand crowded together, wishing peace, embracing, and shaking hands.

"Peace be with you," says the same lady who first spoke to me before the Mass. She turns to me with tears in her eyes, and she tries to smile as she leans over the pew and hugs me.

The priest moves behind the altar and begins the Mass. After more prayers and hymns and kneeling and standing and finally the blessing, the priest walks out in front of the altar and asks us all to be seated. He looks over at Tia, nods, and gestures for her to stand.

Tia moves to her feet and turns to face the mass of people sitting behind us. "Thank you all so much," she says, standing right beside me. Her words are slow and clear and warm. "Our family is so incredibly touched by this tremendous outpouring of love." She stops. She breathes. "There's just no way to express how grateful we are. . . . Although it's Christmas Day—after the Mass, our home will be open to all who want to remember Jordan and share memories, or just be together with us. Thank you all so very much."

Tia sits down, closes her eyes, and I see tears streaking down her cheeks. I put my hand gently on her back and hug her to me. Tia drops her head, bursts into tears, and begins to weep, wiping her eyes with a white cotton handkerchief passed to her from Poppie.

I lean into her. "I'm so sorry," I whisper, squeezing her shoulder. "I'm here," I say.

The sound of Tia's muffled sobs echoes through the packed church.

The priest pauses as he raises his arms and looks out at all of us and says, "Let us go forth into the world in peace."

After, organ music erupts out of wooden pipes and fills the air like a rich, soaring orchestra. Everyone in the entire church stands and row by row begins to file out. The priest goes first, followed by more people in white robes, then the choir, and finally our row. It seems like there is not a dry eye in the entire church. It's so sad. I walk down the center aisle quietly. I mostly keep my head pointing down, but when I glance up, people are looking at me with *I'm so sorry* looks in their eyes. I walk behind Tia, who walks behind her parents, and Dominic and the mom and the dad. Everyone is staring at us, almost hugging us with tender eyes. People reach out and put their hands on my shoulders and clutch and squeeze my arm.

Outside the big wooden doors, on the top of the wide stone steps, the six of us—even Nonie and Poppie—stand as a family and greet people as they leave Christmas Mass. The bells of the church are ringing out. The sun is behind clouds and the air is cold enough to make me shiver in my fancy skirt and sweater. I stand in between Tia and Dominic as a billion people file past us. Some people are crying and some people just stand awkwardly and don't know what to say.

A bunch of teenage girls in dresses circle around me and stare at me with shy smiles, eyes red from tears. "Oh, Gracie, I loved your sister so, so much," one girl finally says. "I can't believe this happened. I'm still in shock. We were supposed to play soccer tomorrow . . . I still have her voice mail in my messages. I can't erase it."

After she speaks, the rest of them are eased into talking—

"She was such a good person, the sweetest!" a second girl says.

"We're so sorry for your loss, Gracie. It's so sad," says the next.

"I'm so, so sorry, Gracie. . . . I can't stop thinking about her," another adds. "When I heard the news, I just couldn't believe it. I'm speechless. I still don't believe it. . . . I was texting her, like, two days ago," she tells me, and her eyes fill with tears.

I swallow. "Umm, thanks," I say weakly, and watch them move on, reaching up and wrapping their arms around Dominic's big shoulders.

A few people say things that are kind of confusing, like an older couple who look at me and say, "Everything happens for a reason. She's in a better place."

And I'm looking back at them, like—*How can not living be a better place?*—when Dominic leans over and whispers in my ear. "If one more person tells me she's in a better place"—he grits his teeth—"I am seriously gonna punch them in the face."

Most of the people are incredibly sweet. A lot of them don't even say one word. A short older lady looks at me and her eyes fill with tears. She just, like, hugs me and doesn't let go. There's something about that kind of hug that sort of takes your breath away. To be held like that. I'm not sure if she is helping me or I am helping her, but I let it happen and I hug her back. I look on as she offers Dominic her wrinkled, outstretched hand.

"Dominic," she says, holding on to his hand with both of hers. Her voice is quiet. He has to bend down closer to hear. "I'm Gloria—Jordan's friend from the elder care center. Your sister visited me every Sunday afternoon. She never missed a day. Never! She was a ray of light, that one." Gloria's face brightens at the memory. She shakes her head. "I don't have words for the pain I feel. . . . I'm so sorry. This must really be hard for you. . . . I can only imagine what you are feeling, dear."

For the first time all day, I see Dominic's eyes well up like, *Someone gets it.*

"Thank you," he says, leaning over and hugging her gently. "Thank you very much."

I ride back to the house with Dominic in the bright-blue truck that has the surfboard strapped on top, which I'm pretty sure is Jordan's. I am pretty sure of this because there are fuzzy pink dice hanging from the rearview mirror above the dashboard and a red soccer bag that's open with a light-blue sports bra and pink-and-white-striped soccer socks spilling out. There are muddy cleats on the floor by my feet in the front seat, and Jordan's school ID is attached to a red lanyard that's stashed in the cup holder.

There isn't a lot of talking.

Every so often I glance over at Dominic. His tie is loosened and the top button of his shirt is undone. He is here but faraway and silent. He reminds me a little bit of Teddy, the way he's broody and quiet and looks like he would rather be anywhere but right here driving this truck down a tree-lined street back to a house filled with people. He pulls up along the curb and turns the engine off and just sits in the front seat.

He doesn't move.

He stays perfectly still.

The reason he doesn't pull into the driveway is that there are a zillion little boys in white untucked button-down shirts, black dress pants, and bare feet outside playing basketball and laughing and pushing and tackling each other.

The two of us stay right there in the truck parked in front of the house and watch the boys through my window. I don't know what to say. And for what seems like a long time, I say nothing until I think of something and manage to speak—"I felt like I hugged a thousand people today," I say softly.

Dominic takes a big breath and leans over, resting his forehead against the steering wheel. There is another five minutes where no words are spoken, then—"This makes no sense whatsoever," he says, his voice breaking. "This just makes no sense," he repeats. Then with his hand he pounds the dashboard, his body collapsing against it.

Hearing Dominic's quiet sobs is just about the hardest thing I've ever done. My heart aches as I watch him.

But I surprise myself. I don't want to leave.

I'm not scared.

I sit back and I'm just there with him. I just have a feeling words won't help make this all hurt less. I stare out the window and watch people walk up the pretty grass-lined stone path, up the front steps, and into the house, carrying trays of food or flowers—a few young moms and dads with sweet new babies and toddlers in their arms. After ten minutes of silence, Dominic finally sits up straight, breathes in deep. He wipes his nose with his sleeve and turns to look at me—his long eyelashes are still wet with tears.

"Thanks, Gracie," he says.

"Ready to do this?" he asks.

I look back into his sad eyes and give him a faint, tender smile.

"Yeah," I say.

50.

DOMINIC WAITS FOR ME TO climb down out of the truck, and we walk together around the side of the house and into the kitchen through a sliding-glass door. There are six or seven ladies busily preparing food, chopping and slicing and stirring and baking. I don't see Tia, but I see the mom, who I hear people call Claudia. She looks focused, sprinkling cheese on top of a large tray of lasagna. She does not look up at us, and I'm kind of relieved. I get the feeling that for her being busy, cooking, is exactly what she needs.

Dominic nods at me and proceeds to disappear into the family room, where the Christmas lights are shining on the tree and, more importantly, where a professional basketball game is playing on the widescreen TV. There are lots of guys Dominic's age and dads with their dark jackets off, ties loosened, top button undone, shirtsleeves rolled up, sitting on couches, laughing and talking and watching the game. I watch a few of them jump up to their feet and greet Dominic with big, strong hugs.

I am about to clear off a space to sit down at the kitchen table, crowded with huge baskets of fruit and cookies, when, without warning, a lady in a dark-blue dress wraps her arms around me and squeezes so tightly my glasses get knocked off my nose.

"Oh, Gracie," she says, finally releasing me and stepping back. "We are all just devastated." The lady shakes her head. "The Mass today was such a beautiful testament to your incredible sister," she says.

I know people mean well and they're trying to be nice, but I don't know what to say back. So I just say a quiet, "Thanks," and try to be brave. But boy am I relieved when I see Tia walk into the kitchen. She's changed into jeans and a gray sweater. Her long, dark hair is down. She slips an apron on over her head, cinches it tight, and smiles at me.

"Gracie girl," she calls across the kitchen. "Nonie is making her famous manicotti. Come throw an apron on and we can help her."

I do put an apron on and I do help all the ladies in the kitchen. It's so busy and crowded, but it feels good to chip in, even if my job is chopping onions and stirring the spaghetti sauce—or gravy, as Nonie calls it. And, wow, there is so *much food*: gravy and tons of pasta are all cooking on the stove. And that's not all—there is a constant stream of people coming through the door, and it seems like almost everyone is bringing trays of food: lasagna, chicken parmesan, platefuls of chocolate chip cookies and brownies, a dish of enchiladas and quesadillas. Big plates of cream puffs and a tray of cannoli with a giant green-and-red bow tied around it.

Tia and I clear off the kitchen table and move all the food buffet-style to the long dining room table. The house is so filled I can barely walk through it. Every room I go into, people come up to me and hug me. Some people smile, some burst into tears. "Gracie, I'm so sorry," they say. Or—"Such a tragic loss."

I nod and say thank you and try to be polite and grateful. I understand it's, like, hard I guess, to know what to say. But I can see in Tia's eyes and in the way her face softens when everyone goes to hug her: it's better to say *something* than nothing. No matter how hard or awkward it is—it feels good to have so many people care.

On my way to get the extra napkins and plastic cups from the back of Tia's car, I pass three little girls in red sparkly taffeta dresses with white tights, black patent leather shoes, and glittery ribbons tied in their hair. They are in a guest bedroom off the kitchen. I stand at the open door and smile as I watch them playing make-believe.

One girl is like, "You're the mom. Your name is Cecilia!"

Another little cutie shakes her head and points to herself. "I'm the teenager!"

A third one giggles. "I'm the baby!"

Outside, I walk down the front path and look over at the boys laughing and passing the ball, and I think about how it's so weird, but so true, how the most horrible thing can happen and life still somehow goes on.

By the time the sun goes down and most of the people have left the house, I am seriously exhausted. I try to help clean up, but the same group of women in the kitchen insist on me sitting down. The mom, Claudia, is still moving, scrubbing, washing, drying, and putting things away. She doesn't stay in one place very long.

"Oh my goodness, Nicole," she tells a neighbor, handing over a tray of freshly wrapped lasagna. "Please, you have to take some of this home. There's no way we can eat all of this." This happens five or six more times, until soon, the house is almost quiet. The tables are cleared. The counters are wiped up. The last of the neighbors leave after more long, tearful call-us-if-you-need-anything hugs. The TV is turned off. One by one everyone in the family files into the now clean and finally empty kitchen. It's dark and no one moves to turn on the lights. The table is warmed by the faint glow of the Christmas tree from the other room. Dominic, the dad, the mom—who looks so tired—Nonie and Poppie, and I all sit down around the kitchen table. Everything is put away except Nonie's sauce, a bowl of pasta, bread, and a salad Tia takes out of the fridge and places at the center of the round table. There aren't a lot of words at first.

I'm surprised when Dominic of all people breaks the ice.

"That was really special. Brooke, I mean," he says, chewing a piece of garlic bread.

The mom nods. "She was lovely—just lovely," she says softly. I notice that she has hardly touched her food.

I see Tia reach under the table and hold the mom's hand.

I glance across at Dominic.

The only sounds are the silverware against the plates.

We sit like that around the table and it is almost calming. Just sitting together as a family. Nobody is even speaking, but the glimmer from the Christmas tree lights softens the quiet. It feels so comforting to be together.

I am taking a bite of salad when Tia leans forward and whispers, "Do you guys hear that?"

Dominic freezes, his fork in the air. "Hear what?"

Tia stands. "One sec," she says, excusing herself and walking to the family room and looking out the large window to find out what is going on.

She walks back into the kitchen and smiles gently at her sister, offering her hand to help her up.

"Claudia, sweetheart—Nonie, Poppie, George, Gracie, Dom . . . I think you better come see this."

51.

WHEN WE OPEN THE FRONT door and stand on the steps, there are probably three hundred kids standing outside under a dark, moonless sky. Three hundred of Jordan's classmates holding three hundred candles lit and glowing, huddled together, the crowd of them overflowing onto the front walk—a sweeping chorus of voices singing "Silent Night." Jordan's soccer team is in the front with their red-and-white jerseys on over sweatshirts, and Dom's friends behind them, tall and handsome, still in their suits and ties from the Mass . . . and more kids behind them, spilling into the street. All of them stand, arms around each other, as their voices lift into the cool night air.

The six of us stay just outside the front door on the steps. We don't walk farther. We stand together and watch all of Jordan's friends, the light from the candles flickering across their faces, gathered on the lawn and spreading out into the street, crying, hugging, singing, and then there is silence and just, like—a hush. The dad pulls the mom into his chest and she begins to weep, muffled tears. There is nothing worse than this. It's honestly the saddest thing I have ever seen. I can't take my eyes off her. There's nothing I can do to make it better. Tia and the dad help the mom back inside. I follow them. There are no words spoken. I stand at the bottom of the stairs and watch this strong, beautiful mom collapse into her husband. Tia has one arm and he has the other, and midway up the stairs the mom suddenly stops and looks back at me, reaching her arms out—

"Gracie," she says, big tears streaking down her face.

I puff my cheeks and swallow hard to stop this awful feeling from leaking out—but I cannot keep it down. I run to her, two steps at a time. And when I reach her, I let her stretch her arms around me. Everything I have been holding in bubbles up my throat and spills out, and I stand on the stairs, sobbing, dripping wet tears. The grief and worry comes out every place it can.

"I love you so much, sweetheart," she tells me, kissing me on top of the head. "I'm so sorry, I'm so sorry. . . ." She speaks so softly into my hair. I clutch onto her with both my arms. I feel her big, wet tears dropping onto me. After a minute or two, Tia takes her sister's arm gently, and with the dad, together, they walk her up the stairs.

* * *

I stand in Gracie's room and look outside the window at the last of Jordan's classmates walking away down the street, still holding their candles, the moon rising above them. I turn away and look over at Jordan's side of the room—

Her perfectly made bed.

Her nightstand.

I notice a small box wrapped in shiny green paper with a red Christmas ribbon. I walk over and pick it up. *For Gracie*, reads the tiny card, in neat print with a hand-drawn heart.

I don't think about what I'm doing.

I sit back onto my bed with Buster watching and rip off the wrapping paper. Inside is a small stuffed bumblebee and a note—

Bumblebee!!! I saw this and thought of you! You are always my sweet little honey bumblebee sister. Promise me you'll always believe in yourself, lady! You can do anything and don't forget it!!!
Merry Christmas! I love you so much!
xxo giant hug, Jordan

I hug the bee to my chest and crumple back onto the bed and wonder how it is possible to ache for someone you have never even met. I curl up with Buster. I snuggle into his warm, black, furry body and try to hide the tears streaming from my eyes. I cannot stop crying.

I place Gracie's eyeglasses on her bedside table and bury my face into the pillow and wonder if I will ever see my family again . . . if I'm ever going to get home. What if something horrible happens to them . . . I'm sobbing now. *How can the world take someone so full of life away? And why?* I start feeling a pain in my stomach and a tight lump in my throat. I just have the worst feeling. I don't know how much longer I can do this. I try to make all these crazy deals and promises—like, *I won't take anything for granted. I won't wish I was someone else ever again.* I don't know what I need to do to wake up as me. I press my face against the pillow and try to muffle the tears. I hear myself cry out loud, "I just want to go home . . . I just want to go home."

A minute later I hear knocking.

"Gracie, honey." It's Tia.

As soon as I hear her voice, the tears fall faster, spilling out of my eyes and dripping down my face onto the soaked pillow. They will not stop. I turn away. I want to be strong. I don't want to cry. *They have already been through so much.* I feel the weight of Tia's body sitting down on the bed next to me. I feel her hand on my back. And I just stop fighting it—

I am crying so hard now. Heaving.

Tia sits with me—she doesn't leave. She is right there

beside me, and after a long moment, I turn my face toward her.

"I'm really scared," I manage to get out.

Tia's wet eyes sparkle. She reaches and touches my face. "Oh, honey—I'm here," she says in the softest gentle voice. "You are not alone. You are safe."

"What is wrong with me?" I say, choking on my tears and snot, sobbing uncontrollably.

"Oh, sweetheart, there is nothing, *nothing* wrong with you at all. . . . Your heart is broken"—she stops and takes a deep breath—"and it's okay to not be okay." A minute or two goes by. "You don't have to be alone," she tells me, looking into my eyes. I feel my insides calm and look back at her and think about how hurt hurts less when you have someone to share it with.

For a long time Tia doesn't say a word, and I close my eyes, and it's like—I can still feel her sitting here with me. I feel her here.

I look up at her sitting beside me.

"Sweetheart," says Tia, reaching out to stroke my hair from my wet face. "I watched you so strongly there for your brother today, and for your mom and dad, for Nonie and Poppie, for *me* . . . and for *yourself*. You are so brave—" She stops, breathes in, and gazes at me for what feels like a minute. "Oh, honey," she says, she speaks so softly. "Yesterday and today were the hardest two days of my whole life. There is no real way to make this hurt less"—a single tear falls down her cheek—"but I promise you, tomorrow the sun is going to come up. It might seem impossible to even imagine right now, but you are going to get through this."

PART THREE

52.

SOMETHING IS VERY WRONG.

I am falling faster than I ever have. I am ripping straight down at a crazy speed, hurtling through the air, like I'm inside a washing machine. It's so scary! I drop down, down, down, faster and faster, and finally crash hard onto a cool lumpy bed with springs poking out of the mattress. I think I am knocked out for . . . well, I don't know how long—but I wake up in a terrible panic, terrified and extremely sweaty. I lie very still, brace myself, and slowly open my eyes halfway: I am alone in a double bed in a small, cramped, run-down, dimly lit room. There are dark curtains over the window by the door. There are no pictures on the plain, wood-paneled walls. I reach out and pick up a tiny box of matches on the nightstand and read the small print: *Flamingo Motel.*

I place the matches back where I found them and begin to really lose hope. *Why am I in a motel? When will I ever get home?* I start to think about my parents and Carmen and Teddy. It's finally beginning to sink in. I might never go back.

My head is hot and I can't stop coughing.

It's hard to breathe.

The pain comes from my chest. My lungs kind of hurt. Also? I find myself reaching under the thin blue blanket and scratching my legs and arms, which suddenly itch all over. I peer under the sheets and notice that I am fully dressed. I am *not* wearing pajamas. I am wearing a too-big winter coat, a T-shirt, and frayed, faded jeans. *Where am I? What is happening?* The second I'm thinking about how hopeless I feel is the second I hear the sound of a door unlocking and feel a rush of cool air—

A woman walks in, wearing jeans and a gray, short-sleeved, stained T-shirt. She has clear, milk-white skin. Her hair is bleached-blond streaked with dark roots and is tied back in a high, tight ponytail. She's quite beautiful. She doesn't look or seem like a regular mom. She's broad-shouldered and tough and really young, and she wears a tiny diamond stud in her nose. She has these super-intense striking blue eyes and a colorful leopard tattoo inked into her skin, starting on her lean upper arm and winding down all the way to her wrist. I get the feeling right away she's the kind of person you would want to *not* be mad at you. She doesn't look like she takes crap from anyone. Ever. But her eyes light up when they connect with mine.

"Merry Christmas, Punky!" she says. Her voice sounds confident and familiar, and her whole face smiles as she looks at me across the room, shuts the door, and locks it.

I go to say hi, but—oh my God, I can't even talk. I'm having a coughing attack! I open my mouth and, like, no sound comes out at all, and when it does it's wheezy and sounds hoarse.

"Merry Christmas," I finally manage, and cough a wet, terrible cough. My throat is sore. It just, like, hurts and also itches. My voice is high and scratchy. I sound like a squeaky little bird, and when I speak, a sharp, burning pain radiates through my chest.

The young blond mom winces. "Oh, Punky . . ." A look of worry spreads across her face. "We've got to do something about that cough." She sits down on the side of the bed, reaches out, and places her palm across my forehead. "You're not burning up, thank God."

The coolness of her hand feels good. I kind of wish she'd keep it there.

I watch her open up a paper bag and pull out a cup that's obviously hot to touch. "I got you some peppermint tea for your throat," she says, removes the plastic lid from the cup, and hands it to me. "I hope it's still hot." She looks worried.

I sit up, leaning my back against the wall, lift the tea to my lips, and take a sip. The hot liquid slowly rolls down my throat and for a moment it soothes the ache.

"It's still hot," I squeak, and then cough a deep, wet cough, dislodging phlegmy snot that I need to either swallow or immediately spit out.

The mom jumps up, runs into the bathroom, and returns with a wad of toilet paper. I spit the green stuff into it and cough some more. When I cough, the mom's face crumples as if she can feel it in her chest too.

"Punky, oh God, I am so sorry to do this to you right now, but—" She stops. She takes a deep breath. "Well, the good news is we got a job." For a split second her eyes light up.

We got a job? I think, and wonder what she means.

"The bad news is—" She stops and glances down at her phone, then looks back up. "We have to leave—like, *now*, if we are going to get there in time." She sighs and looks into my eyes. "I'm so sorry, Punky, I know it's Christmas, but if we ever want to get out of this dump . . ." She looks at me tenderly and takes a big breath. "I'm trying, hon, I'm trying so hard. We need this, we need this bad." She reaches out and pushes the hair from my eyes. "Look, there's *no way* I'm leaving you here all day alone."

I feel a cough coming on and quickly take a swig of tea.

The young mom stands. "Okay—what do you need? What can I do to help you get ready fast?"

"Um—no. I can do it," I say, turning my eyes away from her and getting up out of the bed. I can't stop coughing. When I stand, I am careful where I plant my feet. The motel room carpet is stained and dirty. Not from us. Or I mean, whoever I am or the mom. It's the kind of place it is. It's not nice. It's . . . it's the opposite of Jasmine's room in London times about ten billion. The air smells like old cigarette smoke, and the floor feels damp and grimy against my bare feet.

I step into the cramped bathroom and shut the door behind me. I have no idea where or who I am. The only thing I know for sure is the light in here blinks and buzzes. There is no plastic curtain on the shower, and there is a sign taped to the lime-green tiles that reads *Out of Order*. The sink drips and has mold creeping up the sides, and there is rust on the countertop. The wall is rotted. There is no mirror. The hot water in the sink doesn't work, and the water comes out in a weak, thin stream. I lean over and splash my face. I dry off with my sleeve and sit down on the cold toilet seat. That's when I see it. Straight ahead of me. There *is* a mirror. It's cracked and dirty and bolted on the back of the door and—

I am . . .

Oh my gosh. I know who I am.

Right there, sitting on the cold toilet seat, staring into the cracked mirror with my jeans down and gathered around my ankles, my mouth kind of drops open—

I am the girl from the bus.

The one I didn't stand up for. The one they were so mean to.

I am her.

I am in her body.

My long white-blond hair is tangled and knotty. My skin is very fair and pale. I have wild turquoise-blue eyes. They look so sad. I have pink welts and scabs from bites that were itched and scratched all across my arms and legs. Some are bleeding a little. They hurt. My heart just sinks. I feel so bad for her. I don't even know her name.

53.

OUTSIDE THE MOTEL ROOM THE parking lot is empty, and I wonder where our car is. The air is cold and the sky is gray and drizzling drops of freezing rain. I am wearing the young mom's jacket, the same exact clothes I woke up in. She is wearing just the T-shirt and jeans, her hair still scraped into a ponytail, her arms loaded with a plastic bag filled with rags and brushes and sponges and a bucket full of cleaning supplies—baking soda, white vinegar, that bright-blue glass cleaner, rubber gloves— and a mop. *This job must be cleaning*, I think as I stare at the bucket and then up at her. The two of us walk quietly in the spitting wind. I feel a little guilty that I'm pretty sure I'm in her coat. She must be freezing. But honestly, I'm really, really cold and I don't feel so well. My head hurts and my cough is bad.

We walk together across the vacant abandoned lot, onto a weedy uneven sidewalk until that ends—dart across an intersection and an empty blacktop parking lot. At first I think we are going into a supermarket, until I remember: everything is closed.

It is *Christmas.*

I trail behind the young mom, trying not to cough, and we keep going until we stop at a huge dark-green Dumpster behind a strip mall. I stand there like a scarecrow, holding the mop and the bucket and the bag, and I watch her walk up to the Dumpster, and as if it's a swimming pool ledge, easily hoist herself up with her arms, throw her leg over the side, and begin rummaging through whatever's inside like she's on a treasure hunt. She quickly pulls out a box and holds it up high like a prize. "Jackpot!" she says. "Christmas special!"

She climbs out, eyes shining, and leaps down onto the pavement as if it's nothing. She dusts the front of her shirt off with one hand and presents me with an unopened box of Dunkin' Donuts.

"They are perfectly good!" she says, sounding giddy. "Look, the stickers are still on. They must have put these out this morning. There's a little bit of everything in here—" She pops the box open. "Glazed, blueberry, powdered sugar, cinnamon—all your favorites, Punky!" She closes it again and proudly trades me the box for the bucket and the bag and the mop. Then we walk.

By three blocks I finally get my nerve up.

"So, like . . . where's the car?" I ask.

"Ha-ha! Yeah, right!" The young mom lets out a hoot. "You want a ride on Santa's sleigh?" She smiles at me. "No buses today, babe. We are going to have to walk, one foot in front of the other."

On Christmas Day number five, I am walking on the side of a very busy road with cars flying by. I am cold and tired and trying not to cry. All I want is to just be home. *My home. My room. My bed.* The wind is whipping and the rain is picking up as we hike along the crumbling shoulder. The ground is littered with trash, and we are surrounded by car dealerships—with lots jammed with shiny new cars—gas stations, closed grocery stores, McDonald's, Pizza Hut, shopping malls, and nail salons. I recognize where we are, I've driven by it on the bus a thousand times, but I've never in my life walked along this road. Isn't that kind of strange?

There is no green anywhere.

No sidewalks.

Just cars and trucks zipping by—

The air smells like exhaust.

It's hard to even breathe.

After about a mile or maybe two, we finally see another human being, a fragile-looking silver-haired old man, walking toward us, pushing a shopping cart with an American flag attached to the front. The cart is filled with empty bottles and cans. When I see the guy, my heart begins to race, but I quickly notice the young mom is not afraid.

"Sweet Pete," she hollers, and waves.

I can tell by the way the old man's face lights up that he seems to know her, and I quickly get the feeling she is the kind of person who never passes anyone without noticing that they're there. That they matter.

The old man's mouth cracks into a smile, and when it does I see he's missing almost all his teeth. He looks happy, though. Wrinkles and all. He doesn't seem to mind the cold, or the fact that he's collecting bottles and cans on Christmas morning.

"How about a little breakfast?" the young mom asks, nodding toward the box of doughnuts in my hands.

The old man is quiet, then shakes his head. I glance at him and try not to look away. He has thick white stubble on his chin and a wool cap over his head. He's wearing a black sweatshirt that has the words *Proud Veteran USA* printed in bold gold letters. My eyes travel to his shopping cart, filled with all his stuff: clear plastic trash bags packed with collected empty soda cans. Two folded-up wool blankets. A baseball bat. I stare at it all and try to imagine fitting everything I own in one little cart.

"Okay, Merry Christmas, Pete. You take care of yourself now," the young mom says, and the two of us keep walking.

The old man pushes his overloaded cart past us.

I look up at him—

I let his eyes in. I manage a tiny smile.

"Peace be with you," the old man says, with a sideways toothless grin.

Peace be with you. Oh my God. I just stop walking.

I stop.

I can't believe he said *those* exact words. And right there on the edge of the road, with traffic zooming past me and pelting rain blowing sideways, I am instantly taken back to church—to *yesterday.* By far the hardest day I have ever lived through. I think about Dominic and the mom and the dad, Nonie and Poppie, Tia sitting with me last night. My heart just hurts so much. I picture all of them now, this morning, eating breakfast around the table in the kitchen. I hope they're okay. I try to swallow.

We keep walking single file along the side of the road as big trucks rattle by us, too fast, and too close, leaving a trail of diesel fumes. I glance up at the storm clouds gathered in the sky. It looks like it's going to pour any minute, and I'm having a total coughing fit. I hunch over with my hands resting on my knees and am hacking up green snot onto the gravelly side of the road, and just like that—literally three seconds later—I am completely drenched head to toe! A huge tractor-trailer whizzes past me, barreling through a muddy, grimy, pond-sized puddle. It happens so fast. I feel the wind and the teeth-rattling shake. I look up. I see it. I see it coming. The next thing I know I'm soaked to the bone—my hair, my face, my too-big-for-me coat. Everything slows down—it's like slow motion: I see the young mom drop all her stuff and run for me, pulling me away from the road and hugging my trembling body to hers. Then? She loses it! Her blue eyes flash with rage. Not at me. At the truck—

She cups her hands around her mouth and turns toward the tractor-trailer, which is long gone. "Are you f—ing serious!!!?" She thrusts her hand up and extends her middle finger. "Well, Merry Christmas and thank you very bleeping much!"

Right at this moment, thunder rumbles.

I step back from the whir of passing cars.

The weather is getting worse. There are huge dark clouds following us, and the spitting mist is turning into a steady, sharp rain. I stand shivering and stunned on the side of the road, wiping the muddy gross slime off my face, holding my breath from toxic fumes, and my mind flashes to the peacefulness of the blue lagoon, swimming alongside Niko and the fish . . . riding horses through the snowy forest with Cass . . . Everything about right now is opposite that. It's hard to believe the world has both. So much joy and so much—

This.

The mom looks up at the threatening sky.

"Merry freakin' Christmas!" she screams. She looks so tired. Standing half in the ditch, she hugs my soaked body to hers, and when she looks down at me and the pitiful soggy box of doughnuts in my hands—the second our eyes connect, something just, like, clicks—and all I know is she looks at me and I look at her and we both suddenly burst out laughing. It's like, if you don't laugh, you are going to cry, right? I'm beginning to think sometimes it's just about the only thing you can do. I am standing huddled along the shoulder of a busy road, with muddy puddle juice dribbling down my chin and neck, having a pee-in-your-pants kind of laughing fit. We both are. We just, like, lose it, until we are laughing so hard we are practically doubled over.

ME: laughing uncontrollably, coughing out snot, tears running down my cheeks.

HER: shaking her head, her smile connected to mine, grinning hilariously and wiping away the tears flooding her eyes.

And that's it. We laugh like that until there are no laughs left, and finally our laughter dissolves into a peaceful silence and we gather our bucket and bag and mop and continue walking, finally turning off the busy road and down a quieter tree-lined street. Only one thing . . . I'm still soaked. I'm still wet. I can't stop shaking. I'm still so, so cold. My teeth are chattering.

The young mom takes the soaked-through box of soggy

doughnuts, tosses it in an empty trash can at the end of someone's driveway, and carries everything in her arms. She carries it all. The two of us walk down the middle of the empty, narrow street. I look at the pretty houses we pass by and try to picture the families inside: opening presents, or sitting around a table eating breakfast.

The young mom turns to me and gives me a big smile.

"Things could always be worse, right?"

I nod. *After yesterday . . . I know what she means.*

She stops and shifts the mop and the bag and the bucket all to one side and reaches for my hand. She sighs and looks at me. Her eyes are wet. I'm not sure if it's from the rain, the laughing, or if she's actually crying.

"We are going to get through this, honey," she says. "Things are going to change for us really soon—I just have this feeling." She squeezes my hand. "Can you hang in there?"

I nod and cough and look back at her.

For just a moment the two of us walk in silence, her hand warming mine. "We just need to keep going . . . we just need to not give up," she says.

I'm not sure if she's telling me as much as she's telling herself.

Five minutes later, we turn onto a street with cute family houses and big Christmas wreaths. I look around. *I think I've been on this street before.*

"So where are we going anyway?" I finally ask.

She lets go of my hand and pulls out her phone, glancing down at a map.

"We have, like, half a mile. We're almost there," she tells me, taking a big breath and letting out a smile. She's walking with the mop over her shoulder, the bucket in her hand, the plastic bag looped around her wrist. She must be totally freezing in her thin, damp T-shirt, but she never complains. Her strength shines through her eyes. She's tough. She's strong. And when I'm with her, I kind of begin thinking maybe I am too. I work to keep up. The thunderstorm sounds like it's getting closer. The clouds are turning darker and darker.

"Yeah, it shouldn't be too hard a job. Some teenagers threw a party last night," she tells me, glancing up at the threatening sky, then back at me. "I guess it got a little out of hand. They need some help cleaning up before their parents get back."

54.

OH MY GOD!

I am walking up the brick steps to my own house!

The young mom reaches out her finger and presses the doorbell, looks at me, and raises her eyebrows.

"Honey," she says with a sparkle in her eyes. "Try to picture living in a sweet house like this—" She grins at me. "Believe me, Punky. One of these days it's going to be true."

My heart is pounding when the front door opens and I am looking up into the eyes of my very own brother!

"Hey, Merry Christmas," says Teddy, sounding genuinely happy to see us. He is bleary eyed with crazy, curly bedhead hair, in the same rumpled T-shirt from the last time I saw him and jeans with rips in the knees.

"Hi, I'm Teddy," he says, coming forward and offering

his hand to the young mom.

She shakes Teddy's hand. "I'm Jess," she says, and turns to me and reaches her arm around my shoulders. "And this is my daughter, Josie."

Teddy looks at me straight in the eyes.

"Hi," he says with a big, warm smile.

"Hi," I say to my own brother standing in front of me. I have to work to not, like, throw my arms around his waist. *I'm not me. He doesn't even know me!*

"Come on in." Teddy motions us to step inside. "Honestly, my sister Carmen and I are so happy to see you," he says, shutting out the cold wind. "You have no idea," he says to Jess. "You are literally saving our lives."

Oh my gosh. It's SO weird to be back in my own house!!! I take three small steps in and look all around. In the light of day the house actually looks even worse than it did when I saw it on Christmas Eve. It's a *disaster!* Red plastic cups on the floor and on windowsills, half-filled with who knows what. The smell of day-old vomit is rising out of my mom's expensive blue glass vase. Soda stains and sticky spills on the floor and the carpet, and cigarette butts scattered on the entryway rug.

Jess sets her mop up against the wall and the plastic bag and bucket down on the floor, and the two of us stand just inside the door.

"Wow," Jess says. "Looks like someone had a little bit of a party." She flashes Teddy a mischievous smile. She's tough but incredibly sweet.

Teddy shakes his head. "Yeah. Not one of our better ideas. It got out of hand really fast. We just told a few friends—word got out. Like two hundred kids showed up. It's not what we had planned and—" Teddy stops and looks over at Carmen breezing down the stairway, looking like she just got out of bed. Her long, dark hair is in a heap and held together with a chopstick on top of her head. She is wearing her thick-framed black glasses, a hoodie, and sweatpants.

"This is my sister, Carmen," he says.

"Hey, Merry Christmas," says Carmen, holding out her hand to Jess. "You are seriously saving our lives."

"I'm happy to help," Jess says, squeezing my shoulder. "I'm Jess and this is my daughter, Josie."

Carmen looks right at me, and her eyes light up. "Josie! Oh my gosh, I love that name!" She smiles at me, and then her face quickly changes. "Wait! Oh my God. Did you guys, like, walk here? Isn't it, like, cold and rainy and gross out? You must be totally freezing! Oh my God, you are soaking wet. Do you want some dry clothes to change into?"

Jess looks at me, and then back at Carmen. "That would be really nice, and—"

Carmen jumps in before she has to ask. "You can even grab a hot shower if you want." She smiles at me and then at Jess. "I mean, that's the only way I can ever warm up."

Jess turns to me. She looks so relieved. "Babe, a hot shower sounds good, right?"

I nod. It does sound good. It sounds so nice. I'm so cold. My hands are numb. I try to hold in my coughing.

Carmen is already halfway up the stairs. "Jess, let me run and get you a sweatshirt or something too—"

"No, it's okay," Jess says, looking up at Carmen.

"No, really," Carmen calls from the top of the stairs. "I mean, you are the hero today." She smiles down at us from the banister. "And it is Christmas, after all!"

My heart is pumping so fast. I just stand there in the entryway of my own house, in shock. I'm like, *Is this real? Is this happening right now?* But it is, and after Carmen comes back downstairs and hands Jess a navy-blue sweatshirt, the four of us walk through the house, taking note of what needs to be done.

Teddy leads the way. "Keep your shoes on," he warns. "There's broken glass everywhere." He points to the floor. "Utter mayhem," he adds, shaking his head.

To the right, in the living room, the disco ball light is smashed and shattered into a billon sharp shards scattered across the living room floor. And that's just, like, one thing of a thousand! Seriously. It's bad. We don't even walk into the bathroom downstairs. The four of us all peek inside from the edge of the red carpet. Teddy swings open the door, and a filthy smell like puke and urine fills my nose.

"Ugh," I say, making a face. "It smells so—"

"Disgusting," finishes Carmen.

Jess leans in, then pokes her head back out. "Wow. Looks like someone had some problems aiming for the toilet. And—" She pauses, turning to look at Teddy, lifting her eyebrows. "Apparently, you have some fans."

"Yeah, okay, *that's* embarrassing," Teddy says, quickly turning red.

Even from the door we can all see, written in dark-red lipstick on the mirror: *Ho, ho, ho we love you, Teddy—you are so ho, ho . . . hot!*

Carmen's flip-flops crunch against broken glass. "The kitchen, the living room. It's all a mess. Definitely the stains on the rugs and carpets are the biggest thing that will get us in *huge* trouble." She stops and shoots a panicked look at Teddy, then looks back at Jess. "Our parents are getting home tomorrow, and there's no way we could clean this all by ourselves. We don't even know where to start!"

Teddy agrees. "It's pretty much trashed," he says.

We walk back to the entryway, where the bucket and the bag and the mop are. The four of us stand there for a moment. Jess turns to me. "Honey, why don't you let Carmen show you where to get cleaned up, take a hot shower, and change out of those wet clothes?"

Thank you, I see her mouth to Carmen.

Carmen's face brightens, and just like that, I am

following my own sister up my own stairs! I look back at Jess, pushing up her borrowed navy-blue sweatshirt sleeves. "Kitchen first?" she asks, handing Teddy the mop.

Teddy lets out a small smile. "Let's get after it," he says.

55.

"SO, LIKE, WHERE DO YOU go to school?" Carmen is walking with me up the stairs.

"Redwoods," I answer. It's so crazy to be talking to my sister again.

"No way, you go to Redwoods?" Carmen says, now looking straight at me at the top of the stairs. "Oh my gosh, so does my little sister! Do you know her? Frannie Hudson?"

You should see my eyes.

"Umm . . . ," I stall.

Carmen walks straight for my door, and I get this anxious fluttery feeling in my stomach. Like, I mean—*if I'm here, who is in there?*

"Frannie!" says Carmen, pounding on my closed and locked bedroom door. "Come on, you can stop being mad at me, please! There's somebody who goes to your school out here."

Carmen looks back at me. "So wait, do you know her?"

"Um—" I mumble. *You could say that.*

Carmen turns away from my door, like she's given up. "She has, like, long dark hair and really pretty eyes like you. Do you know her?" she asks again.

"No," I lie.

I can barely handle this. . . .

Carmen grins. "Well, you two should totally be friends—" She stops and looks at me for a second. "It's weird, but something about you really reminds me of her. I think you'd really get along."

I cough. A lot.

"Oh my gosh, poor thing! You are really, really soaked. Let's see if we can find something for you to wear." Carmen walks into her room, glancing back over her shoulder at me standing at the door. "Come on." She waves.

I hesitate for a second. I can't believe Carmen is actually *inviting* me into her room. I mean, she never does this with me!

"Seriously, come in!" She tucks a loose strand of dark straight hair behind her ear and smiles.

I walk through the door to Carmen's room in my squishy wet socks and I'm afraid to sit down and get her stuff wet, but she insists.

"Don't worry—just come sit down!"

I drop down onto the edge of her bed. I cough.

"Oh, dude, that cough does *not* sound good." Carmen goes over to her night table and reaches into a drawer and pulls out a pack of cough drops. "Here—I have some killer cough drops. These are my favorites. The grape ones are the best," she says, handing me the entire bag.

Carmen opens her closet and begins rifling through it, tugging a few things off the hangers and folding them up. Next she goes to her dresser, digs around the bottom drawer, and pulls a few more items out, adding them to the stack.

"So, listen," she tells me. "I have all these clothes that I never wear." She nods toward the neatly folded pile. "This is all stuff I'm getting rid of. Have a look. See if there's anything you'd like—"

I stare back at her.

Carmen pulls out her blue sweater—*that* blue sweater from the bottom of the stack. The same blue sweater she demanded I take off in the kitchen the last day of school before Christmas vacation.

"Ohhhh, try this one on—" She walks over and holds it up in front of me as if she was a salesperson at a store. "Oh, yeah. Definitely! It will look *so* supercute on you. Oh wow, it really matches your eyes!"

"Thanks," I say, sounding slightly shocked.

She's not done. Carmen grabs a pair of jeans from the dresser. "Oh man, I'm so bummed these don't fit me anymore. I bet they will fit you perfectly. I think I wore them every day of middle school." She folds them and tosses them onto the pile. "Oh, here's this old T-shirt I never wear, but I don't know why, it's practically new. This is my favorite track hoodie, but I have, like, three of them." She looks at me, eyebrows up. "Okay," she laughs, folding up a red T-shirt. "This reminds me of my ex-boyfriend. You'd seriously be doing me a favor! Please, take it!"

Then: "Hey, do you like music?" she asks.

"I guess," I say, and I watch her and all I can think is, *This is so weird. Carmen has barely talked this much to me in a year.*

She walks over to her speakers, pulls her phone out of the pocket of her sweats, and plugs it in. "This playlist will definitely get you in the Christmas spirit! I'm, like, seriously *obsessed* with Jasmine," she tells me, pressing play and turning up the sound. "I just love her! She's just got the best vibe, right?"

"Yeah," I agree, and really do smile this time. "Totally," I say, and cough a squeaky laugh.

"All right, well . . . so, I'll leave this on up here. And you can totally feel free to crash in my room after your shower. Lie down. Whatever you want. Make yourself at home." Carmen smiles. "Hey, let me show you the bathroom, and take those clothes"—she points to the pile of hand-me-downs—"they're all yours," she tells me.

My eyes get big. "To keep?" I ask.

"Totally," says Carmen with the sweetest smile. "Honestly, I've been meaning to go through my stuff. Seriously! Take it all."

I look back at her, and I have to remind myself she's smiling at Josie and not me, Frannie. But I'm just so grateful. So relieved. Josie deserves to have warm clothes. I want Josie to have nice things. Also, does this sound weird? I'm so happy Carmen is being nice when nobody is even watching.

Well, not *nobody*.

I am.

I follow Carmen to the yellow bathroom. The same one I share with her and with Teddy. It's the only room in the house besides the upstairs bedrooms that isn't completely a mess.

Carmen flips the light on. "Okay, so do you need anything else?" she asks me.

I shake my head and pop a cough drop into my mouth. Carmen's eyebrows go up. "They're so good, right?"

I nod.

"Oh, wait, let me get you some towels." Carmen reaches into the cabinet and takes two folded fluffy white bath towels out and sets them down on the counter. "All my stuff is right here," she says, pointing to her product-lined shelf. "You can totally use my shampoo or anything you need. Okay?"

I stare at her in disbelief. The last time Carmen found out I used her special expensive shampoo and conditioner she, like, literally, chased me down the hallway, sat on top of me, and punched me in the arm. Hard. I think I still actually have a bruise.

"So you're good?" Carmen asks, facing me, backing into the hallway.

I nod. I can barely speak without coughing. Plus, it's just so weird! I'm having a hard time putting this into words—all of this—*everything*. I'm home but I'm not home yet. I'm in someone else's body. I'm talking to my sister.

She's being so nice. . . .

Carmen looks at me and smiles hugely. Her eyes are gleaming. "Oh my gosh, you are such a little cutie," she tells me. "I cannot *wait* for you to meet Frannie!"

56.

INSIDE THE YELLOW BATHROOM I close the door and lock it and slowly, gently peel Josie's clothes off one by one. When I look down at her skin and her bare arms and legs—I just, God—I feel so bad. There are finger marks from itching, and open wounds from the scabs. Dried-up blood along the scratches.

"Oh, Josie," I breathe. I'm shivering. My lips are quivering as I reach out, open the glass door to the shower, and turn the water on. I let it run for a second, touch it to make sure I get the temperature just right, and step inside.

Oh my God. That hot water feels so good.

There are seriously almost no words.

I lather up a clean light-blue washcloth with Carmen's special rose soap and start from the top of my body, scrubbing behind my ears, in my ears, and along the back of my head. Using the soapy, soft cloth, I do the same with my face and my neck and I just get every inch of me. When I look down, so much dirt is coming off me. The hot water feels so good against the cuts and scrapes and wounds—washing away the itch and the pain. I bend over and scrub my legs, my ankles, and between my toes—beneath my nails.

Next, I get to work on Josie's hair. I lather up my scalp with Carmen's flower-blossom-smelling shampoo, scrub, and rinse. Then I dump her coconut oil conditioner in my hand and massage it into the long, tangled strands. I work the knots out from the ends, until finally I can run my fingers through. Then, with the hot water still pounding down, I just sit—

I sit right there on the shower floor.

I sit and hug my knees with my arms, and drop my head down between my legs. I let the hot water cascade onto my neck and back. I close my eyes. I breathe in deep, inhaling the heat and the calming scent of Carmen's soap. I sit like that, my head slung between my knees, and let the water just pour over me, washing away all of Josie's hurt. I imagine her wounds healing and feel her body—*my body*—warming and waking. I think about everywhere I've been and everyone who I felt closeness with, everyone who made me feel love—Cass, Luke, Rosie . . . Dani, Liam, Max . . . Niko. Tia, Dominic . . .

Jordan's entire family. Jess. With the pulsing water jetting down against my head and neck, I think of the wonder of everything that's happened. How somehow I made it back to my house.

I'm here.

I'm safe.

I turn off the water, step out onto the bath mat, and wrap the fresh towel around my body. With a second towel, I wipe my face and dry my hair. The heat and steam cleared my head and I'm thinking, *How good it feels to be clean and warm.*

Next, I go to work on the wounds.

I tend to each cut and bite and tender oozing scab.

I sit down on the edge of the toilet seat, still wrapped in my towel, and squeeze a little dab of antibiotic cream onto the tip of my finger and start from Josie's feet and work my way up, dabbing the ointment on the wounds and massaging around each one. I open the bottom cabinet door, reach for the box of Band-Aids, and apply Hello Kitty pink bandages to Josie's three worst scrapes and cuts.

I use the towel to wipe the fog off the mirror and take a nice long look at Josie's fresh, clean face. It's so crazy, because I'm looking right into Josie's blue eyes and also, I'm kind of seeing *me* for the very first time. I can't explain it, but it's like I'm seeing both of us: Josie's fragile wild eyes, and this new strong me, in there, inside. It's like, this feeling comes over me like—*I want to be part of the world. I want to be in the world. I want to live.* I take a big deep breath and gently brush out Josie's long, white-blond, tangle-free hair. I smile softly into the mirror—*Taking care of yourself really feels good.*

57.

I WALK DOWNSTAIRS AND INTO the living room dressed in Carmen's fuzzy blue sweater and hand-me-down jeans, smelling like rose soap. My hair is down around my shoulders. I watch for a long minute before anyone sees me standing here. They are all working: Jess, in her borrowed navy hoodie, her hair tied back, is vacuuming up tiny shards of glass. Teddy is near the front door, on his hands and knees, scrubbing the floor clean with a soft-bristled brush and a bucketful of sudsy water. Carmen is standing on a stool, wiping the windows that face the street with a clean, damp cloth, reaching up her arm, starting at the top and working her way down.

Jess looks up at me, smiles, and shuts the vacuum off.

"Feeling any better, honey?" she asks.

I nod and smile quietly. "Yeah," I say.

Carmen glances over her shoulder from her step stool. "Hey, Josie, if you're hungry, we finished the kitchen. You can go in there and help yourself to anything."

Jess's eyes and mine lock. "That sounds like a good idea," she tells me. "Having a little something to eat might make you feel a little better, honey."

"Okay." I nod, and Jess looks relieved, turns the vacuum back on, and gets to work.

I walk out of the living room and into the kitchen and—

"Whoa," I say out loud when I walk through the swinging door into the thanks-to-Jess extremely spotless bright white kitchen. My eyes scan the room. It's, like, cleaner than before the party. I've never seen it so—shiny. The dishwasher is humming and gurgling and working away, and the counters and table are glossy. Everything is put away. It even smells clean. Airy. I shuffle across the newly polished floor wearing Carmen's fuzzy slippers that she usually would never let me wear and stand in front of the open refrigerator door and stare inside at the half-empty shelves. As soon as my eyes land on the carton of eggs, I feel the corners of my lips turn up.

I have an idea!

First, I slip my mom's crisp white apron over my head, tying it snug around my waist. Next, I wash my hands and rummage through the drawers and open the kitchen cabinet doors, looking for two bowls. When I find them I set them on the counter beside the sink. Then, one by one, I gather all the ingredients in my arms: flour, baking powder, sugar, salt, butter, milk, eggs. Just thinking about little Rosie and her big eyes peering down into the mixing bowl makes me smile as I crack the eggs—which are not anywhere as fresh as the ones from the Chicken Chapel. These eggshells are white and the yolks are pale yellow and they break right away, instead of staying all perky. I measure and pour in the milk and the melted butter with the eggs. I get a fork and stir it all together and dump in the flour, baking powder, sugar, and a pinch of salt and mix it up until the lumps are gone and the mixture starts to kind of bubble, just like Cass taught me.

I don't have blueberries, but—*I have to figure out a way to use what I've got.* I find half a bag of chocolate chips in the fridge and sprinkle them into the batter.

I'm not going to lie: I am so proud of myself when I pour the pancakes into the hot buttered pan! You should seriously see my smile. It's big. I can't believe I've never done this before. It's so easy! Plus, I can't wait to surprise everyone. *Helping feels good.*

Okay, yeah. So I burn the first pancake. I throw that one away. *One burnt pancake is not going to stop me!* I think to myself, and laugh. I turn the heat down and try again. The second one is perfectly round and I wait just like I did that day with Luke, until I see the batter bubbling, and then, with the metal spatula I flip it. I repeat this same exact thing twelve times, until I have a dozen golden-brown pancakes, all stacked in a giant leaning steaming buttery-smelling tower. I set four places, plates, place mats, forks, and knives. I pour four glasses of orange juice, and with a fork I poke and carefully lift three perfect pancakes onto each of the four plates.

I want to open the kitchen door and shout, "Grub's on!" the way I have heard Teddy before. But I remember I'm Josie, and that I still have a bad raspy cough. I walk into the living room and just smile until everyone finally looks up.

"Umm—" I look to Jess. It's hard to hold back my excitement. "I made you guys something."

You should see Jess's face when she enters the kitchen and sees the table set and the plates of pancakes.

"You did this?" she asks, beaming. "Oh, honey." She covers her mouth with her hand. "This is, this is . . . this is just—"

"Oh my gosh, this is so sweet!" says Carmen, dropping into a chair and grinning at me through her glasses tipped at the end of her nose.

"Honey!" Jess sounds amazed. "I didn't even know you knew how to make pancakes."

I smile proudly. "I do," I say.

Teddy takes his first bite, and his eyebrows lift. "Dude, chocolate chip pancakes! Are you for real? Why don't you just come live here forever?" he jokes. "These are amazing! You're awesome," he says, taking another bite and shooting me a wink across the table.

Carmen drenches her stack with maple syrup. "I seriously cannot believe you did this!" she says, lifting her fork to her lips and hesitating before she takes a bite. "Oh my gosh—I wish Frannie would get her butt down here and like . . ." She lets out a soft laugh and smiles at me from across the table. "Let's just say she could learn a thing or two from you." Carmen grins sideways at Teddy. "Wouldn't you just die if Frannie surprised us like this? *Ha!*" she hoots. "Not likely!" She rolls her eyes.

"Seriously," says Teddy with a laugh.

For a second some really bad feelings creep back. They start in my stomach. But then—I just, like, breathe, and look at Carmen and let out a tiny smile. She has no idea. It's me. I *am* here. I did this!

I *did this.*

This is really *me.*

They don't have to know. I *do.* I can take care of myself. I can be anything I want to be. *Screw them,* I think, and shake my head.

Teddy grins across the table and raises his glass of orange juice in a toast.

"Hey, Merry Christmas, y'all!" he says with gusto.

Our glasses clink together, and Teddy looks at Jess and then at me. "I don't think I can remember a Christmas where I felt more grateful," he says with a quiet smile. You can see in his face that he means it.

* * *

After I clean up and wash the bowls and the dishes, dry them, and put them all away in the cabinet, I join the rest of them in the living room and try to help. Jess is now on her hands and knees, scrubbing puke stains out of the black-and-white rug. She's so intense, and I can tell whatever she does, she does with all her heart. It's just the look on her face and the way she moves. She's determined. Nothing is going to stop her. And Teddy and Carmen take her direction. We all do. Jess patiently shows us how to treat the stains. And soon we are each on all fours, sunny-yellow rubber gloves on our hands, sprinkling cornstarch, waiting five minutes, and scrubbing dried vomit out of the living room rug with a bristled brush.

By eight p.m. the house looks amazing!

Like, seriously, *amazing*.

When we are done, we walk through it again, checking the bathrooms and every nook and cranny to make sure we didn't miss a spot. Then we all—Teddy, Carmen, me, and Jess—just stand together in the middle of the living room, like, astonished. Everything feels really clean and the air feels clearer. It smells good. It feels, like, orderly and calm . . . Inside the house, and inside *me*.

Carmen says it best. She looks at Jess. "Our house is beautiful. I've never seen it like this before. It's almost . . ." She pauses and sighs. "It's like, right here, right now, everything is right with the world." She looks at me as she says it. "It kind of feels like we're wiping the slate clean. Do you guys know what I mean?"

For Christmas dinner, Teddy—beside himself with relief and gratitude—orders takeout Chinese food delivered to the house for the hungry workers, him included. Carmen gets all in the spirit and sets the dining room table. We never eat in here. It feels nice. She lights a small wax candle that smells like evergreens and places it at the center of the table, surrounding the soft glimmer with special-occasion red place mats and my mom's fancy white plates. Carmen's very serious about it. I kind of feel like Jess's way of doing things has sort of rubbed off on her.

Teddy gets kind of into it too, dramatically taking the white Chinese food takeout containers out of the plastic bag and setting them on the table, calling off each dish he ordered one by one: "Kung pao dumplings, wonton soup for Josie's cough—" He stops and winks at me, then goes on, "egg rolls with hot mustard sauce, crunchy vegetable fried rice, sweet-and-sour chicken, rice noodles . . ."

Right before we eat, Carmen turns to Teddy. She looks suddenly concerned. "Wait—Teddy, seriously, please, will you go see if you can get Frannie to come down? Tell her we got her favorite egg rolls and veggie fried rice. I mean, I'm actually a little bit worried. . . ."

Teddy reaches for a dumpling. "Dude, I tried a few minutes ago. She won't even talk. She's giving me the silent treatment. Pretty sure she's still heated about last night." He shrugs. "I understand, man. We screwed up."

"I'm going to try," says Carmen, already on her feet, but Teddy gives her a look and she drops back down into her chair.

"Just let her be," Teddy says quietly. "She'll come down when she's ready."

"How's the soup, honey?" Jess asks.

"Good," I answer. *It is really good.* The warm liquid feels good sliding down my throat. I eat it all, and even tip the bowl to my lips and drink the last drop.

For a long minute there's no talking. Everyone is starving. The house has been transformed into some sort of magical oasis. It's hard for me to explain it, but—it feels different. Peaceful.

Carmen's eyes light up. "Oh my gosh, with all the cleaning and everything—I almost didn't say it! Merry Christmas, you guys—and like, I am seriously grateful, and not just because you saved us from getting punished for the rest of our lives—" She pauses and smiles, and her eyes literally sparkle in the candlelight as she says it. "I can't explain it," she goes on, "but I just, like, I don't know. You feel like family. I feel like I've known you for a really long time."

Outside the night air is bitter cold and the wind is howling and whipping. It's raining still, but I am leaving the house with a bag filled with the clothes I came in (now washed, dried, and folded), and a huge pile of hand-me-downs from Carmen. She stands just outside the front door and even gives me a hug.

"I hope I see you again!" she says.

Teddy is driving us. He insists. "It's hella cold out. It's pitch black and it's practically hailing," he tells Jess. "There is no way I'm letting you two walk home."

Before we get into his car, he unzips his Princeton lacrosse hooded sweatshirt, takes it off, and holds it up behind me.

"For me?" I ask, threading my arms into the too-big-for-me sleeves and zipping it up. It comes down to my thighs. I look back at my brother and wonder when he turned into some kind of knight in shining armor.

"Oh yeah, rockin' number ten," he says with a big grin, and gives me a fist bump. "Awesome new look."

Carmen does not get into the car with us.

She was going to but she stops halfway down the brick steps and looks at us all.

"Hey, on second thought—I'm going to stay here, you know, in case—" She exhales a long breath that shoots into the cool night. "In case Frannie comes down. I don't want her to be alone again."

58.

"THIS IS GOOD RIGHT HERE," Jess tells Teddy, like a block before the motel.

Teddy glances at her in the passenger seat. "Are you sure?" he asks. "It's raining. Really, I would feel better if I could take you straight to your door. It's dark and it's—"

"Okay," says Jess. She sounds embarrassed. "It's right up there." She points.

"The motel?" asks Teddy.

Jess nods.

It's quiet when Teddy turns into the empty, deserted parking lot. Teddy shuts off the car and immediately gets out. And as the three of us stand outside under the dark sky, the pink neon *Flamingo Motel* sign flickers in the cold rain. Thunder booms and there is a sudden flash of light against the night, and the craziest thing happens—

"Thunder snow!" exclaims Teddy, throwing his head back and smiling at the sky.

My mouth drops wide open. It's snowing! And it's coming down fast.

"Holy cow!" Teddy says. "It's just amazing! It's never snowed here in my entire life!"

Even Jess is grinning. She tilts her chin up and lifts her arms toward the sky. "It's a Christmas miracle!" she announces, giggling.

I look up too. I look up into the blue-black night at the giant glittering snowflakes falling on my face. I stick out my tongue like I did on my way to the Chicken Chapel. "This is so crazy," I say, and think how it feels like I'm in one of those snow globes, and everything has been shaken up.

For a stretch none of us move. We all stand in the snow, smiling at the wonder falling all around us. Teddy extends his hand and Jess shakes it. Then, surprisingly, he pulls Jess into a big warm hug.

"Thank you so much," I hear him say quietly. After he lets go, I watch my brother reach into his back pocket and take out his wallet.

Jess immediately shakes her head and backs away. "Oh, no, no, noooo, you already paid me," she tells him firmly.

"But—please," says Teddy. He takes money out of his wallet, folds it, and holds it out to Jess. "If you knew my dad—" He stops, and the look on his face changes. "Really, Jess, please take a little extra. It's Christmas and you . . . you totally saved us."

"Hey, then we're even, because we had fun too." Jess beams at Teddy as she leaves him standing with the money still in his hand and takes three steps backward toward the hotel door. "And isn't that what we're all here for? To look out for each other?" Jess says, suddenly reminding me of something Brooke said about Jordan yesterday at Christmas Mass. My heart aches. I know I didn't know Jordan, but I feel like she'd totally love Jess.

Jess turns to unlock the hot-pink motel door, and before she steps inside looks back over her shoulder.

"Thanks, Teddy. Merry Christmas," she calls out, flashing him a smile.

I face Teddy as I backpedal toward the open motel door. Snow pouring down.

"Umm—" I say, looking at him as I speak. My heart begins to beat faster and faster. I feel a wave of overwhelming panic. I mean, *Will I ever see my brother again? What do I do? What should I say?* My body moves without me telling it to. I just don't think about it. I run toward him and fling my arms around him. Tight. I want to say, *I love you, Teddy!* I want to say that, but I just squeeze him with Josie's arms, as a layer of snow coats my hair and my nose.

"Thank you," I whisper so softly, I'm not even sure he can hear me.

When I step back, Teddy looks at me kind of surprised.

"Hey, I'm the one who should be thanking *you*. Those pancakes? Amazing!" He winks. Then, with no words, he smiles with his eyes and slips the wad of bills into my hand. "Please," he says, raising a single finger to his lips as if to say, *Shhhhhh*. He smiles at me through the quietness of falling snow. "That's for you and your mom. Merry Christmas, Josie."

Inside the room, I pull back the heavy curtains and watch Teddy's car drive away. I can't believe I might never see him ever again. I feel this heaviness in my chest. For a long time I just press my forehead against the cool glass and stare sadly at the falling snow. Until—I remember I'm holding a wad of cash in my hand. I set down my new bag of clothes and watch as Jess shakes out the sheets and neatens the bed.

"Oh, shoot!" she says, slipping off the navy-blue hoodie. "I forgot to give this back to Carmen."

"That's okay," I say quickly. "I mean, I think she wanted you to keep it."

"Yeah. Maybe," she says, her voice tired.

There is a long pause, and Jess strips off her jeans and crumples into the bed in her underwear and her T-shirt.

"They were really nice kids. Teddy's a really good guy,"

says Jess, pulling the thin blue blanket up to her chin and exhaling the exhaustion of the day.

She smiles at me from the bed. "Hey, how are you feeling, honey? Better?"

I look back at her. "Yeah," I say in nearly a whisper, and out of nowhere I feel this sudden, light-headed flash of hot, this familiar fear in my body. It comes on quick— *What if Jess gets angry that I accepted the money from Teddy? What if she flips out?*

"Um, I—I like . . . I did something—" I say, trying to be brave. "I'm worried you are going to be really mad—" I stop. I walk toward her. I sit down on the very edge of the bed.

My throat feels like it's closing.

Jess sits up. She gives me a concerned look then a quick smile. "Oh, honey." She keeps her eyes on mine— they are shining, and they calm me. "If I'm frustrated, or if you're frustrated—" She pauses for a long moment, reaches out and touches my face very gently, pushing the hair out of my eyes and looking at me, the corners of her mouth lifting. "Honey, whatever is going on, we can figure it out *together*. You know that. You're not going to lose me. Ever, ever, *ever*." Her face brightens. "Even when you feel like you're falling apart. I can take it. I'm with you through it all."

I swallow back the lump in my throat.

I feel so relieved when she says that. I know she's not

even my mom but . . . it just feels so good to hear it. I can't even really explain it. I take a big breath. I lean in and—

"Um, I—" I begin, but then freeze. I don't know what to say, so I just hold out my hand and slowly open it like some kind of magician revealing a white bird. Except it's not a white bird that flutters its wings and flies away. It's a wad of crumpled twenty-dollar bills that falls onto the blanket and into Jess's lap.

"It's from Teddy," I say. "I know you said no, but—he . . . he, like, he really wanted you to have it. He just gave it to me and I couldn't—" I stop and look at her.

Jess's eyes get big and then flood with tears. "Oh my gosh," says Jess in disbelief. "He gave this *all* to us? He really gave this to us?" She sits up straighter and counts out the bills into her hand. "There is over two hundred dollars here!" She looks at me, tears pouring down her cheeks. "Combine this with what we made today . . . and it's—it's enough to finally get out of here. We have enough for our deposit!"

Jess finally breaks down. She is crying and smiling at the same time. Her eyes are wet and sparkling. "I'm going to meet with the shelter caseworker on Wednesday, and if everything goes well . . . we'll get into that new women and children's center on Saint Christopher Street. You know, the one with the playground and the courtyard and the washers and dryers! It's beautiful, and you're going to *finally* have your very own room. . . ." She pulls me in, cradling my head with her two strong hands, and looks me straight in the eyes. "We can get out of here, Punky," she whispers, tears streaming off her face. She is so happy. "It's really going to happen. We can get a new start."

She is glowing.

She smiles.

I smile back.

The tender way she looks at me seems to speak without her having to. There are no words but . . . somehow, she says: *everything*. My eyes fill with tears—good tears—and I hug her tightly and rest my head on her shoulder. I breathe her in. She smells of orange-scented floor polish and salty sweat, and she holds me for the longest time, rocking me, whispering in my ear. "Oh Punky," she says. "Oh my love." And this warm, grateful feeling nestles in my heart. *This is what Christmas is truly about.*

I am so tired.

I don't know how late it is or how long I've been lying wide awake, tossing and turning. I am sweaty and a little bit itchy. I stare off into the silent, shadowy darkness. There is a voice in my head that is running on a loop: *What is going to happen tomorrow? Who will I be?* I don't know if anyone's listening, but if they are, if someone in the universe can read my mind? *I'm really ready to be me. I want to be me.*

I want to try.

Jess is next to me, sound asleep, her arm draped around me. I scooch over a little closer and listen to her quiet breathing and secretly wish she would magically just, like, wake up and make this all feel less scary. I roll onto my side. I try to breathe. *Breathe,* I tell myself. *All you have to do right now is breathe.* I shift my weight, rub my wet eyes with my hands, and exhale loudly, hoping Jess will somehow hear me and—

Right at that second—right then, I feel the weight of her hand lightly touch my arm.

"Honey," she whispers. Her voice is so delicate. So soft. "What's going on—are you okay?"

I turn toward her.

My eyes connect with hers through the darkness of the room. "I—I'm . . . I'm a little bit afraid," I whisper softly. "What if—what if I wake up and . . . I can't do this—" I stop, my throat tightens—*how can I explain this?*

Jess snuggles up closer.

She's, like, six inches away from my face. She smiles at me through the darkness. "I know you're scared, honey. I know this has been so hard. I know how much you want things to change. Is that what's going on?"

"Yeah," I answer in barely a whisper, and wipe my eyes.

Jess is quiet for a long time. "I was so proud of you today," she says, facing me, lying on her side. "You are just—you are just so strong, so wise. There are a trillion things about you that are amazing." Her voice is so certain. So tender. So calm. She looks straight into my eyes and whispers, "Honey, you can handle anything that happens. *No matter what.*"

I breathe. I swallow. I try to inscribe the words inside the part of me that will be gone from here tomorrow. *I can handle anything that happens. No matter what.* I repeat it over and over again in my head. I try to remember. I try to believe her. I have never had anyone tell me that before. . . . It's hard to find the words to say how good it feels. It feels like some kind of suit of armor. A shield. It feels like how I want to be. How I want to feel.

"Punky?" She waits for a minute. "You know that, right? You can handle *anything* that happens. *No matter what,*" she repeats with such certainty. She keeps her eyes on mine with the softest, surest gaze.

I love her so much right now. I know she's not my mom. I know, but . . . I breathe in the silence and smile the softest smile back.

"I can handle anything that happens. No matter what," I say into the hush.

"Anything is possible," she says dreamily, in her whisper-soft voice. And that's the last thing I remember. That and this: "Merry Christmas, love. You are the greatest thing I've ever done. I'm truly blessed to be your mom."

59.

I DO NOT KNOW HOW long I'm flying. But I'm *flying*. Wait. Not, like, in a *plane*. I'm flying with my arms spread out like wings, steering myself through the wind, my smiling face tipped forward like some kind of superhero with goggles, except I don't have goggles: my eyes are wide open.

There is no rain.

No snow.

Only cool, drinkable open air and a beautiful, cloudless blue sky, and I fly into a burst of rosy warm light, over sun-washed farms and lakes, soaring over rolling green mountains, treetops, above sweet, fruity, fragrant fields of wildflowers: pinks and violets, golden yellows. I inhale. The sunlight is twinkling against the sky. A breeze lifts me from behind. There is no spinning.

No twisting. No somersaults. I just glide, free, like an eagle . . . it's like nothing else matters . . . it's so peaceful! I can see *everything*—it's, like, the best view in the whole world. There's so much more than I knew . . . everything looks so small from here—green hills, tiny houses and farms, and the only sound is the wind rushing by me. I feel this openness. . . . I smile and squint into the sunshine. I am in charge of my body. I am in complete control. It feels like I'm swimming but through air, and when I gradually slow down, I don't plummet, or drop, or slam or crash. And I don't feel scared! I float down like the lightest feather and bounce to a soft, gentle stop.

I land facedown.

I don't know where I am or *who* . . . but the first thing I am thinking when I touch down is how good it feels to be perfectly still. How lush the quiet is. How wonderful it feels to be alive. I take a breath and I close my eyes.

I don't know how long I'm out, but when I wake up I am curled into a bed, a pillow beneath my head and clutching a soft blanket. I feel like I slept better than I have in a long time. My eyes are closed and I keep them shut. I mean . . . I know by now. I get it. I might open them and it may very well be Christmas, *again*—

I don't move for a long while.

I am quiet.

I lie very still, and a tiny bit of familiar worries ricochet around my brain. I feel that old fear, that panic rising up, but then, like—

Screw that!

I've changed. I am different now. I am done hiding. I am done being scared. I calm myself down. I take a long, deep breath. On my own count of *one, two,* and *three*—I crack open my eyes and—

I exhale the biggest joyful sigh!

I'm H-O-M-E!

I am in my own bed! I sit up and immediately look out my window. The sky is a dreary gray, but the three plastic reindeer are still planted right where I last saw them in my neighbor's lawn. I smile at them and at Teddy's car parked in its usual spot under the basketball net. The grass looks wet but the snow is gone. I stretch my arms up over my head, whip the sheets off, and stand.

Oh wow.

I feel my feet on the ground. I'm here! I finally made it! I look down. I am wearing the same *exact* clothes I remember wearing on Christmas Eve: my pink glitter heart pajama bottoms and my sky-blue tank top. My next thought is that I'm kind of freezing. I walk over to my dresser, dig through my top drawer, slip on a long-sleeved T-shirt over my tank top, and pull on some socks.

I push my desk away from the door and step into the quiet hallway.

I look left and I look right. Carmen's door is closed. So is Teddy's. I don't hear any noises. I listen closely and peer over the banister downstairs. Everything looks as sparklingly clean as I remember from when Jess and I left last night. The carpet is freshly vacuumed. The house smells good.

I tiptoe down the hall and into the yellow bathroom— the same one I was just in, *yesterday*. Inside I quietly shut the door and switch on the light. I can feel my heart begin to race as I walk toward the mirror . . . I mean, *I am home. But am I me?* I stop. I can't look yet. There's something I want to do first.

I strip off my clothes and drop them onto the floor and run the water just like I did for Josie. This time it's me stepping into the very hot shower. I sink to the floor. I drop my head. I let the water warm me and soothe my neck. I wash my hair and breathe in deep. I stay in there until the hot water begins to turn to warm, and finally stand, turn off the spray, and step out. My toes sink into the bath mat. I wrap myself in a fluffy white towel. Finally, I move to the mirror, reach up and with my hand, wipe the fog away. And, "*Yes*," I say with a huge smile. I move a little bit closer. I'm glowing from the inside out. My cheeks are all rosy, my green eyes are kind of sparkly with bursts of tiny stars, and my skin is clear. The scab I had picked at has healed. My long, dark, wet hair is plastered to the sides of my face and neck. "Hi," I say, and laugh because I am home and already talking to myself. It's me. It's *me*.

"I made it," I say softly. "I did it. I'm here." I smile into the mirror, eyes gleaming, as if I'm meeting myself for the very first time.

And in a way—

I kind of am.

60.

"OH, LOOK WHO DECIDED TO grace us with her presence," jokes Carmen.

She and Teddy are sitting at the kitchen table, eating leftover Chinese food straight out of the carton.

After my shower I fell back asleep for I don't know how long. I have messy slept-in hair when I make it downstairs, stand at the doorway and, like, stare across the kitchen at my sister and my brother.

Teddy looks up and flashes me a huge white smile.

"Frances!" he exclaims, like he's actually really happy to see me.

Carmen rolls her eyes. "Too bad you missed *all* of Christmas! What's your deal? Are you still mad at us?" She shovels in a forkful of wide noodles and smiles at Teddy and then back at me. "Ooh, come on," she says, chewing. "Do you forgive us? Pretty please?" She giggles. Her face brightens.

Teddy looks up from his egg roll. "Seriously, though, Frances, you were right, okay, we messed up."

I have not said a word yet. I just stand there and feel the corners of my mouth turn up. "So wait," I say with the biggest smile. "It's like—it's . . . it's not Christmas anymore?"

With one hand, Teddy grabs a cloth napkin, wads it up, and throws it across the room at my head. "Dude, are you even awake?" He laughs. "*Yesterday* was Christmas and you were on strike, remember?" He shakes his head.

"Yeah," I say. *I do remember.*

I walk over to the fridge, open it, and take out the last carton of Chinese sitting on the shelf. Veggie fried rice. I open the silverware drawer and get a fork. I pour myself a tall glass of orange juice.

"Do you guys want some?" I ask, holding up the OJ.

Teddy looks up at me. "I'm good."

"Yes, please," says Carmen with a puzzled smile.

I settle into a seat across from my brother and sister.

Carmen looks at me hard for a very long time.

"What?" I say, and laugh.

She stares at me for about a minute, peering across the table though her thick black glasses, wrinkling her forehead.

"Something seems different about you," she says.

For a few long seconds I'm quiet. I don't say anything.

"Yeah," I say finally, and smile inside. "Something kind of is."

Ten minutes later, Carmen is in the middle of telling us—well, mostly Teddy—a story about Jules and some guy she hooked up with at the party, when she suddenly stops at the sound of keys jiggling in the door. In an instant the three of us share a nervous glance.

"Hell-looooo!" we hear.

It's my mother.

Carmen shoots me a look as she stands. "Do *not* say anything about—"

"God. I won't," I say, quickly cutting her off.

"Good," she says, shooting me a you-better-not-or-I-will-kill-you look.

Teddy leads the way, and Carmen and I follow as the three of us walk toward the front entryway. My mother has already stepped in and set her small suitcase down inside the door. Her dark hair is rumpled and her face is slightly bronzed and suntanned. She smiles and raises an eyebrow.

"Nice to see the house is still standing," she says with a loud laugh.

Carmen immediately goes up to her and hugs her, kissing her on the cheek. "Oh my God, I'm so jealous of your tan! Did you guys have fun?" Carmen asks in a sugary-sweet voice I haven't heard since yesterday.

I go to hug her, too, but—

My mother pushes me away.

"Oh, Frannie. Please, no hugs, I can't deal with clinging right now. I'm sticky and exhausted and I have a splitting headache. I need to sit down."

I take a few steps back. I have this glazed look on my face and hurt just washes over me. But there's not a lot of time to really feel anything, because at this exact moment my father walks through the front door. He has a suntan too, more like a burn on the top of his head, and he's dressed in a tie, dress shirt, and slacks.

We all kind of freeze and watch his expressionless face as he silently takes off his suit coat, hangs it up, turns and nods at Teddy, and continues walking straight up the stairs.

"Your father has an awful headache," my mother whispers. "There was a screaming baby right behind us the entire flight. She would *not stop crying*. It was hell."

My mother steps a few feet into the house. "Soooo . . ." She lifts her eyebrows, looking all around, her hand on her hip. "The house looks great," she says, sounding slightly shocked. She glances down at the table right by the door. "Where is my vase?"

The three of us are all silent for a second.

"Oh," I say, excited. "I know where it is!" I dart into the kitchen. I remember washing it yesterday with Jess.

I find my mother's special blue glass vase resting on a dish towel off to the side of the sink, pick it up in both my hands, and carefully rush back to Teddy, Carmen, and my mom, and place it down in its regular spot like a trophy.

"Uhhh—I was, like—I was just washing it out," I say, and glance at Carmen, a little bit proud.

My mother gives me a funny look. "You were washing the vase?" She lets out a loud sigh. "I don't think I even want to ask."

I feel Teddy squeeze my shoulder, and I look up at him. He shoots me a wink.

Carmen turns toward me with the slightest smile and a relieved look on her face.

The three of us follow my mother into the kitchen. She walks over to the sink and fills a glass with water, returns to the table, and drops into a chair. Teddy, Carmen, and I sit down at the table too.

"So," my mother says, sipping her glass of water and sitting back in her seat. "Did you guys get along?"

Carmen glances at my mother and smiles. "Of course we did!" she lies.

My mother isn't even really listening. "Is there any food in the house? Did you go shopping? Did you use all the cash we left?"

"Um, yeah," Teddy says, glancing at Carmen. "We kind of treated ourselves to a big Christmas dinner last night."

"Oh, good," my mother says. She takes another sip of

water and sets it down. "Well, thanks for asking," she says, sounding sarcastic. "Your father and I had a *fabulous* time!"

Carmen leans across the table. "I'm totally jealous." She beams at my mom. "What was it like? Was the water gorgeous? Was it that see-through turquoise blue?"

My mother turns to Carmen. "So gorgeous! We swam alongside some of the most colorful fish, and the water was just beautiful, as blue as blue can be—"

"Oh my gosh!" I say quickly, and smile. "I *love* swimming in water like that!"

Carmen rolls her eyes. "Yeah right, you wish!"

My mother lets out a long, dreamy sigh, as if she wishes she were still *there* in Jamaica, and not here with us. She drifts off for a moment, then looks back. "We also rode horses on the beach. It was *wonderful!*"

I smile across the table at my mom. "Oh, my gosh! I *love* riding horses!"

This time Carmen laughs in my face. "Give me a break! You have never ridden a horse in your life."

"Whatever," I say under my breath. I feel the inside of me begin to crumble, but I try to stop it. . . . I pull my shoulders back and I keep my head up.

My father walks into the kitchen, heads straight for the fridge, reaches in and cracks open a beer, and sits at the end of the table, drink in hand.

My mother continues, "Oh, and we went sailing!

Honestly, that was my favorite part—" She turns to my father. "How about you?"

He lifts his beer to his lips and flashes a tight, forced smile.

I sit up straighter. I turn to my mom.

"I love the ocean! I really love going new places!" I say excitedly. "I mean, like, one day, seriously, I'm going to sail to Australia and navigate the boat all by myself, using the stars!" Just the thought of the ocean makes me smile so big. "Oh my gosh, have you guys ever been, like, out at night and looked up and seen the—" I suddenly stop speaking.

My father is cringing at me, lifting both his hands up and covering his ears like a little kid might do.

"Frannie," he says sharply. He does not look at me. "You are speaking extremely loudly." His words are slow and much louder than mine, which makes no sense to me. I freeze. I feel the worst feeling inside. It, like, floods me. I feel it in the pit of my stomach and in my heart. My throat tightens. My whole body does. I look straight across the table at my mom for help, but—

She avoids my eyes. "Frannie, your father is absolutely right," she says, looking away, shaking her head. "You need to work on lowering your voice."

Carmen smirks. "Seriously, Frannie, are you trying to be triply annoying right now?" She glares at me. "Your voice is like a loud, irritating squeal. You need to seriously chill, just, like, seriously, *stop talking.*"

I look to Teddy, but he is focused on his phone—head down, texting.

The whirl of conversation between my sister and my mother picks back up. My father sits back in his chair and clicks the television on. I sit there at the table and try to swallow. My head heats up. My heart just drops. *Nothing is different. Everything is the same.* I bite my lip. I hold back the tears. I stand up. I look right at my mother.

"May I please be excused?" I say, and back away from the table. My voice is shaky. And it might sound like a question, but really it's more like a statement.

I spin around and push the swinging kitchen door. It slams back, hitting me as I walk through it. I can hear my mother call after me as I climb the stairs: "Frannie, you are being ridiculous. You don't need to leave, just stop talking so loudly! You need to lower your voice. I told you your father and I have throbbing headaches . . . and you . . . *blah blah blah blah* . . ."

I stop listening.

I turn it all off.

In my room, I close the door and lock it. I dive directly into my bed, facedown, and pull the pillow up over my head. I'm not going to lie—at first, I really do want to cry. My heart is pounding and I can't even breathe. I feel myself start to shut down. I pull my legs up into a ball and—

Wait. What is that?

I feel a lump under my stomach. Like, a real lump. *Under me.* I reach beneath the sheets and feel around with my hand and . . .

As soon as I feel it, I know what it is.

I pull it out and stare, eyes wide with shock and pure and total delight. I am holding the cuddly stuffed bumble-bee! *From Jordan.* The actual bumblebee is in my hands!

"Oh my God," I say, clutching the furry bee to my face, and I can't hold them back any longer—the biggest, most relieved tears start leaking out of my eyes, and soon I am crying for the billionth time. Happy, fat tears pouring down my cheeks. In this one second, everything that was fuzzy suddenly makes sense. I wipe my eyes and curl up with the soft plush bumblebee. I wrap myself up in my blanket, and I calm myself down with slow, deep breaths. And I hear a chorus of voices in my head, the best ones I could ever wish for—people I love, and people who love me—soothing whispers—*There's nothing you could ever do that would make me leave you.* I hear Cass and feel her holding me tightly. *You are just right. There is nothing wrong with you at all,* says Dani with her twinkling smile. *I feel so lucky to be your dad,* Luke tells me under the sky full of stars. *You are going to get through this,* says Tia, looking at me through her own wet tears. And Jess, her voice whisper soft—*You're not going to lose me. Ever, ever, ever. I'm with you through it all.* I play them over and over again in my head a thousand times. And oh my God, I'm sobbing now. Slowly, it sets in: *I'm not alone*. They're not here, but . . . I can still hold them all in my mind. They are a part of me now. My heart feels like, this explosion of love and warmth. I feel so close to them. I feel safe.

And there's one more voice I hear. *Mine*.

"*You can do this*," I say, wiping my eyes with my hand. "*You are safe. You are so strong . . . just breathe*." I say it over and over and over again in the softest, surest, kindest voice. And if you've never tried talking to yourself like that, maybe you should. Because all I can tell you is that right here, in my very own bed, for the first time in my life—in my own body, in my very own room—I'm taking such good care of myself. I have changed the story in my head. The bumblebee fits perfectly in my hand, and I pull him close and snuggle him right up to my cheek. I inhale the faintest scent of Tia's perfume. I feel a sense of peace that I never had before. They're with me. It lasted. It's *in* me. It's real.

61.

"FRANNIE!"

I hear Carmen outside my door.

"Fraaan-niiiiiie," she sings. She's not really knocking. It's more like pounding. "Come on, open the door, please?"

I sit up in my bed and stare at the closed door and try to decide if it's a good idea to open it.

"Fraaan-niiiiiie," Carmen calls out in her sweetest sugary voice. I can see her slippers through the gap at the bottom of my door.

"Fine," I mutter to myself, get up and walk over and open the door and quickly return to the exact spot where I was. Except I don't turn away and I don't lie down. I sit up on top of my bed, hug my knees, and lean against the wall and look back at her—*she's up to something.*

Carmen stands silently in my open doorway, smiling in her black-rimmed glasses. She's dressed in her shiny peach-colored pajamas. Hair clipped up in her typical chopstick bird's nest.

"What?" I say.

Carmen tilts her head and squints at me. "Um, wow, you could say hi first?" she says, and laughs. "Also, what's up with sitting in the dark? Turn on some lights!" She hits the lights and grins. "Better, right?"

"What do you want?" I ask her. And look, I'm not acting all nice to her back. She's so mean! I'm sick of it.

Carmen suddenly looks past me. "Wait, no way, where'd you get those boots?"

"What boots?" I ask, confused.

"Those?" She points across my room toward my closet. I turn and look and . . . *Oh my gosh.* My eyes pop. My jaw drops open. On the other side of my room, sitting upright, are Dakota's cowgirl boots, the ones I wore on Christmas Day riding Trigger! The brown boots are lined up neatly, as if I had taken them off and set them side by side, right by my closet door.

"Seriously, though, when did you get those?" Carmen asks, sounding almost jealous. "Those are SO cute! I mean, like, I would even wear those!"

I don't answer her. I jump up and pull the boots on. Which is funny, because I'm wearing my pink glitter heart pajama bottoms and sky-blue tank top. They fit perfectly. I look back at Carmen leaning against the side of my doorway, arms folded tightly across her chest.

"I got them from a friend," I finally answer. And I am smiling the kind of huge smile you smile when you have a total secret that is just yours and makes your heart feel all warm and happy.

Carmen raises an eyebrow. "Oh, so does that mean you actually *have* friends? *Ha!*" She laughs. "Good to hear."

I stay silent while I glance back at her like, *Really?*

"What, I'm kidding!" She laughs. "Seriously, they're cute, though."

I look down. The boots feel good on my feet, and they remind me of Cass and Rosie and Luke, not to mention Romeo. I am smiling the biggest goofy grin as I look up and say it. "They're not for just wearing around," I tell Carmen. "They're for riding—" I stop. "Forget it." I say, and shake my head. "You won't get it."

Carmen uncrosses her arms and grins. "Okay, whatever, cowgirl. Listen, are you going to watch a movie with me or what?" She pauses. "Well . . .?" she asks.

I stay silent.

"Are you really going to make me ask twice?" Carmen rolls her eyes. "Fine!" She sighs. "Frannie, do you want to watch a movie together?"

My eyes kind of get big because, yeah. You heard it too! Carmen just asked *me*, *me* to watch a movie with her?!! But I surprise myself by what I say.

"It depends. Are you going to be nice to me?" I ask, and push my hair out of my face.

"Oh my gosh." Carmen flashes me a smile. She walks to the bed and holds out her hand to me. "Just come!"

We make popcorn together in the kitchen. I pop it on the stove, and Carmen pours on the butter. I follow behind her down the basement stairs, and we sit shoulder to shoulder on the couch positioned directly in front of our big flat-screen TV. I scooch over a little closer to Carmen. We are under a bunch of blankets and surrounded by piles of pillows. My pink glitter heart pajama bottoms are tucked into my cowgirl boots, and my legs are stretched out, my feet propped up on the table in front of us.

The lights are off.

The popcorn is in a bowl on Carmen's lap. Carmen is fidgeting with the remote control, trying to get the movie to start. I settle back into the couch and glance at my sister sideways. Our arms are touching. It's the closest I've been to Carmen in . . . in a really long time.

She pops a handful of popcorn into her mouth. "Hey," she says, munching. "Like, how'd you know where Mom's vase was?" she asks.

"Oh, um . . . I just like—" I start, then stop.

"Whatever." She glances at me and smiles. "You helped us out. Good save," she says.

"Thanks," I say, sounding shocked because she is

actually being, like . . . *nice*. Then—

She turns. "Dude, seriously?"

I look back like, *What?*

She scowls at me. "Are you, like, trying to touch every single piece of popcorn when you put your hand in the bowl? You're gross."

I feel my shoulders tighten and take a deep breath.

Carmen yanks the blanket and elbows me. "Also, do you *really* need to sit *this* close to me?" She glares at me until—

"Fine!" I answer, and scoot over at least five feet.

My sister laughs. "I didn't say you needed to move *that* far!"

I inch back over.

Carmen points the remote at the TV, and finally the screen bursts with light and sound. She leans forward, places the popcorn on the table, and settles back. Now our shoulders are almost touching again. She spreads out the blanket evenly over our legs.

"Oh yeah, by the way," she says, looking at the TV as she speaks. "I met the sweetest girl yesterday. She and her mom came over to . . . ohhh—never mind *why*, the point is, I think you guys should hang out. Her name is Josie—she's in your grade at Redwoods, and she's awesome."

"Okay," I quickly agree, and smile. "I'll look for her at school."

Carmen turns and wrinkles her forehead as if she's studying me. She hesitates for a second, and then, "Okay, don't let this go to your head, but . . ."

"But what?" I say.

Carmen shrugs. "You know . . . I'm not sure what happened to you on Christmas or what exactly is going on—but, like, this new spunky you?" She stops and gives me this long, intense look. She has a gleam in her eyes. "I like it," she says.

I keep my eyes straight ahead, but the corners of my lips slowly turn up.

Carmen leans over and grabs the bowl of popcorn and places it right in between our laps. "Now, *shhhhhhhh!*" she says, wiggles closer, and drapes her heavy legs over mine. "It's starting!"

62.

IT'S THE FIRST DAY OF school after Christmas vacation. I step up onto the noisy crowded bus and walk forward down the aisle. My whole face brightens when I see her sitting by herself in the window seat a couple of rows in back of the driver. Her long white-blond hair is parted at the center and pulled back.

I slide into the seat beside her.

"Hi," I say, and give her the biggest smile.

Josie looks up at me shyly. I try not to stare at her milk-white skin and ocean-blue eyes. We are both quiet for a second. The bus swings to a start and Josie presses her cheek up against the window and stares out the glass, and for a moment we both watch the houses and grassy yards flash by. But pretty quickly my heart starts racing because, well—I'm so excited to see her! I glance sideways. I want to ask a million questions, like—*I want to know how she is! How's Jess? Did they move? Are things better?* During the next few minutes of silence, I remind myself Josie has *no* idea who I am. She's never even met me! For a second I begin to wonder—*Who was she when I was her? Like, whose body did she bounce to?* I'm pretty sure everyone who I was bounced into someone else. But that's not something I will probably ever figure out.

The bus rattles around a corner and my body leans with the turn, my shoulder lightly grazing hers. Josie turns and glances at me.

"Hey, um—" I smile at her fuzzy blue sweater. "I love your sweater," I blurt out.

"Thanks," she says in a whisper-soft voice.

"The blue, it like—it goes perfectly with your eyes," I say.

Josie turns again, brightening. "Thanks," she says.

I watch her unreal blue eyes glance at my neck. Her face comes alive. "Is that a real shark tooth?" she asks.

I reach up and wrap my fingers around the shark tooth—I found the necklace in my room the same night my parents got back, along with the red-beaded bracelet from Dani. They were both sitting right beside my alarm clock! Today I have everyone with me. I'm not alone. I have Niko's necklace against my skin, Dani's beautiful ruby-red beads around my wrist, Jordan's furry bumblebee tucked in my backpack. I wiggle my toes in Dakota's broken-in leather boots.

I rub the smooth shark tooth like a lucky stone.

"Yeah, it's real," I say, and smile at Josie. "I got it from a friend," I tell her.

"That's so cool," she says softly.

The bus stops; its doors open. Josie looks up, startled, and immediately drops her head. I can hear them before I see them. Alexis. Whitney, Tay. They are laughing, sharp and loud, like they are in on the same funniest joke as they climb the steep bus steps. I feel Josie's body next to me tense. She's terrified. I can see it in her face. Her hands are trembling. And look, I'm not going to lie to you, I feel a rush of anxiety too. My stomach feels jittery; my heart starts beating very fast. But—I stay.

I sit tall enough for both of us.

I square my shoulders.

I breathe.

I'm safe, I tell myself in my head.

It's okay.

See, there's one more gift. I got it from Jess. It's a shimmery magical force field, made up of one single thought: *I can handle anything that happens. No matter what.* I take a slow, deep breath and I look right at Alexis as she walks by. For a long moment our eyes connect as she giggles, passing by me with her paisley bag slung across her shoulder. And yeah, I'm a little bit nervous, but I'm okay. I don't turn away. I don't drop my gaze. I stare right back until she looks away.

The bus starts up again. I turn and look at Josie. "Oh, hey!" I say with a twinkle. "I'm Frannie, by the way." My voice is soft and easy. There's silence for a second.

"I'm Josie," she says, glancing toward me.

The bus vibrates. Our shoulders bump. I glance down. My faded blue jeans and her jeans line up seam to seam. I don't move away. It takes me about a minute to say it, but I do. "I know this sounds kind of random, but—" I pause. "I was wondering . . . do you want to sit with me today at lunch?"

Josie turns and for a split second we look into each other's eyes.

She smiles.

I smile back.

"Yeah," says Josie, and her shoulders soften. "I'd like that a lot."

63.

IT'S ALMOST SUMMER: MY LAST official day of
seventh grade, and I ride the city bus ten bumpy miles,
zipping down empty country roads that wind through
deep-green farmland—until, finally, the bus stops on the
side of a quiet, dusty lane and drops me off.

The sun is shining.

No clouds.

I wait for the bus to pull away, tighten the straps of
my backpack, dart across the empty road, jump the old
wood-rail fence, and run as fast as I can. *I'm beginning to
learn, being brave always feels a little bit scary at first.* I run
through a meadow of long-stemmed purple wildflowers
and through waist-high grass and down a big sloping hill,
and when I get close—

I stop.

I whistle.

I smile as I watch his head jerk up and his ears perk forward. He gives a little nicker and immediately breaks into a trot toward me.

"Oh, you're such a good boy," I say.

I grab his thick mane and swing up on him, haul my butt up, throw my leg over, and ride him all the way into the barn. Sometimes we run, sometimes we walk, splashing across creeks and trotting and galloping over the flat, open grassy pasture—I can feel his strength underneath me, straddling the horse, leaning forward, sitting tall—so fluid, and free, and he takes such good care of me. His name is Goldie because he's a goldish-reddish Thoroughbred, a big old and perfect first horse. My teacher, Shaina, she's the one who told me about this shortcut to the ranch. She's like, "If you can hitch a ride from the pasture, it's a lot more fun than walking up the road!" And she's right! I'm smiling my big gap-toothed smile, my ponytail flapping behind me, sitting on top of Goldie, in my jeans and my T-shirt and my leather boots. I breathe in the clean air, the green pasture dotted with flowers. I love being the kind of girl who can ride bareback. I love clopping slow and easy right into the barn!

Elk River is a working cattle and horse ranch. Nobody found it for me; I looked it up and rode the bus out here myself. The ranch is big and always busy. It's got a covered dusty dirt arena that's open on the sides, so we can work the horses in the shade or the pouring rain. Then there's a long barn with an entire side of stalls. I work three days a week in exchange for lessons. In the barn, I'm always smiling so big. I love that earthy sweet smell of horse. It's like a mix of leather, fly spray, sweet horse manure, and hay. It's just the best scent. I muck stalls and I help feed. I go into each stall and fill the water buckets and the feed buckets. Each horse gets a slightly different grain. I look at the chart and scoop out feed, half a scoop of pellets and a little scoop of special mix. I move the wheelbarrow around. And I bring the horses in and turn them out, groom and saddle them, get them ready to ride, untack them, wipe them down, and cool them off—putting them in their stall, or walking them back to their pasture. On Fridays I get my lesson.

Shaina reminds me a little bit of Cass, except she's younger. She's got long, curly, reddish-brown hair and surprising green eyes. She's fearless. You should see her on a horse! She makes it look so easy. And she's always encouraging me and telling me that I'm doing a really good job.

After I finish my chores, I look after Shaina's little cutie six-year-old twin girls, Rylee and Teal, who you can usually find running wild on the farm in their pigtails, T-shirts, dirt-crusted jeans, and tiny worn-out leather boots, playing hide-and-seek, looking for snakes, hunting crabs in the creek, shooting rocks with sling-shots, chasing their pet donkey over the golden-green meadow—flowers blooming everywhere—faces beam-ing, squealing with laughter. Elk River's kind of a magical place.

There is nothing I love more than riding. It's a listening, a trust—the closest I can come to flying. When you're sit-ting on top of a horse, being propelled forward—almost floating above the ground . . . you just feel free.

After I ride, I always walk up to Goldie and I'll just wrap my right arm around his face and just pull his head into me and give him a little scratch between the eyes and up and down his nose, and then I kiss him.

"That was great," I tell him.

His ears flick. "You're such a good boy. We're doing it together," I whisper.

Usually after I'm done, I walk down the quiet, winding ranch driveway and hike one mile to the transit stop and take the San Marcos city bus number seven home. But today something different is in the works.

I wait at the end of the dirt driveway for my ride, which I hear coming, because Carmen is driving with all the windows down and Jasmine's brand-new album on full blast. When the car rolls up to me, Carmen smiles when I climb in. Wait. First she scrunches up her face and says, "Oh my God, you seriously smell like horse!" *Then* she breaks into a grin. "Ready for the best night of your life?" she asks.

"I guess," I say, and smile back at her and at Jules, who is sitting up front too.

Next, we stop off and pick up Josie. She's waiting outside their new apartment with Jess. Carmen pulls up, and turns the car off, and we all get out. Carmen and Jess hug like old friends. It's been six months since Christmas, and so they kind of are—old new friends. If that makes any sense. We all pile into Carmen's car. Well, me, and Josie in the back. Jules gets shotgun. Carmen is driving. Jess stands on the sidewalk and leans into the passenger window.

"Okay, be careful, and I'll see you guys at what?"

Carmen checks the time on her phone. "We'll drop these little nuggets off at—midnight or so?"

"Okay." Jess smiles at Josie and at me, strapped in with our seat belts, and then back at Jules and Carmen. "Enjoy! Be safe. Have fun!"

You're probably wondering where we're going, right?

Night begins to fall as we drive to the stadium, park, wait in line, and get in. I walk up the steep metal steps behind Josie, and Josie is behind Jules, and Jules is behind Carmen, who leads the way. The arena stands are packed! There must be thirty thousand people here. Carmen turns around and flashes us all a big smile.

"Nosebleed seats!" she shouts over the crowd.

The lights go down and the speakers boom. A zillion miles away I can barely make her out, but we all can watch her face splashed across the gigantic video screen. She starts off playing acoustic guitar. The crowd goes nuts. The applause is so loud I can feel the rumble in my heart.

Carmen shrieks, "Oh my gosh, Jasmine! I freaking love her!"

We sit packed together tight: Jules, Carmen, Josie, and me. Shoulder to shoulder. Carmen raises her eyebrows and holds out her phone, pointing it toward us. "Squad selfie!" she announces. "Lean in, you guys!"

We stand and dance in our seats and sing at the top of our lungs until our voices are hoarse. At the end of the show, the four of us walk all the way down to the ground level and stand in this crazy-long line, because Carmen has her heart set on somehow sneaking into the meet and greet.

I get goose bumps when I see Dani in a fringed jacket, black jeans, and clogs, standing by the door. Her wavy dark hair is down and loose. My heart jumps when our eyes connect. She looks *right* at me and smiles big as if there's something familiar. Her lips are pink with a hint of shine. I know there's no way. *No way* that she knows *me*, like, me: *Frannie*. But she turns to the security guy. It's not Hank; it's a big refrigerator-size guy in a gray suit. Dani whispers something in his ear, and the next thing we know, the Refrigerator steps aside.

"I guess it's your lucky day, ladies," he tells us as he lets us through.

Inside the meet and greet, about thirty other lucky fans are standing in line to get their pictures taken with Jasmine. We wait. The four of us stand in line and kind of stare. Jasmine has definitely been transformed by the glam squad! She's wearing a shimmery blue dress and her hair is curly and fluffy and awesome, with glittery streaks of gold on the tips just like on Christmas. There are huge platters of food on the tables, drinks, plates of sushi, fresh fruit. Large arrangements of bright flowers. Flashbulbs are flashing. Fans are standing back and nervously whispering.

Carmen just gazes at it all. "Oh my gosh, it's so ultra-glam," she says under her breath. "Can you imagine rolling like this?"

"I don't know," I tell her. "I think it's harder than it looks."

Carmen nudges me with her elbow and laughs. "Oh, Frannie, you crack me up."

I see Movie Star/Supermodel, impeccable from head to toe: perfect posture, honey-blond hair, glossy red lips, in an all-white dress, pretending to be charming and polite. I spot Hank, dark suit and tie, serious face, standing at the door, eyes shifting around the room. My heart kind of speeds up. It's so crazy! I never thought I'd see any of them ever again. I want to run up to Dani and get one of her heart-to-heart hugs so bad. But I don't, of course. That would be kind of weird! But something does happen. Something a little bit unusual. Something amazing!

First, Movie Star/Supermodel steps into the center of the room. The place goes absolutely quiet. She thanks all of us for coming and suddenly announces that Jasmine must leave early. They are late. As in, *thanks for coming, but good-bye!*

I can see Carmen's face go from all smiles to a big, sad frown. But then—

Jasmine. Yes, *Jasmine*, looks up, walks straight across the room and right toward me. *Me!*

Oh my gosh, is this happening? Yes, it is!

"Hi," she says, flashing me her beautiful smile and reaching out her hand for mine.

"I'm Jasmine," she says. "So nice to meet you!"

"I'm Frannie," I say, and almost giggle.

Jasmine just stands there smiling at me. She can't take her eyes off me.

"Hey, have we met before?" she asks, tilting her head and kind of studying my face. "There's something about you—" She stops, steps back, and crosses her arms, looking me up and down with her signature bright, bright smile. "Cute cowgirl boots!" she tells me, eyelids glimmering.

"Thanks!" I glance down at my well-worn leather boots and look back up, returning her smile.

Carmen clears her throat loudly and pokes me with her elbow.

"Oh, umm, Jasmine"—I turn to my right—"this is my

sister, Carmen, her friend Jules, and . . . my best friend, Josie."

"Hey!" says Jasmine, flashing a smile of perfect white teeth and giving them each a quick hug.

"I just, like—love you!" Carmen blurts out, obviously starstruck.

"Ooh, that's so sweet," says Jasmine, lifting her hand to her heart. She turns back to me and grins again. "Frannie, I don't know why, but there's something about you. . . . Are you sure we haven't met?"

I shrug and smile. "Well, maybe, like, in another life?" I laugh softly.

"Yeah." She laughs a little too. "That must be it." Jasmine stops talking and looks at me for a long second. "Well," she giggles, and her face lights up, "I'm pretty sure we were friends."

"Yeah," I say as our eyes meet again, "I'm pretty sure you're right."

64.

BY THE TIME CARMEN DROPS Josie and me back off at Jess's new apartment complex, it's almost midnight. Jess runs out and meets us by the curb with hugs, and the three of us walk under a sky full of stars down the quiet sidewalk and up the stairs to their new amazing apartment. The apartment is at this place called Hope House for Women and Children. It is gorgeous and brand-new, and it has a playground, a community center, a courtyard, and a vegetable garden.

When we step into the apartment and Jess flicks on the lights, Josie and I sit up on the high stools in the kitchen and Jess serves us each a plateful of mac-and-cheese and a tall glass of lemonade. I love it here. It's small but it's cozy and clean, happy and full of light. It's cheerful. There's a built-in reading nook with piles of pillows in a big window. The fridge is covered with photos of Jess and Josie, and I even made it up there: a picture of me and Josie and Goldie at Elk River. Ever since pretty much that first day back at school after Christmas, Josie and I have become best friends. I can't imagine not knowing her. I love her so much. She's the sweetest best friend I could ask for.

On days I don't have my riding lesson, or that I'm not working at the barn, I come over after school to Josie's and we sit on the tall stools and do our homework on the kitchen island. I sleep over here almost every weekend. And it's so awesome because I get to see Jess as *me*! I get to hug her! She's so caring and kind to me. I mean, she has no idea like—yeah, you know . . . about anything that happened. She's just nice to me because that's who she is. She is just a really caring person. She's doing really great and she has a new job waiting tables, and in the fall she's going back to school to become a nurse. She's going to be the best nurse ever.

Just like Jess promised, Josie has her very own room with a bunk bed, a tucked-away pullout hidden desk, and her very own window that looks out onto the courtyard. Tonight, though, Josie and I drag our blankets and pillows up to the rooftop deck. It's late spring and the air is warm. It's like a little oasis up here: a secret garden terrace of potted plants, a smooth wood-planked floor, a bench, a birdfeeder, and a tiny birdbath. The railing is strung with white twinkly Christmas lights—even though it's June. It's so cozy, and we're safe, right outside Jess's room.

Sleeping on a rooftop right under the stars feels like magic. For a few minutes, the two of us giggle and whisper and talk and talk. We giggle about Josie's secret crush, this sweet redheaded boy in our grade named Nolan, and we whisper about my top-secret crush too. He's on the swim team. He has tight, curly dark hair and caramel-colored skin and big brown eyes that shine when he smiles. He kind of looks like—

Yeah. *Him*.

Josie falls asleep pretty quickly, but I stay awake. I stretch out on the roof deck, under my blanket, and gaze straight up into the night at the thousand pinholes of light—stars, big and bright, flickering in the darkness above me. It's so beautiful . . . it takes my breath away. For a long moment I just feel the night breeze and watch the stars. I search for the Southern Cross rising in the starry sky . . . I think about everyone who I got to be and everyone I miss.

It's so peaceful.

So silent.

If I'm really being honest, there are moments where I still hurt. A lot. It's still really hard to be in my house sometimes. My dad still yells. It's scary. My mom is—yeah. My mom. Nothing has really changed—

But I have.

Don't miss Megan Shull's

"I don't get it," I say.

Actually, I keep saying it over and over again. "I don't get it. I don't get it."

I'm pacing across the small nurse's room, from one cot to the other, back and forth, like that is somehow going to change things.

Worse, Freckles is starting to cry like a total girl except—

She's me.

I have never seen myself cry.

This is unreal.

"Freckles!" I say, realizing I don't even know this girl's name. "Dude, you've got to stop crying, you know? You're freaking me out!"

Ever since Christmas, I know a whole new way. I am different. It's hard to even put into words. I mean, I can look people in the eye now. I'm less afraid. I'm braver. I know I'm not alone. And when things feel hard, I can make myself feel better: I snuggle up with my bumble-bee, or I take a hot rose-scented shower, put on comfy warm clothes, make something good to eat, or just get outside and breathe. If none of that works, I tell myself, *I'm okay. I'm safe. I can handle anything that happens. No matter what.* I repeat that to myself a hundred times. And every night before I go to sleep and every morning when I wake up, I take a few slow, deep breaths and I think about Jordan—on *that* Christmas Day, everything got stripped away, and I remember thinking: *If I ever get the chance to be me again, I'm going to really live.*

The bounces were the best thing that ever happened to me. I can't stop thinking about all the people who I love and who loved me. Sometimes, when I think about it, it's like, by knowing them, I learned how to be myself. And I keep on getting stronger. There's just a light in my heart now that I hope never goes out. Cass, Luke, Rosie, Dani, Max, Liam, Tia, Jordan's whole family, Jess and Josie—I am never going to stop loving them, or looking for them in the stars. And I hope if you're reading this, you know that kind of love really exists. It's a gentleness. It's in you and it's out there too. Don't stop till you find it.

"Yeah, well, your nose is killing me!" she says, snorting back sobs. "What did you even do to your face?"

I look back at her, I mean—

I look back at *me*. I look pretty banged up. "This is unreal," I say, staring back into the mirror. "It's like I'm living in a movie!"

More hilarious hijinks by award-winning author
MEGAN SHULL!